And I saw it was filled with graves,
And tomb-stones where flowers should be:
And Priests in black gowns, were walking their rounds,
And binding with briars, my joys & desires.

"The Garden of Love," William Blake

Madness Heart Press
2006 Idlewilde Run Dr.
Austin, Texas 78744

This is a work of fiction. Names, characters, places, and incidents either are the product of the author's imagination or are used fictitiously. Any resemblance to actual persons, living or dead, events, or locales is entirely coincidental.

Copyright © 2025 Charles R. Bernard
Cover by Waclaw Traier

All rights reserved. No part of this book may be reproduced or used in any manner without written permission of the copyright owner except for the use of quotations in a book review. For more information, address: john@madnessheart.press

First Edition
ISBN: 978-1-967517-00-8
www.madnessheart.press

CHARLES R. BERNARD

A Madness Heart Press Publication

PRIMARY EDUCATION MANUAL | MORALPOL IDEOLOGOGRAM A03.01

For distribution to politically literate students (see PAMPHLET A03.01)
For oral recitation as instruction to younger age groups or problem students: in these latter categories, it is advised that you employ the provided educational aids (see HAND PUPPETS A03.01)

A03.01 | THE KING'S POCKETS

Nature's thorny thicket once grew dense with choking, noisome things. Things which one would not call human, not exactly, though they walked around in human skins and wore human faces over their true selves. The first King had a Wise Council, just like the one our King has today. Just like today, some Wise Councilors were warriors, and some were great landholders. Some were the owners of big factories that made many things, and others were teachers or philosophers. Others still were scientists, engineers, or mathematicians.

In the Kingdom, those were violent days and bloody times, those early years of our first King. Not everybody recognized His Majesty yet, and he had to keep the peace both in the lands he'd newly conquered *and* at home. Many subjects proved themselves to be loyal, hardworking, pure, and honest; just like all of *you* will be one day! Some of the King's subjects, however, were not like you or me. They were the most dangerous, the evilest, the *wickedest* men you could imagine. They caused great pain and fear among the King's loyal subjects, who were close unto His Majesty's heart. Think of how much *our* King loves *us*; that's how much the first King loved *his* people. He said to his Wise Council: "Come! Let me hear you all address this problem, and soon we'll solve this problem for time and all eternity."

First, the warriors announced their plan. "These weeds have thorns," they said, "and thorns are useful. We can use them to defend our garden's boundaries and scratch those with no regard for 'thou shalt not.'" The King, who loved all acts of service and abhorred unneeded waste, immediately made it so. But as the warriors learned quickly, these wild-grown briars refused to be bound. They scratched both friend and foe alike, and often one choked each another's quest for air and light, given half a chance. And still the garden filled with weeds, and city streets still teemed with beasts in human skins who slunk about in human masks.

Next, the landholders and factory owners had their say. "We always need more workers," said the priests of commerce, "planters and reapers; assembly lines and slaughterhouses must be kept roaring night and day. Send us all those idle hands, and we shall give them work to do. The Kingdom will reap the reward, and we'll save money with the sweat of guilty brows." This plan, too, was tried, and it, too, failed. What the foremen saw as "good habits" couldn't be conveyed to those the foremen saw as "bad men." Not when they refused to learn, and even less when brutal structure was imposed through slavery, which teaches naught but evil to anyone. The Kingdom's greatest owners were defeated by the slippery knot of human evildoing, and admitted as much to the King. And still the garden filled with weeds, and city streets still teemed with beasts in human skins who slunk about in human masks.

To the surprise of the Wise Council's teachers and philosophers, the King waxed impatient with them.

"*This* question," said King Cleon, "has solely been the province of your most august representatives since humanity's dawn. I ask you only one thing, to which you may respond only yes or no: have you anything new to say?" To their embarrassment, the teachers and philosophers could only answer "no." The King was satisfied then, and reassured them that their input on other questions would no doubt prove most valuable.

Lastly, the King turned to the Council's scientists, its engineers, and its explorers of strange new technologies. "You could be my last hope," said King Cleon, "and I crave your answer. How would your convocation tend this garden? I am more intrigued, I'd note, to hear *your* proposition than any other." Their proposition was deceptively simple. "Mighty King," the speaker for their Council said, "you need not wait. We have the answers to your questions. Our convocation has discovered new technology; the greatest scientific advancement and the most invaluable technology yet placed at your disposal."

King Cleon was as patient as you all are. You remember "patience," yes? *Very* good!

King Cleon waited for the scientist to go on – and he did. "Your body is the bodies of your people, Lord, and your mind theirs," he said. "Your waistcoat is built of the vaults and catacombs where the Kingdom's mighty store of gold resides. Your armor is the strength of every wall and border." King Cleon was well pleased by this; he recognized the thoughts of Thomas Hobbes, called by some the Monster of Malmesbury. The King approved, nodded affirmation, and the man continued.

"We have discovered that the garments of your kingdom – the lands obtained by might or majesty, and now protected by your shadow – they're *far* vaster than we had suspected. Your garments, King Cleon of House

Skousen, happen to have *pockets* now."

"Pockets," asked the clever King, "large enough to hold our troubled friends? Land enough for weeds to grow as thorny as they like?"

"Just so," said the convocation representative, and the King smiled.

"That's not all," continued the speaker for the convocation. "We propose a course of study on these undesirables. Nature seeds them, and for now we can but weed. However, we have other new technologies. We invented some of them while searching for your pockets. We propose to learn why these weeds grow and how to look behind the masks of monsters." This, too, made the King smile, and he said, "Let it be so." Privately, our kindly King (long may he reign) was much amazed. He had learned about the hidden places in our kingdom, the secret, frightening places where he could put our problems. In today's lesson, we'll begin to learn about those places, too!

And in the next section, you will learn how we began to understand the weeds and their thorns, the monsters, and their masks. Humanity discovered a new science. It studies what makes you yourself, and the rest of us ourselves, too. It's called chromatic-geometric psychogrammar, and it helps the King's loyal servants see the shapes and colors of your dreams.

```
                    MORALPOL|APPEND.01
          Disruptive pupils will receive this
     presentation again during a CGP evaluation
     session. Watch for radiance spikes of <100°
  in RGB 255,255,0 and flag for further
                                monitoring.
```

1.
THE THIRD- OR FOURTH-COOLEST CRIME

Skunk considered himself a patient man, and to this end he gave Eichmann two strikes. That was two fumbling, soft-handed tries for the binoculars. Twice that the sunburned little German got to repeat his inane question – *are you sure, Skunk? It's Frank this time, Skunk?* The third time, Skunk turned, and, finding nothing else to hand, pried a good-sized rock out of the acrid dirt and caved in Eichmann's skull.

The first blow was enough to knock Eichmann to the ground, swiftly on his way to dead if not already there. As slow to regain his composure as he was to wrath, Skunk took off the binoculars and set them carefully on his kneeling-blanket before resuming his dispute with the fallen man. By the time he'd finished, Eichmann didn't have much of a head to speak of above the lower jaw; just a clotted spray of busted-pumpkin skull and bloody brain, artistically framed on its lower edge by a gleaming row of teeth. The upper teeth must have been pulverized in the frenzy; that, Skunk reflected, or the convulsing German had swallowed them somehow.

No matter. Skunk wiped his bloody hands on his uniform pants. The ragged trousers were beyond filthy;

colorlessly dark, stiff, greasy sheaths that gave off a stench matched only by the sweltering and malodorous lower body stuffed into them like so much rotting meat. It wasn't the first layer of loathsome lacquer he'd applied to his long-befouled garments, and it wouldn't be the last. Skunk's full name, inasmuch as any man in Arson had one, was Skunk Pussy. Like other Arsonists, he'd left his old name behind when he'd been transported to his new home. His name was not self-applied, and amounted to a rough approximation of how other Arsonists described his signature bodily aroma.

Skunk's general demeanor was just as unappealing to the other senses humans are cursed with, though, to be fair, few in Arson had the bad luck to be able to describe Skunk's taste. He was clenched and squashed of feature, beadily blue-eyed, and blonde enough that every trace of oil and bodily detritus shone in his long, filthy hair as though it were a brushstroke on a clean canvas. Never a scintillating conversationalist, it was only after the contents of the milk-pale German's cranial commode had been strewn across the sunbaked dirt that Skunk answered the dead man's question.

"Yes, it's Frank." Skunk turned back to the cliff, to the broad view of the forbidden and abandoned valley below, its long stretch of blacktop and the semitruck powering westward, straight into a sunset like a vast tick smashed against the heavens. Straight toward Arson. He picked the binoculars back up and lifted them to his scrunched-looking eyes. "Do you know *another* truck that's painted pussy pink?" He paused, lowering his spyglasses. "Matter of fact, you know another truck that can come within one hundred miles of this fucking place?"

Eichmann couldn't name a one.

It was *their* fault, Uncle Funny would tell anyone who

could stand him once he had a pint of the Jolly Rancher's mule vinegar in him. It was the Board's fault that Arson grew faster than it could keep up with new inhabitants. After all, who *wouldn't* want to live in a place named after the third- or fourth-coolest crime? "Leave it to the bureaucrats in pointy hats," he'd gibber, eyes darting and a little dilated as the mule vinegar bit, the sensation much like booze but cranked out sideways-like. "They even fucked up picking a boring acronym, and that is an ex-tra-*or*-din-ar-i-ly" (he pronounced every syllable) "*difficult* thing to fuck up." He had a point, as manic and mangled as his thoughts so often were. Arson – or ARSO:N, if you wanted to be formal – *did* sound a lot cooler than Area for Registered Sex Offenders: North. That sounded so *clinical*.

Regardless, the name had nothing to do with their predicament. The fact Arson's population grew faster than its resources wasn't a matter of massive inmate influx. Newcomers were a rare delicacy in Arson. It was the fact that every passing year saw less and less to go around. Less of everything; fewer uniforms to replace the ones that wore to shreds, fewer building materials to patch the paltry shanties most Arsonists had built for themselves; worst of all, it meant fewer Board hearings. Fewer chances for Parole. That was the worst to most of them, anyway. The ones who dreamed of Parole.

This was another ticklish point for Uncle Funny. "What kind of low-down, rat-shit, rotten fucking way to run a show is *that*?" he'd sneer. "When a grown man with the sky bright and blue over his head and the sun hot on his face; why, when a *natural* sort of man begs for Parole, it's…" And here he'd usually stop himself before he said *that* word; the word that, more than any other, promised you deep shit in Arson. That word was *sick,* and it wasn't one that got tossed around lightly. Men had died for calling other men that, died under that bright blue sky, and then the hot sun was the only warmth left in them. Uncle Funny liked his jokes, but he watched his step just like the other long-timers.

Clothes, timber, Board hearings; all of these things could be had but twice a year. They came with stingy but reliable regularity. Men were hauled off for Board hearings in the order they requested them, and goods were given out first come, first served. These semiannual infusions of resources were never enough to ensure comfort; hell, they weren't enough to guarantee that every man slept beneath a board or scrap of tin. On rare occasions, these shipments included newly minted Arsonists, freshly shorn and shriven of their past, and often shivering with disorientation at their first sight of their new home. If nothing else, the shipments were predictable.

The same could not be said of Arson's *other* source of goods, but the treasures that the big pink semitruck brought were well worth a year – hell, *two* years – of the Board's new boots or plywood pallets fit to patch the moaning gaps in Arson's miserable dwellings. Let the wind croon lunacy into their slumbering minds on windy nights. What *really* mattered was what came in the pussy-pink truck; that cargo was, to them, more precious than sweet water. The pink truck was the one and only smuggler's rig in Arson, the fountainhead of contraband. It didn't come with any regularity. The truck's appearances were not mechanical, like the rise and fall of Arson's sun. The precious contraband appeared at the whim of a single figure, like the malevolent whimsy of a trickster deity or the incomprehensible agenda of an alien god. Though it always arrived at sunset's reddest hour, the pussy-pink truck came only on the days deemed proper by its owner, operator, and keeper of secrets; Frank Blank.

Skunk descended the dead dirt slope behind the cliff face with the grace of a controlled avalanche. His filthy blonde hair streamed behind him in half-dreaded locks like a trail of sausages tracing the meatball comet of his face. Skunk was not particularly gifted in the arithmetic arts, but necessity and practice had taught him a facility with approximate distance and estimated rates of travel that might even draw an impressed whistle from a physicist. Skunk calculated that he could make it down the slope by the time Frank's truck cleared the ring of bones delineating Arson's border. Skunk could then make it past the Woodpile (where he'd alert Funny, who'd alert anyone he fucking felt like) by the time Frank hit the big incline leading to Arson proper, at which point the light would be like blood. With any luck, Skunk could then hit his shanty, unearth his barter, and make it back to Ardor Street before Frank even popped the hydraulic brakes. *First there, best shit*, Skunk thought in time with his shambling strides, and soon he was even chanting it under his breath as he ran.

"First… THERE… best… SHIT!"

Skunk hit the hardpack at full tilt, and his precipitous rate of descent caused his boots to disintegrate on impact into flapping, flopping tatters of canvas and shreds of thin rubber. *Fuck*, he thought eloquently, but didn't slow his pace. Skunk's feet, like those of most Arsonists, spent as much time wrapped in foot-rags or nothing at all as they did clad in boots. This pair had been on their last legs (so to speak) before he broke into a run, and as with all natural things, entropy's sword had hung above them from the moment of their construction. It wouldn't do to mourn a goddamned pair of boots, not now that Frank was back. Boots were high on the list of wished-for luxuries in Arson, but they didn't rate jimmy-jack shit against the sort of delicacies that Frank's pussy-pink truck held within its secretive, seductive interior. Traveling barefoot and hell-bent-for-leather, Skunk thundered over the hardpack and toward the lengthening shadow of the nearest structure.

Nobody in Arson could say for sure (or, for that matter, gave a shit) when exactly the Woodpile had first opened its door to customers. Not doors, plural: it only had the one, a flimsy particle-board flap slapped more or less in place over the rectangular hole that constituted its entrance. The Woodpile was crudely framed and poorly made; a large, enclosed, off-square porch that grew like a distended tumor from the humble host organism of Little Billy Fingerwidth's trailer. Little Billy was usually in a chemical stupor until dusk stirred the sky with swollen, purple fingers, so Skunk was not surprised when he barreled into the Woodpile and found it empty save for Uncle Funny. The scrap-constructed bar and barbican barely kept the murderous sunlight out; in fact, the roof admitted random cracks of crimson radiance, laser-like in their intensity within the Woodpile's gloom. As the door banged open and Skunk's stench came rolling in like a dead tide, accompanied by the bloody flux of sunset's sullen glare, Uncle Funny visibly recoiled.

Funny was a half-head taller than Skunk, and much thinner. Everything about the man was thin, from his face to his long and slouching frame. His hair, which had receded to a decorative fringe around his bald pate, was thin, too. Where Skunk's mane was blonde and fetid, Funny's fringe was neat, close-clipped, and the color of tarnished silver. There was something uniquely unhealthy about his complexion, a pallor that wasn't so much tempered by sallow jaundice as with a vaguely bluish hue, as though he were perpetually on the verge of asphyxiating on some toxic vapor that afflicted only him. Funny didn't shun the light the way Little Billy, Howling Andy, and some of the others did, but Skunk could tell from the way the pale, lanky man reacted to the light that he'd been at it in the Woodpile all day. Knowing him, things would continue their acceleration all night long. When Uncle Funny decided to bite the mule, he'd usually keep going until he seized up and someone (often Billy) dragged him back to his dugout to recover.

"What in the *fuck*-" Funny barked.

"Frank." It was all Skunk needed to say. He'd barely made it ten steps past the Woodpile before Uncle Funny came crashing after him. Funny did the classic mule vinegar strut, as overenergetic as it was uncoordinated. Skunk didn't bother to turn around, but by the sound of it, Funny made it all the way to the fork in the path. There, some sort of disagreement about which way to turn evidently broke out between his legs. A spate of slurry, rapid-fire curses from the slender man accompanied some sort of crashing calamity, but Skunk had already hightailed it to the right without looking back. He sailed on bare feet and filthy, sausage-casing legs past the Jolly Rancher's reeking chemical fields, where great, noxious clouds of ammoniac piss-stench shrouded his shallow, bubbling chemical pools and scoured the shine from the chicken-wire mesh enclosure in which he kept his blumpkin burrows. Skunk was almost home free.

He referred to it as a shanty, but Skunk Pussy always thought of his small sleeping-space as his *nest* in his own, for-private thoughts. He'd set it up just past the boundary of the Jolly Rancher's territory. JR agreed that Skunk's nest was far enough away from his Ranch House that Skunk's aroma would not trouble him. Skunk's shanty-nest consisted of two wide wooden boards leaned against one another to form an inverted V. A-frame pig shelters Skunk's heavily-edited mind had whispered when he'd built it, but, like most semi-recollections cut adrift, the whisper summoned no memories from the blank void in his past. He'd carpeted the nest with an old tarp, atop which Skunk had wadded a bedroll made of linens too soiled to be sand-washed and reused by anyone else in Arson. It made for bedding that was as malodorous as it was comfortable, and though Skunk may have been the worst-smelling man in Arson, he was most likely the best rested.

Skunk considered it a pretty sweet set-up. He got to stay close to the blumpkins that so fascinated and enticed him, and his closest neighbor was the closest thing he had to a friend. In truth, the Jolly Rancher was the closest thing *any* Arsonist had to a friend. Or a mayor, for that matter; even Uncle Funny only had pretensions that he served as town crier and court philosopher. Skunk had deliberately allowed Uncle Funny to be the one to tell the Jolly Rancher that Frank was back; he'd assumed that was where the slender, mule-bit man would head, and he was right.

As he dug beneath his tarp (oh-so-careful to dig around and beneath the buried bear trap without springing it), Skunk could hear Funny breathlessly reporting Frank's arrival to JR. That was good. Uncle Funny didn't need to worry about being first in line for barter; he didn't have sweet, sainted fuck-all to his name to trade to Frank, anyway. What he *did* have, thanks to this timely tipoff, was the Rancher's good will – and that was worth a squirt or two of mule vinegar when the chips were down and things got dry. Skunk realized he was getting distracted and palpated the chunky, disturbed soil until he found what he was looking for; the shredded remains of a plastic grocery bag wrapped around a folded rectangle of oil cloth. Should he take the time to find his rubber flip-flops in the bedding? Fuck no, time was of the essence and he needed to run faster than those sandals could flip or flop. With his dubious treasures in hand, Skunk squirmed back out of his lean-to and hauled himself back into a full-tilt run for Ardor Street.

He made it with at least half a minute to spare, in which time the Jolly Rancher and Uncle Funny managed to catch up. The three of them stood at the crumbled foot of a long, featureless stretch of asphalt. To say it was the only paved road in Arson would not be accurate, because it wasn't *in* the settled part of Arson. In fact, the furthest boundary of Arson's populated area began where that bright black ribbon of pavement ceased to be. *The end of the road*, thought Skunk for the thousandth time, just as pleased with his witticism as he had been the first time, *literally* and *figuratively*. Beyond Arson, the blacktop stretched away from its terminus and back into the valley of sun-bleached bone and sand toward the distant, dreaming mountains; the no-man's-land that separated them from everything they'd left behind.

"Well, d-a-a-ad *gum!*" As happy as a hyena and as sunny as the smile on a sadistic sheriff's face, the voice of the Jolly Rancher rang from just behind Skunk. "Has it been a *minute* since that rascal Frank has come round here, or has it been a gosh-darned *minute!*"

Crimson soaked the western sky. To the east, dusk was just beginning to pour the sweet wine of nightfall. Skunk turned to greet his friend with an ugly smile, but only because those were the only smiles his squashed-up face could manufacture. By this standard and many others, the Jolly Rancher couldn't have been more of a contrast to Skunk if he'd made a study of it. Not that he had, however; the nature of Skunk was one of the few things the Rancher *didn't* seem to make a study of.

Arson was an eclectic mix of mostly-damaged, mostly-ageless-looking men. Skunk, for example, could have been either a hard 40 or a chemically preserved 70. By contrast, the Jolly Rancher was as spry as he was smooth of skin, though he had a seedy sort of smarm that Skunk both basked in and distrusted. JR's hair was as black as motor oil, and the way it was slicked tight against his skull, that may have been for good reason. His skin, though sun-kissed from his frequent exertions at the Open O Ranch, didn't have the same weathered quality which many Arsonists developed from the feral lifestyle forced upon them. The Rancher's black irises matched his hair and his neat moustache, though Skunk doubted that the Rancher dyed his eyes with motor oil. If he had, it probably would have dyed the corneas, too.

"Hey, JR." Skunk looked past him at Uncle Funny's wheezing face and tried to meet the grey-haired man's zig-zagging gaze. "Hey, Funny. Can you guys hear Frank's rig?"

They could. So could the other skulking Arsonists, more of whom began to gather as the throaty roar of Frank's engine filled the playa. They heard, and they came running at the sound. Even the ones like Howling Andy that couldn't come for one reason or another sent proxies to meet the pussy-pink truck and barter for the dainties there on offer. These placeholders would take a cut of said dainties in payment, naturally, since they'd not only gone to the trouble of hauling their asses down to

Ardor Street, but had thereby become part of a gathering crowd. If there was one thing most of Arson's denizens disliked more than the settlement itself, it was their neighbors. Garrulous sorts like Uncle Funny were rare; Skunk sometimes suspected that even the Rancher only tolerated other Arsonists with such sweet good cheer because it made for better networking, better gossip, and a better market (and pool of test subjects) for the many fine concoctions and distractions he experimented with.

The line began to fill in behind Skunk and the two acquaintances to whom he'd given early warning of Frank's imminence. Box Spring came sauntering up, and Prod and Pinetop right behind, holding hands like always. Balloonman, Salty, Pharaoh; soon the whole community was packed into the end of Ardor Street. Save for a few notable absences, that was.

"Where's Eichmann?" Uncle Funny asked, scanning the grime-smeared, gathered faces for the wet-eyed little man. "I thought he was watching the road with you today."

"He was," Skunk replied, as cool as Arson's starless night. "I killed him."

Funny's lips twisted in a leer, as much a mule vinegar spasm as a sign of mirth. "Did you, now?"

"Yeah. I beat his fucking brains in with a rock. His body's still up the cliff." Skunk's ugly smile this time was full of genuine warmth and bonhomie. "He went down like a sack of shit. I'd probably still be up there picking teeth out of the goop, but, you know..."

"Yes, yes, first here best shit, I believe you've said that before," Uncle Funny replied. He was trying to hang on to the convulsions of mirth that threatened to overtake his skinny body. "Caved in Eichmann's skull, did you? Oh, me, oh that's *good*, Skunk. *Oh.*"

The rising rumble of the engine soon drowned out any further repartee. Toward the back fringe of the crowd, a few of the more difficult Arsonists jostled. They thumped each other to avoid the stigma of last place, but they needn't have worried; Eichmann won that prize by default. The truck's snarling advent was like the predatory charge of some great, ravenous beast. The grille, the tires, every part of it was a pornographic, princess pink, and shiny like it hadn't just crossed a beige expanse of dust-blown highway. Funny thing, that. Frank drove through that same worthless desert every time, and every time, that truck of his arrived looking as shiny as a freshly-peeled piece of hard candy.

Skunk could remember flashes of hard candy. He also knew trucks. More accurately, he could still remember "truck" – the concept, a bit of how they functioned, altogether enough for him to suspect that at some point before Arson he might have had something to do with them. As a job, maybe. It was hard to tell; every resident of the colony had a ham salad of shredded, mashed-together memory, unrefrigerated and quickly spoiling in the heat and the denuded desperation of Arson. If anyone could hold onto a few fragments like "pancakes" or "driveway" or "sentenced to transportation," they shared them with the others. Many things were trade- or barter-only in their tiny world, including some forms of information: gossip, or reports like the one Skunk had given Uncle Funny. The remnants of *before*, however, were not in this category. They were worthless on their own, hoarded and gnawed in isolation. To better understand their situation, Arsonists had created an informal and constantly-updated oral history of *before*. Frank Blank and his smuggled treasures were a huge part of how this history evolved. Skunk, like every Arsonist, adored Frank for his efforts. Still, Skunk's memory of "truck" meant that he noticed certain strange details.

Frank's pretty pink truck wasn't your usual eighteen-wheeler (another term which Skunk had contributed to the settlement's evolving lexicon). It had a lot more than eighteen wheels, for one thing. Skunk tried to count them, once or twice. Their configuration was strange and inexplicably repulsive, and he'd have sworn that the axles and wheels switched positions and moved when he wasn't looking. It made him feel dizzy and a little sick. Nor was Frank's rig a truck that could have feasibly cleared any overpass short of an elevated interchange; the top of his truck had to stand twenty-five feet if it stood an inch. It didn't line up with "truck" as Skunk knew it, in other words. He had managed one murmured conversation with Frank in which Skunk had conveyed two things (that he knew Frank's "truck" was not exactly a truck, and that he hadn't told anyone, nor would he) and Frank had conveyed two (his gratitude and the wisdom of Skunk's decision). That had been the beginning and the end of it.

The pussy-pink behemoth rolled to a menacingly majestic stop, its engine's cataclysmic thunder as loud as sustained gunfire. The Arsonists knew what came next, and so they stuffed their fingertips into their ears. Right on cue, Frank's truck engaged the hydraulic brakes with a vicious, earsplitting hiss that must have been audible for miles. If anyone had been around to hear it but the bones and the blumpkins, that was. The engine cut out next, and the silence was as sudden as the brakes and twice as resonant for its eerie clarity. Ordinary trucks' engines, Skunk knew, could sometimes ping and pop as they cooled. Frank's truck was not quite so subtle in its repose. Its outsized, one-story engine gave off violent

BANGs as it settled down to slumber. These bangs were so violent that they made Skunk imagine some strange tribe of mutant engineers, trapped forever in Frank's engine, whanging away with their wrenches in a pathetic bid for freedom. He wasn't sure what to make of the kinship he felt with the strange, imaginary captives.

Frank let the moment build. He was good at that kind of thing, and Skunk would never dispute it, dim as his sense for showbiz was. When the suspense seemed unbearable and the sun sparkling on the glass and the pink metal became too succulent to suffer, Frank popped the latch on his door with a heavy *CH-CHUNK* and let it swing gently open. One grimy, khaki-colored work-boot hit the top step of the makeshift ladder of steel bars welded to the truck's cab and four thick, tan fingers folded over the door's top edge like the slow, confident tread of a tarantula. Frank Blank craned his head over his grip on the door and surveyed the Arsonists gathered to plead sufferance at his rolling shrine.

Frank Blank, first and foremost, looked like a desert creature. Though no Arsonist could say from whence he hailed, that much seemed self-evident, at least. What little skin he showed the world consisted almost exclusively of his lower face and his hands below the wrist; all else was concealed beneath a wardrobe that was only slightly more mutable than the worn-out uniforms of the Arsonists. Frank wore boots and blue jeans. He favored western shirts in shades of plaid drawn from the red-to-brown spectrum, each interchangeable change of clothes bleached by the sun and frayed by countless years of use. He wore a leather belt with an unassuming round brass buckle. His hands and face were brown like rich, tanned leather, and despite the hard look of his flesh around the mouth, Frank's exact age was difficult to pin down.

Frank's getup had a sole remarkable component; a flamboyantly large, cream-colored ten-gallon cowboy hat graced by a broad leather band. He wore the hat tipped very low, and the center of the band was decorated by a large oval of glinting amber, in which were suspended a half-dozen or so tiny, wilted flowers, eternally preserved in the slow throes of their death.

Nobody in Arson had ever seen Frank Blank's eyes; not even once. Frank only showed the world his low hat brim and its softly luminous band-buckle. Early in his tenure, the first fight Skunk had witnessed which had led to bloodshed had taken place inside the Woodpile, and had spiraled out of this very topic. Someone – Uncle Funny? Balloonman? – had ventured the opinion that Frank had no eyes, and that's why he kept his hat so low. That was also why when anyone tried to sneak a peek or, hell, even glance in the direction of the shade pooled there, your eyes got sucked into the black hole of those dying little flowers. It wasn't just some of them, after all, it was *all* of them. Don't be stupid, someone else had shot back, of *course* Frank had eyes, he drove a fucking *truck*, didn't he?

Back and forth it went, with others venturing theories about Frank. The mule bit deeply that night at the Woodpile. It had only been a matter of time until someone got stuck or choked out or, just hypothetically speaking, brained with a rock. In this case, the lucky winner had lost a wrestling match and been plain old beaten to death; unoriginal, sure, but he supposed that some means of murder were timeless classics for good reason. Skunk couldn't remember who'd been killed that night.

Frank now stood high above them with his hat

drawn low, and he turned his unseen (and perhaps – contentiously – nonexistent) eyes across the misbegotten throng. His frown relaxed half a notch, which was as close as he came to a smile. When he spoke, it was Frank's same old voice, one part whisky warble, one part smoke, and three parts pure desert dry.

"Got a different kind of merchandise for you this time, boys. Custom made. Something special for everyone. Gonna take me a little while to set up. Mule vinegar's on me tonight." General acclaim greeted this, but Frank talked over it. "Should be ready by dawn. Go have fun until then."

Frank waved lazily at the dissolving cheers as the assembled throng retreated to the Woodpile to pound mule vinegar into themselves until they couldn't move. Frank spoke as the groups receded, pitching his low, sandstone voice so only those frontmost within the ranks of the congregation could hear him. "JR, Skunk. A moment?" Uncle Funny lingered, too, as though he also expected to be invited, but soon the call of the mule overrode his umbrage and he staggered off to finish the self-pickling process he'd begun much earlier. Frank watched Funny scuttle off, and soon it was just the three of them.

"Skunk," Frank said. "New blood."

So, just the *four* of them, then. "What in the fuck are you talking about 'new blood,' Frank?" Skunk's irritation was plain. "*Everyone* comes in the same way, by-"

Frank cut him off. "Not this one. Not this time. Be a good boy. Name him, if he needs it. Take him on the tour. Get him a glass to drink." Skunk stared at him with scrunched eyes, but even he – one of the meanest and most violent sons of bitches in Arson – never argued with Frank. Without another word, Skunk crossed the broad, matte-pink grille of the truck to the driver's side, and there began to clamber up the seven-odd feet of crude rungs welded there until he could grab hold of the passenger handle. He climbed like a graceless ape: quickly and in odd, lurching counterpoint. He seized the ancient handle of Frank's cabin door and hauled it open. His efforts were rewarded by a cantankerous squeal of ill-oiled hinges. *Frank*, Skunk noted, unsurprised, *does not take on many passengers.*

The cab of Frank's pussy-pink truck was the same libidinal shade as the rest of the vehicle. As far as Skunk could determine, every facet of it from the semi's screws and tire-stems to its windshield wipers was the same hue. The interior of the truck smelled the way it always did: bad. Skunk didn't mind bad smells. One might even say they were sort of his *thing*, if one were so inclined. He had a great nose for funk, and had anyone asked him, he could have told them precisely what Frank's throne-room-on-wheels smelled like. One part unwashed body crevices, from the crack of the ass with its distinctive, shit-dappled musk to good, old-fashioned armpit funk. This was strange because Frank Blank himself never smelled like much of anything besides dry desert rock. Another part of the smell was old, dried cum – but *very* old, like an adult theater that had been closed for a decade in the hot Arizona sun. Skunk paused. He had no idea what this last association meant – didn't know "cum," "adult theater," or "Arizona" – but he knew that it was accurate. Such strange half-thoughts were common currency among those shriven of the world from whence they came.

A new addition to the smell on this particular day rose from a crumpled rag of a man who lay unconscious on Frank's seat. This aroma was fascinating enough that it arrested Skunk for several moments as his imposing olfactory epithelium parsed its strange mélange. *Not formaldehyde*, he thought (Skunk knew "formaldehyde"), *but something similar.* Under that, a spicy scent like ginger and the telltale, stormbound kiss of ozone. This exotic medley rose from the unconscious man in great, intoxicating sheets as he slumbered on the passenger half of Frank's pink vinyl seat. This wasn't difficult: Frank's truck was disproportionately, monstrously large in every regard, and the front bench seat was as broad and long as a queen-sized mattress. *Frank must perch on the edge of that chair like a fucking vulture when he drives*, thought Skunk, not for the first time. "Upsy daisy," he grunted at the rag-man, and grabbed the unconscious form by one bony ankle, hauling him into the dying light.

The newcomer was a skinny fellow with a head as bald and smooth as a ball bearing and smooth, unblemished skin as black as the Jolly Rancher's oil-dark hair. Skunk didn't find it remarkable that the man had arrived in a state of deep somnolence; the noble folk of Arson tended to arrive with their cerebral eggs well-scrambled, so to speak. The newcomer, Skunk noted, had no eyebrows or eyelashes, nor a hint of stubble on his face. Strange, but nowhere near as strange as some Arsonists (a brief vision of Howling Andy flitted through Skunk's mind, and he shivered).

"Let's get you to the Woodpile," the blond gargoyle told the insensate man. "I think I'll name you on the way there. Then we'll wake you up and get a pint or two of mule vinegar into you. Does that sound good?" The man offered only boneless nonresistance in reply as Skunk draped him over one shoulder and began to descend the truck's rungs.

"Skunk Pussy you fucking bastard!" The shrill

scream split the cooling evening like a scalpel. Such a lamentation could only have one source, and it made Skunk smile. Sure enough, when he stepped off the last rung and landed, barefoot, on the hardpack, Eichmann was waiting for him. The diminutive German had a right to be pretty pissed, Skunk reasoned; the man's furious eyes and pale face had reconstructed themselves completely, but the preceding deconstruction had, no doubt, been quite unpleasant. The only sign that Eichmann skull's had recently been reduced to chunky stew by Skunk's wrath was a wide band of gore soaked into the fabric of his tattered uniform, a patina of his blood which sprawled from neck to waist like a carmine apron.

Arson was a strange place, and it ran like clockwork to the peculiar rules laid down by Dr. Gayle. These weren't rules of the variety the Board cared about; these were the rules of reality. One ironclad commandment may as well have been handed down by stone tablet or hammered into Arson's worthless dirt in yard-high letters: THOU SHALT NOT DIE. This wouldn't have been a warning or an order so much as a reminder, had such signs existed. When one was exiled to Arson, one stayed where one was put. Death was no escape. No matter how often Arsonists died – poisoned by mule vinegar or any of the Jolly Rancher's other lethally potent intoxicants, stabbed or hacked with crude weapons, head smashed in by a stone – they'd wake again within a few hours, whole. Bloody and disheveled, to be sure, but physically restored. The only exception was Howling Andy, but how *he'd* wound up such a mess was a tale in and of itself.

"Hello, Eichmann," Skunk said. He faced his murdered, resurrected friend with the slumbering newcomer slung over one broad, greasy shoulder. "No hard feelings, right? Come on. You didn't even miss anything; Frank's setting up a special surprise for us right here on Ardor Street, and it won't be ready until tomorrow. Come to the Woodpile and help me name this new guy. Vinegar's on Frank." Eichmann tried to keep his frosty stare fixed on Skunk, but eventually he averted his eyes and muttered a resentful concordance. The three of them – Eichmann, Skunk, and the new fellow – left Frank's truck behind them in the eerie glow of late desert twilight and headed for the Woodpile.

Meanwhile, Frank turned his unseen eyes toward the Jolly Rancher. The Rancher's smile stayed oleaginous, but a brittle shine of fear lit the back of his eyes. Frank's regard was never a comfortable experience, no matter how often one trafficked with him. The desert trucker raised one hand with three fingers extended, then folded down one after another, miming a silent countdown. Three, two, one…

CRACK-**BOOOOOOOOM**

The sonic boom rolled through the shimmering air over Arson like the drumbeat of a dawning doom. Arson's crude and scattered habitations trembled. A few of the less well-constructed shanties collapsed outright, including Skunk's improvised lean-to. Skunk would curse mightily about this later, but at that moment, he was too distracted by Frank Blank's unexpected living cargo. The boom, for all its wrath, was no great mystery. It was a sound that everyone in Arson was intimately acquainted with, for good or ill. The Jolly Rancher knew it well. It was the sound of judgment, which meant that it was sometimes the sound of mercy, but more often the sound of cruelty. It was the clarion that signaled the arrival of Arson's tormenting angels. It was the sound of Parole, and the sound of Parole denied.

It was, in short, the sound of a Pocket Protector breaching the Area for Registered Sex Offenders: North. Which meant that the Board – or, more accurately, Dr. Gayle – had come to deliver something. News, most likely. Bad news, likelier still. After all, that was really the only kind of news there was for any of the sons of that benighted place. As though to confirm this, Frank Blank leaned close and clapped one dry, unlined palm down on the Rancher's shoulder. He spoke in a conspiratorial tone: "You're all fucked."

The Rancher nodded sagely, and soon he and Frank fell to murmured conference. After less than five minutes of this hushed counsel, the Jolly Rancher – brewer of potions, possessor of strange passions, and Arson's de facto mayor – jogged off to the hardpacked desert wastes to meet their visitor in person. As the Pocket Protector streaked down the leaden sky from its entry point miles above, it left a trail of burning smoke like the puffy, ill-tempered pucker of a badly healed scar. Frank watched this for a few moments, then turned, hands on hips, and gazed up and down the crumbling length of Ardor Street.

He sauntered to the asphalt's terminus, squatted, and took a pinch of meager, toxic dirt between his thumb and middle finger. Frank sifted it slowly, allowing each jagged grain to slip through his fingers and fall back to the still-warm ground. He lifted the last of it to his nose, inhaled, and contemplated the feel of the place around him for a moment. The ancient flower buds entombed in amber on his hatband muttered to him. They were wise, those venerable travelers from a distant time, and they had seen much. He listened attentively, then frowned agreeably and nodded.

"This will do fine," said Frank Blank. "Yes, I think it

will do just fine."

```
ICON INTERNAL MEMO | INTERSTITIAL
CONTROL 112.01.01
DO NOT REPRODUCE | DO NOT TAPENOTE |
DO NOT KEEP
FROM: Susan Knave MS ICON Junior Engineering
Staff
TO: Arthur Kusunagi PhD ICON Reification
Engine 23 Senior Engineer
```

Senior Technician Kusunagi,

This is my third and final warning on this topic. You can also consider this my resignation, effective immediately. I understand the pressure you're under, Dr. Kusunagi, but this isn't a question of career or reputation. Public safety isn't even at issue; it's much more than that. We can't measure what might be at stake. I mean that in a literal, scientific sense.

From an institutional standpoint, I find what Dr. Gayle is doing to the fabric of the Pockets under their jurisdiction distasteful in the extreme, but those are criminals and a reasonable person might be persuaded to believe in their vision of justice. This isn't about that. It's about the unresolvable mass and energy numbers. I've repeatedly submitted reports indicating that the error outputs in Reification Engine 23 are not random. They're not a result of electric or magnetic fluctuation at the Mount Elbert facility, and they're not coming from the computers. We have an external factor influencing our control of the King's Pockets.

Kusunagi, I cannot convey how much this scares me. You know as well as I do what we're talking about when we say "output errors" and "an external factor." Something outside of the Pockets is getting into them;

maybe more than one something, based on the exotic psychogrammar waveforms we've tracked. We simply don't have strong enough barriers in place around the interstices, and if something can get into them from wherever they're coming from, and we can get in and out of those same interstices from our own macrocosm…

This is too important to leave to you, Kusunagi. I'm going to your supervisor with this, and then I'm going to whomever will listen and help me get the word out. What you're doing here is an unlocked door in the middle of the night, and something is quietly trying the handle.

With regrets,
SK

*From the hand of His Majesty Cleon, Third of His Name, **A DECREE:** Will no one rid me of this turbulent junior engineer? - **HMC VI*** FORWARD Susan Knave TO Jacqueline Ketch-14-3 FOR IMMEDIATE AND SUMMARY EXECUTION

2.
GHOULS AND BEASTS

The first thing Executioner Jacqueline Ketch noticed (and subsequently flagged and notated in her memory tape) was the Interstitial Control facility's abundance of marble. *Unnecessary expense*, she tapenoted, and: *determine value and flag budget item for elimination.* Her combat boots were loud against its polished surface, and that suited her just fine. She found it expedient to announce her approach by whatever means she had at her disposal. That made people afraid, and that suited her even better. Frightened people, she'd found, were rarely clever people. She'd hardly passed five paces into the ICON entrance atrium when she was met by a fierce woman with predatorily patient, owl-like eyes. Her features were severe and brutally beautiful, and she wore her hair shorn tightly against her shapely skull. Ketch noted the woman's presence and her white jumpsuit, its red piping marking her apart as Interstitial Control's Archdirector of Research, one Dr. Kinsey Freund. The Archdirector's welcome was brisk, bordering on brusque: "Royal Executioner Ketch, welcome. I'm Archdirector Freund. Please follow me."

Ketch wore a uniform as well, of course: black combat boots, black gloves, and a black jumpsuit with black piping, in her case, accompanied by a close-fitting black cowl that disguised her entire face save for kohl-rimmed eyes. Besides the kohl, her eyes were unremarkable; placid, unexcitable, and brown. They displayed no special cruelty or taste for blood: they could have been the eyes of any of the King's subjects. But, then, that was the whole point of an Executioner, wasn't it? To be a cipher, blank but for the duty and the Royal will; just as every Executioner took the name Jack or Jacqueline Ketch when they donned the cowl. The identity of the King's Executioner was immaterial compared to the function they embodied. To see the King's Executioner was to see the King's most secret eyes and ears, not to mention a headsman's axe held by the King's hand. Ketch was nothing more and nothing less.

Archdirector Freund, by contrast, was every inch the individualist. Her face, though untroubled by cosmetics, bore two small tattoos beneath her left eye (a red, bloody tear and a tiny blue crown – quite patriotic). Her hungry, haughty features were arranged in a cold mask of superiority and self-assurance. Her hair, though close-shorn, was a dandelion blonde and her delicate ears bore two tiny diamond studs in each lobe. *Professional*, was Ketch's rapid assessment, *and proud*. That notation went into her tapenote log, as well.

Freund offered a chilly smile. "I'm afraid we haven't really set things up for, um…"

"A layperson?" Ketch replied. "That's fine. I wasn't expecting-"

"Neither were we," the Archdirector interrupted frostily. "We could have set up one of the student interfaces for you, you know. It would have done some of the translation. We've found out over many, *many* years that the processes and data are too complicated to be understood on a mathematical level."

That was interesting. "I tend not to trust that which is not quantifiable, doctor. It's why-"

"Oh," interjected Dr. Freund, "it's all perfectly quantifiable. It's all perfectly mathematical, too; the neural maps and relational territories have been pinned down precisely. It's just too much for humans to process on a *purely* mathematical level. That's why we employ symbol-systems."

"Yes. Why you and your sibling developed… I beg your pardon; I specialized in political ideoplasty in my own schooling. You developed what, again?" This mild lie was the Executioner's attempt to lure Dr. Freund from her doubtlessly well-rehearsed and puerile patter.

"We developed chromatic-geometric psychogrammar. CGP." The pride in Freund's voice was crisp and dry, a flat declaration of a generational achievement. *No braggart*, Ketch tapenoted.

"Right." Though Ketch's smile was hidden by the cowl, the tight fabric moved enough to convey the general idea of good humor to Dr. Freund. "In the overview course I had, we called it-"

"Let me guess." Freund sounded weary now, not proud. "They probably called it 'color class' or 'color crap,' depending on how crass your instructors let things get."

"What's your first name, Archdirector Freund?" asked Executioner Ketch with an abruptness that was decidedly *not* friendly. Any trace of smiling friendliness had vanished. Her mild brown eyes may as well have been painted on for all the emotional insight they offered.

This sudden change in the Royal Executioner's affect

caused Dr. Freund to pause for the first time in their brief acquaintance. She hesitated, then replied; "It's Kinsey."

"Archdirector Kinsey Freund, you have interrupted every sentence I have uttered since I entered this facility." *That* brought a twitch of nervousness to Dr. Freund's proud, tattoo-embellished eyes. It wasn't fear, but it was a start. Ketch went on, her tone as shorn of rancor as it was of mercy. "This is His Majesty's facility, Archdirector, not yours. You think it your sole province; yours and your sibling's. It is not. I am unaccustomed to announcing my visits, Archdirector, and I understand your displeasure at my unexpected arrival. But I am ill-disposed toward the ill-mannered."

"Your pardon, Royal Executioner." Dr. Freund bent a knee briefly, bowed her head, then met the Executioner's eyes again.

Ketch nodded, mollified for the moment. "Where is the other Dr. Freund?"

"They prefer 'Dr. Gayle.'" A pause. "I try not to take it personally. They're preparing your transport to the King's Pockets right now. In fact, while they do, now might be an opportune moment for you to observe my work, as you requested? I'm ready for you."

Straightforward, Ketch tapenoted. "Of course!" the Executioner replied brightly. Then, a moment's hesitation. "Ah. Dr. Freund, it's been a long time since my course in CGP. Is there any chance you have-"

This time Ketch allowed the doctor's interruption to pass unremarked. "Certainly. We've faced this type of situation before." A pause. "Although not with the King's Executioner, obviously." This was followed by a nervous laugh. *Better*, thought Ketch, though she didn't bother to tapenote the observation. *Closer to fear.*

Archdirector Freund led Ketch past a security

checkpoint populated by unmoving guards whose features were obscured by helmets with reflective faceplates. The pair continued on through a long, tall, narrow hallway. More marble. Who had authorized these siblings – admittedly geniuses – to adorn their facility in marble like an ancient temple? *Create file KETCH TR-41*, the Executioner thought, tapenoting the marble and flagging the file *AUDIT*.

Partway down the hall Freund ducked into a subordinate's office and plucked something from a crowded shelf. It was a slick, softcover book, which she handed to Ketch. The tome was thin, more study guide than textbook. Its cover was a pleasant and unthreatening amalgam of vague pastel polygons, with **CHROMATIC-GEOMETRIC PSYCHOGRAMMAR: A REFRESHER AND LEXICON** stamped in businesslike white text.

Ketch began rapidly leafing through the section marked **BASIC VOCABULARY** as the Archdirector silently and swiftly led the way with quick, economical, and echoing steps. At the hallway's terminus, a brushed steel door waited for them. Freund pressed her talcum-pale palm to the security door's metal surface. It opened smoothly, emitting a weak draft of chilled air that smelled like new electronics and old blood.

Beyond the security door, the hallway maintained its height but spread itself wide enough for four to walk abreast. *No more marble*, tapenoted a pleased Ketch, and deleted the *AUDIT* file. A lavish lobby which presented the most highly prized jewel in the King's scientific crown to the uninitiated with such splendor was no waste of funds; far from it. This secure area's contents were the stuff of legends, superstitious dread, scientific curiosity, and skepticism in equal measures, but despite that, the functional corridor Ketch now saw was remarkably unremarkable.

Grey tile floor, impeccably clean. Doors to the left and the right, about a dozen of them. The doors themselves were nondescript but, Ketch noted, even more heavily reinforced than the security door which guarded the corridor. Given the lengths one had to go to in order to even learn of Interstitial Control's existence, let alone *find* ICON's physical location, some may have considered this level of security overkill. Ketch was not among them. *Initial assessment: secure,* she tapenoted.

Dr. Freund stopped before a doorway; indistinguishable from its kindred to the Executioner's eye. "Even in the stone age of the psychosciences," the Archdirector explained, opening the door with a thick, peculiar keycard, "researchers noted that paraphilias are rarely isolated. Where you find one, you find clusters. Like grapes, if you like."

"I don't," Ketch replied, and her candor drew a slight smile from Freund. "But do go on."

"Quite." Archdirector Freund led the Executioner into a broad, bowl-shaped room. The space consisted of a cool, dim dome, softly lit by glowing, golden ripples from some unidentifiable source. The effect was like candlelight in a basilica. On the chamber's spotless floor, bundles of neatly tied and color-coded cables and wires ran from banks of quietened machinery down to the bowl's rim and converging at its base. The cords were like an orderly, synthetic nest of serpents, thought Ketch. Every surface in the room was sterile steel and antiseptic circuitry, framed by matte cream ceramic. Executioner Ketch's nondescript eyes traced the cables' paths down to the lowest point in the chamber, deep in the center of the bowl.

A man's head, visible from neck to crown, was the

centerpiece of this arrangement. There, immobilized and bound beneath the room by wires, monitors, and restraints up to his neck, was Subject SOPS-E305. He'd had a name, once. Then again, he'd also once had eyelids and the topmost portion of his skull. As Ketch watched with unashamed fascination, a tiny, clicking, arachnoid mechanism clambered gently over Dr. Freund's grisly trophy, misting exposed brain and peeled eyeballs alike with some doubtlessly antiseptic mist.

Archdirector Freund waived Ketch toward a plush seat placed before an interface that looked deceptively simple at first glance. The console consisted of light- and shape-projecting holographic lenses and a pair of slim, slick haptic gloves. Ketch sat down, but continued to page through the manual like a student cramming desperately before an exam. *Appearances*, she thought with a chilly inner smile that did not touch her eyes or hidden face, *are deception's best friend.*

For all her innate brilliance, Dr. Kinsey Freund was bound by the restrictions which accompanied the privileges of rank. For example, ICON's ranking personnel were barred from receiving all cerebral enhancements, be they pedestrian or the more advanced, experimental models hinted at by whispered rumors. It was part of the honor and curse that was her calling, and Dr. Freund accepted that tradeoff with grace. His Majesty the King couldn't have his top technologists and theoreticians hacking at and cramming circuitry into the meat of their oh-so-valuable minds, after all. Accidents and side effects related to such augmentations were, while rare, always a possibility. The Freunds' experiments in cerebral modification excluded self-enhancement and were confined to tinkering with a wide variety of test subjects.

Executioner Ketch, by contrast, had no such bars on biotechnological enhancements, and now took full advantage of her mind's suite of interpretive and analytical routines. Moments later, Ketch was rapidly digesting every morsel of the textbook's psychogrammar. She was glad she had. Psychogrammar had become much more advanced in the decades since she'd dabbled with it in her Royal schooling.

"SOPS-E305 has a cluster of paraphilias we often see together," Archdirector Freund said in a naturally warm, detached, and professorial tone. She took a place behind the broad master interface control that jutted out over the room's bowl-like declivity; a vision of a watchtower coupled with an orchestra conductor's stand. "Splanchnophilia, or sexual arousal by viscera. Hematolagnia, or sexual arousal by blood. Necrophilia, or-"

"*That* one I know," said Ketch.

"Quite," said Freund crisply. "Usually, people with this cluster of paraphilias are also classified as sexual sadists. They're torturers, or rapists. *Beasts*, in short. SOPS-E305, however, is missing the sexual sadism component of the paraphilia cluster. That leads to a different set of Undesirable Social Effects; USEs that are less destructive to human life but pose an extreme danger to moralpol. E305 is a *ghoul*, not a *beast*."

"Aren't ghouls just a type of beast?" asked Ketch, watching Freund's face for microexpressions with her own visage concealed by her tight cowl. Her anodyne brown eyes were shallow, lifeless pools. *Second Degree Seditious Compassion?* the Executioner tapenoted, careful to double-note the question mark. Such things were to be watched for, but it rarely did anyone any good to jump at shadows.

Kinsey Freund didn't deign to respond. Instead, she began gently turning a large, intricate, multi-layered dial. "I'm bringing E305 up to consciousness. Not *all* the way up, mind you, but some degree of higher processing is necessary for this exercise." As the dial gave off a slow, steady series of clicks, the composition of the light that spanned the chamber's dome-like roof shifted from a dull, muted gold to a lovely sunrise sorbet of slowly dawning yellows and rose-tinting reds. Ketch glanced back up at the dome when she realized that its surface was directly in the fixed, unblinking eyeline of the man grafted into the devices in the room.

The Archdirector trilled a bright "Good morning!" It was seven in the evening.

"*Good*. Morning!" came an inhuman voice. Had Executioner Ketch not been a person who had, earlier that very day, poured a crucible of molten lead into the ears of a wretch who'd overheard (but failed to report) sedition against His Majesty, her skin may have crawled. As it was, she watched with interest and craned her black-cowled head forward for a better look.

SOPS-E305's face was clearly visible, at least to any visitors (like Ketch) in attendance on the observation tier overlooking his interment. This was thanks to a magnifying mirror placed before him and directed upward. It was fixed in place, and so was he. E305's body was invisible below the level of his chin, which jutted out of a low, pyramidal platform on the floor, the neck of which was amply padded. Ketch knew that, below that, an oddly-shaped metal sarcophagus held the rest of the man's frame nutritionally fed, benumbed, and tightly bound. Ketch had no idea (or interest in) what sort of abbreviations and modifications had been made to whatever was left of the man inside his metal tank. She had a vague memory of hearing that it was more of the subject's body than you might suspect, given that their minds were the subjects of study, but that was only the case if you were relatively ignorant of the components involved in that slipperiest of ontological fish: thought. Prisoners at ICON were confined with certain glands and vessels and responsive organs intact in some cases, for example. Ketch considered that downright humane, when you thought about it. It wasn't as though ICON subjects were some ghastly curiosity like severed heads in jars, for goodness' sake.

This prisoner had a strange, ruddy complexion, no doubt a side effect of the influx of psychopharmaceuticals used to bring him out of his inactive daze. E305's exposed brain was coated in a thin layer of shimmering jelly, into which sterile cables and disinfected cords plunged like hungry worms. The hair on his doughy face had been permanently removed, just as the briefing said: eyebrows included. The subject's teeth were an incongruous, sparkling white, and his eyes were like kites with popped strings sailing joyously through an eternal windstorm of induced and inborn madness. The mist sprayed by his scuttling arachnoid companion lent him a permanent and subtle seep of tears which gently trickled down his cheeks in twin gleaming trails.

"E305, I'd like to introduce you to someone," said Dr. Freund. "This is Executioner Ketch." Her honeyed voice was like a Youth Battalion Mother's comfort offered to a homesick child away at the barracks for the first time. It made Ketch's teeth clench behind her cowl. She removed the question mark from her previous tapenote about criminal empathy.

"*Ah!* Ah. Hello. Executioner. *Is-today-to-be-the-day-then?*" This last, jangling handful of words came out in a manic rush, a marked contrast to the lurching cadence of his previous locution. It took Ketch a moment to process exactly what the peeled man had said. When she did, she smiled.

"No, E305. Luckily for you, it is not."

"Luckily!" The peeled man's lidless eyes rolled wildly. His laugh was like the sound of a blood-sick raccoon choking on a chicken bone. They'd had those, where Ketch grew up. Raccoons, that was. It hadn't been the animals' fault that they often went rabid. That didn't mean they didn't need to be put down. Compassionately, if possible.

"You are guilty of a Sexual Offense, Political or Social," the Executioner said, softly but firmly. "You exist solely at His Majesty's pleasure, and for the moment, his pleasure is that you continue to contribute to Archdirector Freund's important work. So that there won't be any *more* of you, E305. And won't that be a better world for *everyone*?"

"I. Suppose. So."

Ketch realized that she had adopted nearly the same Battalion Mother tone that the Archdirector had. It was something about the prisoner's wired-up, misfiring brain, she supposed; it was enough to elicit a healthy level of sympathy from anyone with proper moralpol. That sympathy applied to E305 as he currently existed, at any rate. Whomever you were before you landed at Mount Elbert, that person was, well, *shriven* was the word that ICON used. Ketch added the emphatic question mark back to her earlier tapenote, ruminated for a moment, then deleted the tapenote entirely. "No more talking," she said quietly to Freund. "I'd like to see the show, please."

"Yes, Executioner."

Ketch and Dr. Freund both slipped on the mesh haptic gloves attached to their respective consoles. The material was cool and weirdly devoid of texture, until they came online with a palpable series of throbs, flicks, and sandpaper pulses. The lens system in each console flickered briefly, flashing the display arc with a rainbow of mellow pastels and sharp, pickled neon shades. The colors faded to a dull, milky glow like foggy moonlight. The lemony sunrise of the dome slowly faded to a creamy, neutral off-white, as though it had suddenly become polished marble. Ketch felt the adjustment in her gloves as a series of smoothing strokes, as though she were sliding her palms along a freshly laundered sheet to flatten it out.

"We'll stick to a simple demonstration," Archdirector Freund said, her gloved fingertips dancing in the air as she typed a series of commands on an invisible keyboard. Overhead, the muted, marbled white began to stir with color. "One of the associative networks we've almost completely mapped is the stilpophilic nexus."

"Layperson," Ketch chided her gently.

"Your pardon, Executioner. The word is derived from Greek and denotes a fixation on glossy or shiny surfaces. It's the associative network that links attractions to viscera, polyvinyl chloride fetishism, and the like. Due to the common use of fabrics with a silk or satin texture in the manufacture of women's undergarments, an entire branch of stilpophilic fixations have emerged as USEs." The sequence tapped into the Archdirector's aetheric keyboard began its transmutation of the dome above E305's unblinking captive gaze. Through the haptic gloves, Ketch felt the ripple-click of the program unfolding like a mechanical cat with a centipede's worth of clockwork joints beneath its silky fur. As Dr. Freund's chromatic psychogrammar program loaded, a series of sinuous shapes and obscene colors began to flow across the dome overhead, writhing and folding in upon themselves in a vermiform aurora.

"Ah. *Ahhhhhhh….*" E305's jaw went slack and drool flowed freely down his chin. On the dome a glistening nest of colors and textures squirmed seductively like bright, shiny, plastic-wrapped, and living guts. Ketch watched the prisoner's face in the magnifying mirror with mild, brown-eyed interest. She could feel the shapes with the help of the haptic gloves; a deeply unpleasant and repellently sensual roil of slick, hot surfaces. *Fascinating*, she thought. For the benefit of the record, she also thought (and tapenoted) *validity of methodology confirmed, high commendations for scientific daring above and beyond standard progress.* That notation would have pleased Dr. Freund, had she known about it. It all but guaranteed ICON a substantial budget increase, should the rest of the visit proceed apace.

The console before the Executioner came to life with a muted, electronic murmur, and a protean, holographic mass began to take shape before her eyes. The computer models were processing E305's active brain response in real time, with the infernally complicated mathematics of neural network interactions rendered legible as shapes and colors. The psychogrammar Ketch had rapidly absorbed before the demonstration flicker-flashed through her mind, accessed by her cognitive implants, and she could suddenly read E305's mental state in the ripple of smooth or jagged shapes and strange, rotten colors swirling before her. *Fascinating*, she thought again. The psychogrammar developed at ICON had put paid to (or provided proof for) theories in the psychosciences which had been hotly debated for more than a century. This display demonstrated one such proof: namely, that splanchnophilia was a symptom of an Undesirable Social Effect-related nexus.

The sort of gruesome display now tantalizing E305; the specific colors, shapes, and textures of viscera, activated a disgust reaction in ordinary, virtuous subjects. Such revulsion was a gift from the untold eons of evolutionary branching which had, in their blind, ghastly grasping, birthed humanity. However, the stilpophilic nexus in the pertinent portions of *E305's* brain reversed this revulsion. The swarming geometry of sickly colors that danced on the dome (and slithered through Ketch's fingers) would induce a spectrum of spiked shapes and fearful colors on the console readout in an average adult human. The rotten-fruit ripple on the console before her was a clear demonstration of a USE Nexus in action. "And what," Ketch asked, "have you learned from the paraphilias E305 *doesn't* have?"

"*Ahhhhh…*" sighed the peeled man.

His exhalation had a disconcertingly sensual tone that bordered on the obscene. Archdirector Freund noted this with a wrinkle of her eyes that made her tattoos jump, and began to turn the display back down with another series of resonant clicks. E305's eyes lost focus as the soporifics in his blood chemistry were increased and the swarming, squirming display faded to the same mellow sunset glow which had greeted Ketch on her arrival. The quietening of SOPS-E305 did not take long; as Dr. Freund resubmerged the subject in his silent anesthetic stupor, Ketch peeled off the haptic gloves with a sensation of palpable distaste, as though some noisome fluid had seeped into them.

While she did this, Freund spared a glance and noted –

just as she'd suspected – that Executioner Ketch had worn her black gloves beneath the haptic gauntlets. Freund wondered for half a moment if this was a function of the Executioner's psychology or her royal office (or if, indeed, there was a difference). Then she, too, stripped off the tactile feedback gloves and led the way back out of the cool quiet of the observation chamber.

"My sibling should be ready for you now," the Archdirector said over her shoulder, her shoe heels' tapping tarantella on the grey tile quieter than it had been on the marble in the lobby. Dr. Freund led Ketch through a mazy span of nondescript corridors and to a final, dead-end hallway. The door at the terminus of the hallway was unlike its brethren. A blazing band of angry red lights abutted its perimeter; a clear enough warning that even Interstitial Control's cellarful of secrets had its own subcellar. Supplementing this chromatic warning were stenciled signs shrieking alarums about security clearance and exotic radiation, not to mention the toxicity of many of the Reification Engine's components. As the doorframe's spectral, electric red saturated the clinical white of her uniform, Dr. Freund stopped before the door and placed her palm flat against its surface. Ketch expected a theatrical rumbling of bolts, and perhaps even a theatrical curtain of thick white vapor. Instead, the door responded to the Archdirector's palmprint by swinging open, slowly but with silent ease.

"Through there, Executioner," said Dr. Freund. "Hard to miss my sibling; there's only one way in or out, so they can't exactly escape you."

"You're not coming?"

Kinsey Freund chose her words with exquisite care. "While my working relationship with my sibling is both professional and highly productive, our mutual understanding is that we work best at a remove."

This wasn't worth tapenoting; the Freunds' peccadillos were better known to greater numbers than the content of their research. Dr. Freund and Dr. Gayle's fallings-out were so operatic that they had, at one point, led to Dr. Gayle's change of surname. All of this had been exhaustively reported by loose-lipped former technicians who could understand most of the pyrotechnic disagreements but almost none of the science or, indeed, the projects' goals.

"Understood," Executioner Ketch said, and stepped over the infernal, glowing threshold of ICON's sanctum. *No*, she corrected herself, *not a sanctum. A mysterium. A mysterium mysteriorium*. In these halls nothing was hallowed, but many mysteries were kept.

The red-lit threshold opened onto a featureless grey hallway of brushed steel. It was short, as hallways go, and at its other end an identical door opened before Ketch like a courtier bowing before the King. The space on the other side was nowhere near as large as the enclosure which held SOPS-E305, but Executioner Ketch knew enough of Dr. G. Ruzicka Freund's work at ICON to know that such confinement was, to them, largely illusory. If Dr. Kinsey Freund harnessed her genius to plumb the depth of His Majesty's subjects, Dr. Gayle used theirs to redefine what space and distance meant – if anything at all. The concrete and ceramic box that made up Dr. Gayle's experimental space, for example, used most of its already-confined space to cram enormous cable bundles cheek-by-jowl with murmuring transformers, along with banks of interfaces and attendant monitors.

"Executioner Jacqueline Ketch 14-3." A flat, tenor voice echoed in the confines of the concrete box, unlovely and titanically indifferent. "I'm Dr. Gayle."

Dr. Gayle was a difficult person to read. Though technically Kinsey Freund's twin, Dr. Gayle looked older by untold years and weathered by travails unnumbered. Their face had deep creases that were absent on their sister's, and though their eyes were unseen behind tiny, socket-cupping goggles with small, smoked-glass lenses, the dark beads of their gaze radiated a great sense of depletion that had its own peculiar gravity and gravitas; not unlike a matched pair of black holes, Ketch supposed. Like their sister, Dr. Gayle wore the white uniform of an ICON Administrator with its red trim, though on their sister it looked somehow clinical, while on Dr. Gayle the same garb seemed as utilitarian as a mechanic's jumpsuit. Ketch tapenoted the appellation *Dr. Gayle*, confirmed a file regarding the working relationship between the Freunds, and nodded with a spoonful of respect.

"Well, Executioner." Their voice was flat as hammered tin. "Come on."

They turned to show Ketch the way. Dr. Gayle's laboratory was as cluttered as Archdirector Freund's laboratory had been sparse. Despite the clutter, Gayle's space was sterile in its own way. True, the air within that concrete box possessed a stuffy and acrid quality, as though the oxygen were static-laden wool. Despite that, the smell of sterilizing fluid was strong, the power junctions and thick cables spotless, and no speck of dust was evident. *Facility maintenance upkeep verified* Ketch tapenoted.

"If you're making notes on that roll of mnemonic tape in your skull," Dr. Gayle said, glancing back over their shoulder in a way that was eerily reminiscent of their twin, "I wouldn't do it in the King's Pockets. Any notes you made before or make after our visit should be fine, but the properties of my research preclude the use of any recording media, including artificial mnemonics."

That was an unexpected and unwelcome twist. "Why? I wasn't notified."

Dr. Gayle paused, searching for words. "Electronic media within the Pockets have been… unreliable of late. We've experienced anomalous flux in our reification. Nothing to worry about. We're in the process of isolating the malfunction in Reification Engine 23, and should have it fixed in short order."

Executioner Ketch nodded. Her mild brown gaze met the twin black holes of Gayle begoggled regard, and without breaking stride as they descended a short stairway, Ketch drew a small, leatherbound notebook and a stub of pencil from one pocket. Like the entirety of her regalia, the notebook's cover was jet black, as was the graphite stub she nimbly flipped into her black-gloved fingers. She jotted down her appraisal and added a note about recording equipment in ICON's mysterium.

Dr. Gayle's lab was significantly more compact than Dr. Freund's, Ketch noted. Whereas Freund's seemed to take up an entire stadium's worth of scattered laboratories and linked banks of computers, Gayle's mysterium appeared to be comprised of one sparse rectangular chamber. Metal scaffolds scampered up each side, occasionally bridging the entire laboratory's width. Equipment ranged from humming generators and dense cable bundles to stacked machinery that was incomprehensible to Ketch. All of this surrounded a strange, bulbous metal structure.

The Executioner had read the few details available about the process she and Dr. Gayle were about to embark on and thus possessed a vague understanding of the process percolating in the great, gleaming gargoyle which they now approached. Per the scanty files, the better part of the preceding day had been spent culturing a complex pseudorganic sheath inside that metal mold. Nestled in the center of this mass, the transportation capsule she and Dr. Gayle were to use on their field trip waited for them. The rearmost portion of the transit pod ended in a tether. The massive length of tether slept in its own housing in a separate section of the complex set aside for miles of carefully coiled cord.

Both capsule and cable were forged from the same physics-defying alloy, and both were as close to unbreakable as the sorceries of modern science would allow. Nonetheless, the sheath was vital to the violent process of entering one of the King's Pockets. This was for the sake of capsule passengers and Pocket-dwellers alike; the transit pods came in hot and they came in fast. This led to the adoption of the first-colloquial, then-semiofficial term "Pocket Protector" to describe the whole assembly. It was widely known that inasmuch as Dr. Gayle displayed strong feelings on any subject, they *hated* the term.

By all appearances, Dr. Gayle and Executioner Ketch had the echoing rectangle to themselves. The evidence of Gayle's subordinates' efforts were scattered everywhere. Broad tables covered in schematics bristled with half-finished devices and, curiously, a scattering of old-style analog pocket watches. Strangest of all was a disassembled marionette, its glass eyes pried out of its pale ceramic face. The puppet didn't mind, to judge by its unmoving smile. Before the Executioner could interrogate these oddities, the pair had swept past them and were closing on the metal mold. It towered overhead, a repellently asymmetric idol to the godly power of human invention.

The doctor led the King's murderous factotum through a cramped metal hallway terminating in an open cabin door, a thick, sealed thing like that of a passenger jet. Ketch still remembered passenger jets, back in the muted distance of her childhood. "Get in," said Dr. Gayle in their flavorless way. The words were neither question nor command, exactly. After Ketch stepped aboard, the goggled Gayle got in and closed the hatch behind them. It sealed with a meaty *CH-LUNK*.

The Executioner hid her surprise at how comfortable the conveyance was. Not in a plush way that she might have jotted down in blurry pencil; this wasn't luxury, just a simple matter of clean, inoffensive fabrics, muted tones, soft carpet, ergonomic niceties, and reasonable accommodations. Things like drinking water and a discrete toilet suite, neither of which would be available where they were headed. *Mercy and cruelty are strangest and most savage when they become two sides of the same ribbon*, Ketch jotted down in a mode more contemplative than official.

The understated reassurance of the cabin was nice, but it couldn't hide the essential strangeness of the transportation pod. After a moment's consideration, the Executioner determined it was at least in part the smell that attended the capsule's innards; a cooked, simmering smell of smoking metal and atmospheric combustion. Ketch knew there were aspects of interstitial travel that were still poorly understood, and had no doubt that some form of truly horrific and as yet undiscovered energy hung attendant around the capsule like the malefic aura of uranium. This didn't worry her overmuch. People in her line of work weren't known for long, peaceful lives.

There were no steering mechanisms in the transport capsule, seeing as it had no more need to steer itself than did a yo-yo. Dr. Gayle hunched in their seat opposite Ketch, beaten fingers crossed over bony knees. They seemed engaged in a silent, heroic effort to dredge up the lost habit of small talk. Ketch did not take pity on Gayle, and watched their discomfort with mild amusement.

"Not much of a view," the technician finally managed. It was true: the thick, shatterproof windows that surrounded them were doubly obscured; first by the thick pseudorganic gel, and then completely by the tight-fitting metal mold.

"I suppose not," Ketch replied, pleasantly enough.

"That's just until we Intersect, you understand."

"I do not, actually," said Ketch, pouncing on the opening like a hungry cat. "I have next to no idea how any of this works, Dr. Gayle."

"Well." They shifted uncomfortably. "King's prerogative, red files, you understand."

Ketch nodded placidly. Her expression was invisible behind her black Executioner's cowl.

"The Intersect will shunt us directly into one of our more interesting Pockets. We'll be visiting the Area for Registered Sex Offenders: North," Gayle said. "It's primarily nonviolent offenders from the Political and Social subset."

"Primarily?"

Dr. Gayle offered Ketch a strange, puckered smile. It pushed at the edge of their lips and exposed just the barest tips of their front teeth like a litter of pearls in a quivering red mollusk. "There are some ongoing experiments that I'm very excited for you to see. For *anyone* to see, let alone *you*, Executioner Ketch."

"Experiments." Ketch didn't care for this sudden spurt of enthusiasm. It was like watching an electrical current temporarily reanimate a dead frog's legs.

"You have a reputation for thoroughness, 14-3," said Dr. Gayle. "I have no doubt you studied my curriculum vitae. There's an addendum to that CV that few know of, however. Did you know, Executioner, that I'm a licensed Moral Philosopher?"

Ketch silently and glumly contemplated the fact that the day likely held more murder. Dr. Gayle kept up their display of ghastly, pearly teeth. The capsule began to shiver, then tremble violently; then the violence stilled. There was a sensation like a blade slipping into fruit, and the entire universe vanished around them.

```
ICON INTERNAL MEMO | INTERSTITIAL
CONTROL 112.08.01
DO NOT REPRODUCE | DO NOT TAPENOTE |
DO NOT KEEP
FROM: Kinsey Freund MD PhD PsyD ICON
Archdirector
TO: Dr. Kerik Goetz  Jur. Dr. Habil. King's
Prosecutor East
```

Honorable Justice Goetz,

Executioner Jacqueline Ketch 14-3 just paid me a visit. She is a quite insufferable person. As is to be expected of one in her line of work, I suppose. I wanted to let you know as soon as I could type this up securely. As legal liaison and Juridical Philosopher for the Nullity Project, you understand better than anyone in this Kingdom that we're balanced on a knife's edge right now. Literally and figuratively.

The good news is that Ketch 14-3 left with a favorable view of my side of things here on top of Mount Elbert. I showed her our Potemkin patient (SOPS-E305), and she ate it up. Ketch doesn't even suspect the existence of the Pit, as far as I can tell. I was surprised she didn't insist on seeing one of our Criminal Violence offenders. A stroke of luck, that. She seemed much more concerned with Ruzika's freak show. I'm not surprised that Gayle's grottos are getting the spotlight. One would have to be some sort of Axis II aberration not to see the sheer utility of Ruzi's project. I just hope Ketch gets a good look at *everything* the illustrious Dr. Gayle has been up to down… in.. *out* there, or however the hell you want to think of it. I suppose that's as good a word as any for it, incidentally; Dr. G. Ruzicka Freund's hell. Well, it seems they have a Dante now. A Dante in a black mask who scared the absolute *piss* out of me.

Now look. I wish I were writing just to tell you that Abyssus was in the clear, but we have a problem. A significant problem, actually. One of the Mysteries, a Morrison Spare, is alive. I know that's quite impossible, but it's also quite true. And it gets worse. I need you to put your hounds on this as quickly and viciously as possible and find him for me, no matter where he goes to ground or who is helping him. It's not important that I get him back alive, but listen to me carefully, Honorable Justice. I require that Morrison Spare's head be returned to me intact. Be as vigorous as you like in apprehending him below the neck; the recovery of his head – his *intact* head, sir – is a must.

To sweeten the deal, you can expect a delivery of our latest developments by this afternoon in the standard manner. These should render quite unpleasant interrogations – or whatever application you see fit to put them to – without the inconvenience of bruises, let alone more photogenic and propaganda-supporting disfigurement. Have *fun* with them, Honorable Justice Goetz. I don't think I need to give you any advice on how the phobia technology is applied, do I?

Your steadfast friend,
KF

FW: ROYAL POLICE FORWARD COMMANDER FRANZ ZIMBARDO

Let's see how tough those black-flag-waving antiroyalist cockroaches are now. Start with the anarchists.

3.
A DEATH OF JR

In his most discordant, jingle-jangle fits of mirth, the Jolly Rancher would sometimes refer to himself as "Arson's leading citizen." His companions never understood why this phrase tickled him so. At the Woodpile, his giggles only drew confused glances. After all, who among them did not rely on the Rancher in one way or another? His reeking chemical fields, the mule vinegar, the strange relationship he enjoyed with the blumpkins and the way those unusual creatures had let him semi-domesticate them in their burrows; as far as anyone else in Arson was concerned, the Jolly Rancher *was* their leading citizen. JR himself would have found it difficult to articulate in concrete terms why that sobriquet seemed such an ill fit, or why it amused him in such a bitter, biting way that the other penitents trapped in Arson's cesspool seemed to look to him for leadership.

The silly geese of Arson were one thing. It was another thing entirely in JR's book to be trusted by Frank Blank. A terrible calling like the Rancher's ambassadorship to the pilot of the pussy-pink truck sometimes felt like a death sentence more than an honor. A death sentence, he thought, and cold hate filled his belly like the memory of water. As though such a thing were possible without the Board granting you Parole. He dearly wished for a way around that bureaucratic purgatory, yes sirree. More than dearly wished. They'd tried their damnedest, he and Howling Andy, and with no results. Or rather, as Andy's condition after their experiments demonstrated, no *good* results.

He caught himself mid-rumination and tried on a smile. Whenever this bleak humor took him, the Jolly Rancher smiled. The smile had nothing to do with how he felt, for his thoughts were ever a tarry tangle of ink and razor wire, but the smile could always rise from the mess like a dead fish on a poisoned lake. By eliciting this whimsical thought, the smile reified itself. If there was one thing the Rancher knew and loved, it was poison.

The Pocket Protector fell through twilight like some celestial being cast down for pride, magnificence manifest in brightest form during its infernal fall. The transit pod itself wasn't magnificent; as always, *that* conveyance struck JR as unnecessarily fast and bulbous. However, its thick coat of gelatin was colorfully aflame from the stresses of punching a hole through the fabric of everything and into a discrete pocket of something-other-than-everything. It burned like a brand in the burgeoning darkness.

Some distance up (it could have been thousands of feet or a few miles; JR had no idea) was a hole in Arson. It looked a bit like a crack, he supposed, but a crack with more angles and dimensions than it ought to have. It had depth, width, breadth, and something else that felt hard to see; like looking at two contradictory things at once. The lines of this fresh breach in the stuff of philosophy were brilliant, lovely things that shone like coruscating, pregnant rainbows.

Of course, it wasn't a hole into Arson, the miserable collection of shanties and feral folk that called itself a town. It was a hole into ARSO:N, the tiny reality inhabited by the Jolly Rancher and his ilk. JR didn't know how he knew this much. Hell, he didn't know why anyone remembered what they did. Some people remembered a bit while others remembered next to nothing, dropped into Arson like they'd been flushed out of a cosmic refuse chute. Which was not far from the truth. The sole common factor among the diverse populace of Arson was that none of them had kept their names, their past lives beyond a few shreds, or, most importantly, remembered what they'd done to merit their exile to this place.

Trailing behind the polychromatic fireball was a shining line of jet black. At this distance, the cord was thin as a spider's thread against the evening sky, but visible in whipping whorls wherever the setting sun's blood-light hit it just so. The Rancher increased his pace to a hearty jog as slabs of burning, iridescent gel peeled off the capsule. JR knew the gel would burn up as it descended, and fall as an imperceptible sifting of harmless, organic dust, but his irresistible impulse as the Board rained down burning sulfur was always a primitive urge to flee that he transmuted into his shit-eating grin and his hearty, "HOWDY!" jog. He didn't even know if they could see him from inside of that technicolor meteor. *Whatever I did*, the Jolly Rancher thought furiously, *and whoever I was, I don't deserve this shit*. He had to resign himself to the fact that the Board, whoever they were above and beyond Dr. Gayle, would never know what sort of courage it took to run *toward* that weird, wiggle-in-place hole in the sky instead of *away* from it.

JR, despite his eloquent overtures of friendship, took

a dim view of Skunk Pussy's inner life (not to mention the ungodly reek that had led to the man's obscene sobriquet). Had he known of Skunk's stray thought about his hair being slicked back with motor oil, the Jolly Rancher would have felt no flush of shame, but he would have been a little irked that half-cracked Skunk had hit the proverbial nail on the slick, black head. The oil felt like a second scalp by now. Thanks to its anointing touch, every strand of JR's coiffe stayed in place as he took in the sight of the pod entering the final few hundred feet of its descent, and thereby buffeting him with a bellows-breath of hearth-hot wind. By now the cable had kicked in with a gentle extension that slowed the capsule's descent and the sheath had sloughed and burned off like a vast skin shed by a fiery serpent god. The pod descended the last threescore feet at a pace so slow it became regal. The Rancher slowed his high-spirited jog to a more dignified trot, and still made it to the landing site before the smoking capsule touched the dry, dead dirt of Arson.

The Jolly Rancher was a proud man, in his own way, but practicality was his chief virtue. That's what made him – *no laughing that jingle-jangle laugh in front of the visitors, now,* he reminded himself – Arson's leading citizen. Thus, he greeted his visitors on his knees, with his head bowed. He didn't know why they were here, but he didn't doubt that it was to say or do something horrible. *You're all fucked*, Frank Blank had told him, and he'd nodded. Sure, they were fucked. How could you get *more* fucked than they were? Food, water, medicine, decent shelter, the ability to die endowed by Mother Nature – they'd been fucked out of just about everything. Now, however, Frank's words began to sink in through a different membrane, and they metabolized a different understanding. *How* can *we get more fucked than we are?* JR wondered, and this time the question was speculative, not rhetorical.

The Jolly Rancher fixed his friendliest smile in place, knelt, and prepared to learn the answer from the emissaries of a world which had cast him out. The capsule rested on a patch of black-scorched dirt, and with his eyes down JR watched the diverse colors of the transport pod's dissipating exotic energies. He couldn't remember how many times he'd done this over the years, nor how long he'd dwelt in this place of sideways time. Nobody did. Soon enough, the door to the pod opened with a *CHUNK* that spoke of serious seals in a serious bulkhead, and two figures stepped out.

One of them, he recognized: Dr. Gayle, the haggard absentee warden of this uncanny penal colony. Gayle looked like they always did, in JR's estimation: like a snowman missing their carrot nose and coal-cobbled smile. A white, hunched uniform crowned by a snow-pale face with two smoked-glass goggle-lenses for eyes. "Well, *gosh darn!*" the Jolly Rancher exclaimed. "Dr. Gayle, I presume?" It was the same joke he made every time; a calculated dimwit's idea of good humor. JR bugled a good-natured dipshit laugh and turned to the other, unfamiliar figure.

JR beheld a woman. He remembered "woman," but only dimly, and experienced a flash of curiosity as to why that was. She stared at him with bored eyes, taller than him by half a head and built like an athlete. She was dressed in all-concealing black that fitted her closely from her masked black cowl to her black gloves and combat boots. "And *my goodness!*" JR continued, pausing to try on a grin that showed his teeth like a jeweler flashing a padded tray of precious stones. "*Who* have we *here?*"

"SOCV-B1, chosen name 'the Jolly Rancher,' or 'JR.' I am His Majesty's Executioner Jacqueline Ketch," she said. Her voice was devoid of passion or even the barest hint of madness. This immediately put the Rancher on high alert. In his experience, few were more dangerous than the fully sane.

"It's a pleasure to meet you, ma'am," he replied. His charm began to recede like a tide. JR began to suspect that Parole was about to be granted to some applicant. He wondered who would disappear forever this time around, and why Dr. Gayle had felt the need to drag a Royal Executioner to Arson to collect her prize.

"You will address me as 'Executioner,' B1. Do you know why I'm here?"

"I reckon I do, Executioner."

Ketch continued to eye him, then did something curious. She reached into a pocket, withdrew a tiny notepad and stub of pencil, and made a note. Then she slid it back, and asked "And why am I here? The way you 'reckon,' that is."

The Rancher laughed. It was a tired laugh, but genuine: a worn-out, battered bank note of a laugh. "There's only one reason an Executioner goes *anywhere*, isn't there?"

She smiled behind the tight cowl. He could see it in the way the fabric moved and tightened. "You reckon correctly, B1."

"Who do I need to fetch?"

"You don't need to fetch anyone, B1. You're right here."

It pierced his numb shell more quickly than Ketch would have suspected. "Now wait a goddamned *minute*. You just *wait*."

"Do you remember what you did to end up here, B1?" Ketch's question was bereft of affect and enunciated quietly, but her words ripped the guts out of JR's outraged alarm like a cougar's claws.

"You don't," continued Ketch, and her voice was softer still. "None of you do. It's part of what they do at ICON. You surrender everything, even the memory of your crime. You come here with what we give you, nothing else. So, you don't remember. It's all right to feel frightened, B1. You have to have wondered. Everyone does. What did you *do* that was so awful someone would put you in a place like *this*?" Ketch paused, and her stare – though steady – had no more depth than a muddy streamlet near a river's reedy banks. "Would you like to know, B1?"

The Rancher's mouth felt very dry. "No," he admitted.

Ketch nodded. "A coward. I understand. Area for Registered Sex Offenders: North, subject SOPS-B1, I am executing the sentence suspended at His Majesty's pleasure, as that pleasure has been formally withdrawn. Prepare to meet death."

He almost felt like laughing. Nearby, Dr. Gayle looked on through their small smoked-glass lenses and said nothing. Their lined and glacial face displayed a species of sad resignation.

Ketch sighed; with the formula completed, her formality relaxed a bit. "Do you know how this works? Got anything to hand?"

"I… What?" JR wondered briefly if he'd been wrong about her sanity.

"I'm the King's Executioner. His hands. I don't carry a weapon; it is forbidden. The world is my weapon. As a courtesy, I'll ask again, slowly. Do you have any weapons to hand that might make this quick for you? I know you're quite restricted on materials here, but I'm sure you've all managed to improvise weapons in one way or another, right? Do you have a blade? A bludgeon?"

The Jolly Rancher shook his head numbly. Strictly speaking, this wasn't true, but he didn't feel like he could speak, had he wished to.

"Very well."

The Executioner was on JR before he could begin to process what was happening to him, let alone plan or react. Her gloved hands were around his smooth throat in moments. He collapsed to the ground and the wind rushed out of him as she straddled his hips, locking his legs with hers and leaning inside the flailing reach of his arms to wrap her hands around his throat with a terrible and inhumanly strong implacability. They weren't gentle, those hands. Ketch locked her thumbs over the Jolly Rancher's trachea and crushed it as she steadily increased the pressure. It was as agonizing as a glass snifter giving way inside his throat. He felt something softer inside his neck burst. Then there was a resonant *KRAKK,* and-

Frank Black's human cargo, Morrison Spare, woke from dreamless sleep and vomited profusely before his eyes had even fluttered open. His entire body felt like a pile of tainted cat food save for his head, which thudded and thundered like a caldera moments from exploding. A piteous moan attempted to slither free from the pit of his gut, but it emerged from Spare's dry lips as a rattling exhalation. Against his better judgment, he opened his eyes.

It was as though opening the barbican of his eyelids allowed his other senses entry as well. He tried to focus, tried to orient himself. Wherever he was, it was dark; save for an uncertain, sputtering light that revealed to

Spare a shanty roof of barely-cohesive scrap. The air was so foul that Spare would have vomited immediately if he hadn't already paid homage at that bilious altar. The space swam in an overpowering reek of unwashed flesh, mingled with an eye-watering chemical tang that coiled, cold and oily, on his tongue. He heard a sound both strange and vaguely familiar. It came from just beneath and to one side of his aching head, the same vicinity in which he'd vomited. Carefully, as though his brain were a beaker of nitroglycerine, Spare turned and looked down.

Three men were eagerly lapping up his vomit. Their hair was long and unkempt, greasy grey-black mops distinguished vaguely by minor differences in length and texture. They seemed as desperate for liquid as for solids, and were tonguing every drop of juice and gobbet of half-digested scrap that had been in Spare's stomach when they'd… he'd…

He turned his head the other way, away from the hellish wretches at their grim repast, and vomited again.

"*Manna from heaven!*" someone screamed. It was the voice of a television puppet from a children's show filmed inside the mind of a depraved creature, perhaps a cannibal with a taste for human veal. "*'And it did not stink; neither was there worm therein!'*" The second half of the first syllable in "therein" unknit the rest of the word in a ragged "*Heh! Heh! Heh!*" The ratcheting report was more mechanical misfire than laugh. Morrison Spare had no wish to see the face to whom this awful, creaking voice belonged. He could hardly ignore the interlocutor, either. He raised his head (a motion which birthed a cobweb of sick pain in his skull) and tried to focus on the speaker with his dry and aching eyes. Even as he did this, he could hear others shuffling forward on the dirty floorboards to batten at the fresh bounty Morrison had gifted them from the granary of his guts.

Spare had regained consciousness in what appeared to be a bar. His body was laid out lengthwise on a splintery picnic table whose bench seats had been pushed against the ramshackle walls. 'Hovel' seemed too grand a word. The place was little more than a pile of loose boards and tin held together with wire and the occasional nail, propped against the ruins of a trailer that should have long ago been condemned (or simply burned). *Where*, he tried and failed to say. He licked his lips, swallowed with a sandy throat, and hauled himself shakily upright. Then he tried again. "Where am I?"

The voice's owner leaned crazily against a broad bar, on top of which were several cracked and jagged jars of an oily, thin black substance. He had neatly cropped silver hair which fringed a bald, dust-dappled pate. He was pale and anoxic-looking. Alongside his thin and lanky frame, everything about him communicated a discomfiting level of torqued-up nervous energy. His pupils were dilated and antic, darting in his bulging eyes like blowflies jostling for a prime spot atop a spill of something vile. He was clad in a ragged, paper-thin prison uniform, discolored to a more or less consistent grey, save for a pastiche of greasy stains around the armpits and around the neck. Glancing down at his prone frame, Spare realized that he was clad in an identical garment, albeit one that was sparkling new compared to the puppet-voice man's. The fabric was slick and unpleasant against Spare's skin.

"Let me explain some things," the manic man said. He scrambled from the bar toward Morrison on stiff, unsteady legs, bearing two cracked jars of the black liquid. It looked like a condiment. Soy sauce, perhaps, or balsamic vinegar. Spare felt the urge to back away from the man, but his body was weak, aching, and nonresponsive, and the man was on him in a trice. Fortunately, all he wanted was to lean in close and bathe Spare in his unspeakable breath as he rambled in a rattling, uneven, and unceasing stream.

"Name's Funny, Uncle Funny, and *you'll* need a name, too. None of us know our names, see, just like *you* don't know *yours*, right? And lots of other stuff, too, right? Missing brain compartments. Luggage got jostled. Happens on your way into Arson, and that's where you are, Arson, if you don't remember that either, some people don't. You'll need to get settled, but don't worry, Uncle Funny will help you and also the Jolly Rancher will, and I think you've met Skunk Pussy, he's a hard-assed bastard but he won't steer you wrong so let's just get you a name and…"

Uncle Funny, which was a strangely appropriate name for the fellow, broke off in mid-tirade and stared down at the two jars in his hands in horror. "*Oh! Oh!* But how could I? You've been through hell just now, what with the transfer, right? Did they work you over on the way here because I've heard they did that to me and I know they do it to some of the others but, hey, listen to me go on. I'm talking problems and world wars and famines and I've got the solution right here, friend, I've got the remedy, so just drink up and then we can get you a name." Following this flurry of incomprehensible verbiage, Funny thrust the less-cracked of the two jars into Morrison Spare's hand so insistently that Spare promptly took it from him just to shut him up. Funny lifted his glass and drained it as Spare inspected his.

It was some sort of intoxicant, that much was evident. Spare raised it to his nose to give it an experimental whiff. He wondered if he could link it to one of the great liquor dynasties: the Rum family or House Whisky, perhaps, even if the contraband product was a branch of such a family fallen on comprehensively hard times. It was *not* alcohol. Spare recoiled from the jar's contents like he'd inhaled hydrogen sulfide. His eyes bled burning tears. His nose went strangely numb and streamed mucus as freely as drool from a slackened jaw. Spare turned his head and coughed hard enough to see stars.

All of this struck Uncle Funny as deliciously amusing, and he cackled as Spare wondered for a moment of wavering consciousness if he were about to die. Then, once he had a grip on himself, Spare realized something. His silver-haired, non-vomit-lapping companion had quaffed his measure as if it were as anodyne as milk. "What the hell *is* that shit?" gasped Spare.

"That, my bee-*yoo*-tee-ful young man, is mule vinegar. The fabled drink of fallen kings and dead souls."

Spare hesitated. He didn't *feel* dead. He felt like shit, and he had the distinct impression that being dead meant you didn't feel much of anything. "I'm... *not* dead," he stated. Funny, living up to his name, cackled yet again. "No, my friend. In fact, that option has been taken off of the table. You are now a proud citizen of the Kingdom's Area for Registered Sex Offenders: North, and here you shall stay until someone somewhere decides otherwise."

"Area for..." Spare's mind reeled. He could remember *everything*, no matter what this strange man with his too-loquacious, too-performative nature might say. He could remember his schooling, then his apprenticeship at the ICON laboratory; the experiments, the incredible *progress*, and then the King's fatal decision. The black-clad tide of death. Redemption at the eyeless hands of his new guardian. Had Frank Blank abandoned him here?

"Look," said Uncle Funny in an unexpectedly

reasonable, I-really-must-insist voice, "just drink this, okay? It will straighten you out. Help you roll with the proverbial punches."

In the end, it was all too much. The bestial men with their grey mops of hair slurping at the remains of his last meal (a seafood chowder, he remembered, and his stomach barrel-rolled again); the fetid, stifling air inside the Woodpile; Uncle Funny and his torqued-up, zigging blowfly eyes; whatever the last straw was, Morrison Spare succumbed and took his first slug of mule vinegar. Instantly, he regretted his rash decision. His muscles locked and cramped, his blood burned, and he was wracked by a trembling, petit mal seizure that lasted for almost half a minute. However, once his muscles relaxed again, once the mule started kicking, Spare was introduced to one of Arson's great, secret joys.

The mule bit deep that night.

It was decidedly *not* liquor, or anything *like* liquor, that much was certain. It had an amphetamine buzz as it kicked in, and shadows at the edges of Spare's vision began to twist and crawl in a hallucinatory tango as an added bonus. He lost touch with his distant hands and misfiring legs. He found himself laughing, overcome by the desire for someone to hit him in the face as hard as possible. Despite this, Spare also felt pleasantly, ecstatically numb. Uncle Funny's chattering mouth kept saying that he'd give Spare a new name, since everyone in Arson had an Arson name, and didn't it only seem right that Spare adopt one himself in the interests of parity? Spare was uninterested in this line of reasoning and gave the matter of a new name short shrift.

Or he did, until the ugliest man Morrison had ever seen in his life entered the Woodpile, made a beeline for Uncle Funny, and clouted him across one side of the head so hard that the mule vinegar jar Funny had been about to slurp from broke over his cheek and lips, shredding both. Uncle Funny went down wordlessly and, wisely, stayed down. The brute's fist looked as big as a small pumpkin to Morrison. The ugly man – a blonde troll with a squashed face, cornflower blue eyes, and an unimaginably vile stench attendant to his soiled rags – stared down at the writhing form of Uncle Funny, then looked up at Spare, who recoiled from the stare.

"You're Morrison Spare," he said in a belligerent, bully-brawler's cocksure baritone. "That's your name. My name is Skunk Pussy. You can call me Skunk if you want to." He paused, as though waiting for a thank-you for this tremendous largesse, then continued without rancor. "Frank wants to see you, so you're coming with me now."

Frank, Spare thought, *Frank is here*. He seized on that thought like a well-anchored root on a steep and crumbling slope. He was eager to accompany the reeking man, but Skunk grabbed him by one arm anyway and hauled him toward the Woodpile's dark doorway with a grip like the clamped jaws of a prehistoric reptile. Skunk hauled hard, and Spare had to step lively to avoid trampling the vomit-slurping derelicts still battening on his regurgitated crab marrow and cream sauce. Stepping lively turned out to be both more and less difficult now that he'd ingested Uncle Funny's libation: his gait was animated by an abundant, herky-jerky energy, but he had trouble directing his strutting legs precisely where they ought to go. Skunk made up for this by steering him, and before long, Spare was gulping the cold, clean, dry night air of Arson.

The night was dark. Every night was dark in Arson; a pure, stifling darkness unleavened by celestial ornamentation. Arson's ebon sky was ever unpolluted by the light of moon or stars. Despite this handicap, Frank's truck wasn't hard to spot. Skunk led Spare past the three- or four-story machine, so vast it made a mockery of practicality. Then, without preamble, he stood before Frank Blank and his confusion and uncertainty no longer mattered. Frank spoke, and he spoke for both of them. Morrison Spare listened, and marveled at the things he heard. Most marvelous of all, Frank showed him; what he'd built on Ardor Street while the mule vinegar had bit and the cannibal puppet-man had laughed. The beauty of what Frank had brought to Arson and the special role Spare was to play in it… it took his breath away.

Hours after nightfall, a hunched and bestial figure sallied forth from a dugout in the hardpacked waste. He crept atop a low rise overlooking Ardor Street and, beyond, the scattering of Arson's shanties. The beast mewled in its solitude, a cry for succor in the sandy night. It mourned, it raged, and most of all, it begged for death. These jagged shards of whimpered woe became a bright bouquet that left his split, stitched lips at last. The sound became a chilling and unearthly howl.

Howling Andy had the black fire in him that night. He howled, and howled, and howled.

Inside the knockdown pile of sun-bleached boards and aged tin that was the Woodpile, drinks were served and drained. Worthless but highly animated soliloquies ensued, and conversations ranged both far and wide in their abundant incoherencies. Men came, men left. Men began to lose their grip on the reins of consciousness and slumped on picnic benches or half-broken chairs. They lolled, and snored, and seized up dying where they lay.

Dawn broke over the horizon like a rotten, bloody

yolk.

Dawn broke over the horizon like a rotten, bloody yolk.

The Jolly Rancher's stiff, cold body lay where Executioner Ketch had left it overnight. The Executioner and Dr. Gayle were seated on camp chairs near the transport pod's hatch, sipping instant coffee. Their plastic mugs smoked faintly in the crisp desert morning air. Ketch's tepid brown eyes were turned to the sky, where the breach in everything was lit by sunrise. The transport pod was tied to it by its long retrieval cable, and the interstitial rift shimmered with unearthly colors along its many shifting angles. It was not, Ketch reflected, as though they'd broken through a pane of glass. The rifts from Arson's violation spread in three (or more) dimensions, and each facet seemed to have sub-facets set at complex angles. A metaphor for their nest of brilliant, questionable activities? Out came Ketch's notebook and black stub of pencil as she scribbled that alongside other observations. While the thought of metaphors was not a technical notation, it might add color to her final report when she submitted it to His Majesty on her return.

As though triggered by Ketch's fleeting thought of "return," a ragged gasp broke from the Jolly Rancher's gaping mouth. His body trembled violently. Ketch was fascinated, and stepped closer to her victim to observe Dr. Gayle's regenerative subroutine in action. The Executioner heard a series of subtle clicks and crunches as the ruptured tissues of the Rancher's neck bound themselves back together and undid the damage she'd so expertly wrought. She still held the notepad in one hand

and the pencil (now little more than a nub) in the other, and scratched notes furiously as JR choked, coughed, spasmed, and, at last, sat up.

His eyes were bloodshot and bleary. To the Executioner's fascination, even the vivid, hand-shaped bruises on his throat faded before her eyes like smudges washed from a tablecloth. The Jolly Rancher made a deeply unpleasant noise in his reconfigured throat and spat a wad of something black and glistening onto the hardpacked dirt.

"You must be a gosh-darned *fool*," said the Rancher in a grating voice. When he spoke again, its timbre had already smoothed itself, and he was back to his slick, friendly self. "You should have hauled me out of Arson first, if you wanted me to stay dead."

"Oh, I know," said Ketch, pocketing her notebook and what was left of the pencil. She extended one gloved hand. The Jolly Rancher stared at it unbelievingly, then took it and allowed the Executioner to help him to his feet. "I am not a fool," she went on, "but I *am* a skeptic, you might say. I believe that verifying a phenomenon firsthand is important." JR's oily hair was still spiked in strangulation tangles, and he looked crazed as he regarded Ketch. However, he was the mayor of Arson (*and* its leading citizen) for good reason. After a beat, he nodded and began to comb his hair back into place with his fingers.

"Heck," he said affably, "I don't suppose that means I've served my sentence?"

That drew a laugh from Ketch and, more notably, from the dead-faced Dr. Gayle. JR joined them; it felt good to have a giggle, and he'd had no illusions on that subject, anyway. A memory wandered through the Rancher's mind as he chortled: Frank Blank, gnomic desert trucker, murmuring *you're all fucked*. That, and the new fish arriving in Frank's custody rather than with the impassive Dr. Gayle. When the prisoner and his jailors finished their laugh, the Rancher asked the most important question with practiced nonchalance.

"So… New residents? Supplies?"

This time it was Dr. Gayle who responded. "Our parameters for the Area for Registered Sex Offenders: North have changed, B1. From here on out, you'll be on your own. But we'll be watching."

"…'on our own?'" the Rancher repeated. He didn't quite comprehend what that meant, but already the visitors from a better world were folding their chairs and returning to the transport pod. Ketch turned to face him, her placid brown eyes the only human facet of a featureless black uniform.

"That's correct, B1," she said. She closed the pod door with a hefty *CH-LUNK*. As JR tried to assimilate these words and their implications, the transport pod rose silently from the barren soil, its retrieval mechanism activated. The hole in everything slurped up the gleaming black line eagerly, and their ascent gained speed. It was a process much less spectacular than entry, but still one that monopolized the Rancher's attention every time. Hell, according to the woman who'd just murdered him, it was going to be the *last* time.

Up and up the pod sailed, ascending on its line to rejoin the universe denied the Arsonists. When it reached the hole in everything, it should have vanished like a blown-out candle flame. Instead, as the JR watched, something went profoundly wrong. The multifaceted cracks in the sky burned bright as the sun for an instant, causing JR to flinch and shield his eyes. Moments later, a thunderclap blew outward from the flash. When his whitewashed eyes could see again, the Jolly Rancher let out a low, appreciative whistle. The residents of Arson might be fucked, but evidently so were Executioner Ketch and Dr. Gayle.

Judging by the explosion which hung in the bright morning sky like a squid made of smoke and flame, that was.

C01.23 | THE MORAL FOUNDATIONS OF OUR KINGDOM

Our Kingdom is a good Kingdom. What do you think about when you think about our good Kingdom? Or when you think about His Majesty the King? We all know what *good* people think, because we are *all* good people. We feel safe. We feel loved. We are like children, well cared for by a wise and noble father. This is why we have no crime, no immorality, and no unhappiness. It is why our Kingdom is a good Kingdom.

Do you ever have thoughts you shouldn't have? Yes, you do; we know you do. We all fail our King. But we try, don't we? To be obedient. To love our Kingdom, and our King. We fail but we try again and we never, ever complain, because what is a complaint? A thought you shouldn't have. And we try to be obedient. To love our Kingdom and our King. It is why our Kingdom is a good Kingdom.

Good people listen when the Kingdom tells them to do the right thing. When your Youth Battalion Mother or your Youth Battalion Father tells you what to do, it is the right thing. When they are told what to do by the Senior Group Leader, it is the right thing. And so on, all the way up to His Majesty, the King. We are all part of a great project, the project of perfecting our people and our Kingdom. We do the right thing; we do what we're told. It is why our Kingdom is a good Kingdom.

And what do we do when we see someone causing

problems? Do we hit and hurt and hate them? Of course not. Do we let them continue to cause problems and lead others astray? Of course not. We tell our Youth Battalion Mother. We tell our Youth Battalion Father. We help that person, because if they are causing problems, they are not happy. And if they aren't happy in our Kingdom, why, the King can pick them up – just like that! – and put them in his Pocket with other people like them, where they can all stay. And then we can all be happy. It is why our Kingdom is a good Kingdom.

We are good people. We are safe. We are loved. It is why our Kingdom is a good Kingdom.

PSYCHOGRAMMR MATRIX|MODULE.2c.3
For use with chromatic-geometric
psychogrammar subprogram C01.23. During
subject's timed reading period, monitor for
radiance spikes of <45° in RGB 238,75,43 and flag
for immediate interstitial transfer to child custody in
ARCO-PS:E

4.
WELCOME TO THE OPEN O RANCH

Archdirector Kinsey Freund reclined in a sterile laboratory chair in her private quarters, gazing at the glowing ceiling as an aide tattooed her face. The aide's name was Robert Flanagan, and he had lovely green eyes and a smooth, shapely, hairless skull. She was unsure whether the heat she felt was entirely the needle or, in part, also the warmth of his thin-gloved hand. She hoped so. She studied Flanagan as he worked with care to add a second, blood-red teardrop next to its extant twin beneath Freund's eye. While she did not have many *visible* tattoos, her red-trimmed jumpsuit's surgical white concealed more than most would suspect. Her eye did not so much as twitch as the aide plunged the buzzing needle into the sensitive flesh less than an inch below her eyeball. Freund was not perturbed. In fact, she found the physical sensation a welcome aid to her silent contemplation.

Judging by the output from the transfer capsule's cameras, Freund's sabotage had worked as well as she could have reasonably hoped. This wasn't the first time Freund had killed in cold blood; the blood drop being stitched into her face was, after all, her second. However, this marked the first time she'd drawn blood from family, let alone her twin. She was fascinated, in a strictly clinical, psychoscientific sense, at how little she felt at perpetrating the betrayal, and what that said about her own mind's peculiar axes in relation to the Kingdom's dictated moralpol. The first time Freund had slain a human, it had been to snuff a rival to the ascendancy of the Freunds. That struck her as moral, a necessary sacrifice of private moral standing for the public good. She was more qualified for the position her rival had been granted, and the incompetent man's regrettable (and, for all anyone else knew, accidental) demise had ensured a brighter future for the ICON program. The ICON program which, after all, her and her sibling's research had helped forge.

For a time, it had all gone splendidly. The fall from grace had been born of Gayle's terrible mistake: they assumed their sister would forever leave them to their own devices. The Archdirector didn't work that way, and had routinely monitored Gayle's project notes. Freund had a ringside seat to the battle between Gayle's prodigious genius and their essential degeneracy; a condition not uncommon in those trained as Moral Philosophers. Freund had documented Gayle's decline exhaustively in CGP workups and documented radiance spikes.

What had pushed her twin over the edge was no mystery to Kinsey Freund. Thanks to ICON's secrecy and autonomy, and thanks to their further isolation in the King's Pockets, Gayle became the administrator of, essentially, an officially sanctioned realm of eternal punishment. Then, Ketch. Executioner Jacqueline Ketch, with her mellow, murderous eyes and black cowl – and that fool, that *megalomaniac* Gayle had thought they'd, what, explain the anomalies in ARSO:N to Ketch? Show her a blumpkin?

The aide finished the tattoo with the snap of its electric motor's cessation, then held up a small mirror so Freund could inspect his handiwork. Freund nodded, and the aide bowed and vanished. She watched him go and savored a brief, itchy throb of desire, and made a mental note to invite him back to her chambers after he'd performed his duties for the day. For seventeen seconds, Freund stared up at the viewscreen ceiling, which displayed a personalized reel of chromatic-geometric stimuli; a vision not unlike a vast field of gold and crimson sunflowers rippling in a mild breeze.

She had to think this over carefully, and measure all her options. Freund was under no illusions that her problems with Gayle or Ketch had been solved by the transportation pod's "mishap." For one thing, there was the absurd regenerative algorithm which Gayle had cast over the ARSO:N interstice like a malign conjurer's necromantic curse. Without another pod insertion, Gayle and Ketch were trapped in deathless perpetuity. And therein lay Freund's biggest problem, she mused. There were many of His Majesty's officers whom Archdirector Freund wouldn't have hesitated to drop into Gayle's cosmic crypt before she bricked it up forever; that was just the way the great game of the court was played. The Royal Executioner was not one of those officers, however. An explanation more plausible than a "malfunction" was required to explain the disappearance of Jacqueline Ketch.

Dr. Freund's most private laboratory was secluded past a labyrinthine set of hallways and offices, deliberately designed to bewilder and mislead. Freund – who had designed the layout of the entire facility herself – knew shortcuts and secrets that no other soul in the Kingdom did. It didn't take her long to work her way, unseen, from her private rooms to a simple, brushed steel door, one of many lining a particular corridor of test subjects. Freund was not superstitious by nature, but she was not an especially didactic materialist, either. Working with the human mind, and then with the cosmic anarchy her sibling had unlocked, she listened to her instincts intently, though she liked to think she tempered them with reason. The subject behind the door before her, VSOSeSa-A01, was not "evil" in the sense that he was gifted with preternatural powers or inhabited by some malefic, disembodied entity. He was certainly *not* capable of chilling the air that hovered just before the door to his cell, Freund reminded herself, despite the evidence of her frigid fingers.

The Archdirector took a deep breath, dabbed at the ointment-coated tattoo that branded her a siblicide, and opened the chamber that held the man who was her guide, the Virgil to her Dante, and the best material resource yet recovered by ICON related to the Pit.

Thunderous enough to topple shanties and dislodge loose boards, the explosion which greeted the unlovely dawn following Frank Blank's arrival would have shattered Arson's windows, had the settlement had any glass to shatter. It *was* loud enough to make the windshield of Frank's pink truck shiver; though it, like everything that composed the sum total Frank Blank phenomenon, was built from substances more esoteric and invulnerable than appearances implied.

Four figures stood on Ardor Street. Three of them

– Morrison Spare, Skunk Pussy, and Uncle Funny – started at the sound and craned their necks to gawk at the explosion hanging in the clear morning sky. The fourth was Frank, and he did not deign to look. Frank's hat brim was, as always, drawn low to conceal his hypothetical eyes. "Skunk," he said placidly, "go check that out." Skunk woke from his hypnotic fascination with the spreading stain of flaming smoke, nodded his matted blonde head, and trotted off to investigate.

It was a morning of wonders. The populace of Arson, wrenched by the concussion from deathlike sleep or sleeplike death, either fell back into their stupors or wandered out into the rutted path to gaze up at the blast and its attendant meteoric shower of burning debris. After Skunk left to check on the explosion and the fate of the Jolly Rancher, the trio of Frank Blank, Morrison Spare, and Uncle Funny were the only souls neither slipping back into unconsciousness nor rapturously taking in the sight of what, by all appearances, was a fuckup of literally cosmic proportions. Instead, Frank's little group stood on Ardor Street and leaned against the back bumper of Frank's truck.

"Back bumper" was, Spare observed, a bit of a misnomer. The misbegotten monstrosity that Frank Blank drove – what Frank often called his "pussy-pink truck" – was three times the size of the biggest semitruck Morrison had ever seen. In the process of unloading his unusual cargo, Frank had unfolded the machine's titanic back gate. The interior of the truck's voluminous trailer was shrouded from the general public by a heavy black curtain. Frank hadn't told Spare or Funny what was in the trailer, if anything, and they didn't think to ask. They were too wonderstruck by what Frank had constructed as the night swept over Arson in its yawning, terrible freedom.

Ardor Street, previously an empty stretch of crumbling blacktop, now sported a neat line of eight varicolored structures. Frank referred to them as "sheds." In the darkness just before the dawn, while something nearby howled, Frank had spoken to Spare regarding what the desert trucker had constructed with such astonishing alacrity. He'd answered some of Spare's questions and explained a few things, too. About how people *actually* wound up in places like Arson, for example. About what places like Arson *really* were, and what the ICON laboratory was *really* dedicated to, and why Frank had been forced to bring the Mystery named Spare to such a place. When Frank talked with his unseen eyes and narcotic charisma fixed on Morrison, Spare lost track of velvet words and dust-dry desert sense. What stayed with him was the simple knowledge that he was here to help Frank help the people of Arson, and that was good enough for him. After what the King had done to the other Mysteries, that was *more* than good enough.

Uncle Funny was the first. This was in part because he, unlike the lightweights crashed out at the Woodpile, was still riding the mule when dawn oozed over the wasteland. He happened to shamble-strut past Frank's new installation, and took note. "Ex-*qui*-site!" he screamed, and "*Frank!* Frank the man of mystery and magazines!" (*Magazines?* Morrison wondered.) Funny let his botfly eyes crawl over the sheds. They were identical in all details but color. In order from the shack nearest Frank's truck to the one furthest from it, they were black, red, orange, yellow, green, blue, indigo, and violet. His garrulous theatricality slipped for a moment, and Uncle Funny staggered closer to inspect the sheds one by one. In his mule-bitten state, he had to inspect them carefully with one eyeball at a time, as the two were having a hard time coordinating their enthusiastic efforts.

In front of the indigo shack, Funny lost his steam. He stared at its unprepossessing door and its plain handle, painted the same vivid indigo hue as the rest of the structure. It possessed a few windows with tightly-drawn indigo shades which masked the shack's interior. The shacks possessed a presence in their neat line there on Ardor Street, an aura mixing menace and mystery, gift and challenge. Frank Blank stood impassively and let Uncle Funny feel the charge in the air; the strange, pregnant electric potential, vital enough that it seemed to lend a certain lively sparkle to the dead, denuded soil around each shack.

"What." Uncle Funny's tone was declarative, but Frank Blank understood his query well enough.

"There's a hole in the bottom of the sea," Frank said. His voice was grave, though undershot with wry amusement, and as dry as the ring of bleached bones that surrounded Arson's far perimeter.

Uncle Funny took a hesitant step toward the indigo-hued shack. He still couldn't make out a damn thing beyond the opaque drapes. He touched the painted doorknob with one questing finger, and gasped as a thrill of electric pleasure rippled up the length of his scrawny arm in a delicious, short-lived flutter, a ribbon blown through Funny's nervous system by a strange, sensual wind.

"Careful now," murmured Morrison Spare. Uncle Funny whirled to face him with a sneering snarl upon his lips, but the sight of Frank's new visitor stopped him cold. When he'd first glimpsed the newcomer, laid out and unconscious in the Woodpile on a splintery tabletop, the new fellow seemed ordinary enough. Molasses skin, smooth and as-yet-untouched by Arson's unforgiving sun and wind. Fresh new uniform (which Skunk, at Frank's direction, stopped the other inmates from poaching for patches). Spare woke as all transported convicts did; sick near to death. The one strange detail had been his lack of hair. Not so much as one solitary follicle dared to raise its stubbly head from the man's flesh: not even an eyebrow or an eyelash. Uncle Funny now thought he had the answer to at least one mystery about the stranger.

Morrison Spare gazed at Funny through dreamy, unfocused eyes as an indigo halo wove itself around his head in an unwavering crown of light. Though bright enough to draw a pained wince from Funny, the halo's light, he noticed, cast no shadows.

"He's right," said Frank. The sound of Frank's gentle rasp startled Funny. Somehow, he'd forgotten Frank was there; the desert trucker tended to blend into the wasteland like a chameleon when he so desired. "There's a *lot* packed into that little place," Frank continued, and gazed with unseen eyes around the broad, desolate scrapscape of Arson as though to make a point. "There's a lot in that shack because it holds everything they took from you. Memories. Certain passions and predilections. All the dark and dirty treasure that your King and your King's servants say does not exist."

Uncle Funny listened to this speech with a slowly climbing sense of vague and impotent outrage. "What the hell are you *talking* about, Frank?"

It was Spare who answered. His voice was a milder, dreamy drone than Frank's smooth, stony timbre. "Frank and I want to give you back the parts of you the Board took away. We're going to sort out everyone in Arson.

The Board has always just been Dr. Gayle, and they've decided to exceed their remit. We're here to offer, well, not balance. More like the resolution of a paradox." Uncle Funny looked at Morrison like the smooth-headed man had just released a mouthful of pebbles from his open lips. Ignoring the new fish, Funny directed his question at Frank Blank. "So, the shack. It's full of, for instance, photos? Old records? Things meant to jog my memory? That's not going to do the pro-*ver*-bi-al trick, Frank. It's all been erased. It's not waiting in a pretty *shed* for me." He voiced a despairing puppet giggle, then said, "I know that's not the way it works, Frank, and that means you *def*-initely know that's not the way it works."

"Hoboken," said Morrison Spare.

The word hit Uncle Funny like a gunshot. He flinched so hard it practically bent him in half, and a haunting school of jellyfish memories, only half-seen and half-solid, flitted through his mind and then were gone. "*Jesus*," he gasped.

"It's time for you to take leave of Arson," Spare continued in his whetstone-whisper sleepwalker's voice. "But only for a moment; if that's what you want." The indigo halo burned, its light intense and diffuse like a fire in a fog bank. "But you've got to accept it. Frank isn't in the same business that the Board and the Kingdom are. Neither am I. We don't do *shriven*, for one thing. Do you want to know, Uncle Funny? To have it back?"

The man with the neat, balding grey pate and lean face contemplated his situation miserably for a few moments. His nod of concordance was firm and certain. "It's not *Parole*," he sneered, "right?"

"Oh no," said Frank. His voice almost concealed the smile hiding inside of it. "*Far* from it. Parole means they haul your ass back up the cosmic pipe to Dr. Gayle's lab, where they'd give you to their sister. And then, after a bit, you'd wind up dead. Paroled. But you knew that; just like you know that what we're at here isn't death, and isn't any game of Dr. Gayle's."

Uncle Funny liked the sound of that. "Let's be at it then, shall we?"

Spare extended one hand, forefinger-first, and laid it against the locked doorknob. With his other hand, he grasped Funny's wrist. For the lean, mule-bitten man, the instant that followed was one of terror and displacement. The unmoving, hardpacked dirt beneath them did not visibly shift, but gravity's grip became abruptly slippery, like the whole damned continent from horizon to horizon had tipped to the east or west a few degrees in some titanic rebalancing. From below the indigo shack – *miles* below, from the sound of it – came a tremendous, clattering cacophony. Richly layered sounds of opening. Funny heard a vast unclasping of doors, drawers, cupboards, nightstands, and who knew what else. It sounded like an entire mansion's worth of spaces, from tiny to titanic. Then, as the surrounding atmosphere subtly downshifted to the baseline strangeness deeply woven into Arson, the indigo shed's doorknob clicked, and its bright, painted door swung slowly open.

Uncle Funny stepped over the threshold without hesitation and, on his first step, he vanished.

I should have stopped to find some fucking boots, Skunk groused to himself as he sprinted unshod up a gentle slope of scree and to the place where the Jolly Rancher always met the mysterious Board representative. Skunk's bare feet were, honestly, as callused and thick as the soles of any Board-issued footwear. Hundreds (maybe thousands?) of feet above, the crystalline cracks in everything continued their slow healing, sealing reversal. It was like watching ice crack, only reversed and slowed to a crawl. Skunk remembered *ice*.

He crested the low hill and spotted the Rancher, who stood staring off in the direction that the flame-swathed debris from the explosion's fallout was beginning to rain down. He seemed relaxed and in good humor, good old JR. Skunk had just started to let his guard down when he was rocked by a shift in gravity and equilibrium, a wave of disorientation which flowed over him like an unexpected tide. The wrenching change was powerful enough to send Skunk stumbling to his knees, but he recovered quickly. Glancing up, he saw JR stumble uncertainly as well, so at least he knew it wasn't something messing with just him. *Whatever the fuck* that *was*, he thought with practiced practicality, *we'll deal with it eventually. One flaming bag of shit at a time, I always say.* He reached the Jolly Rancher, where he staggered to a halt. He'd run hard, and with his hands braced on his knees he heaved great, loathsome breaths as a simmered stench rose from his body. At last, he raised his squashed face with its belligerent blue eyes to regard JR. Skunk's blonde brow and tense lips were both creased in distressed confusion.

"JR," Skunk asked between panting breaths. "What… the *fuck… happened*?"

The Rancher scuffed a toe against the dirt and measured Skunk with his oil-black eyes. "*Well* sir," he said affably, "Dr. Gayle came down. Had an Executioner with her. And I'll be *dad blamed* if she didn't wring my neck like a prize fryer!" JR held his own hands up and twisted with a theatrical "*KRAAAAAACK!*" to demonstrate the general idea. Skunk goggled at him. "It gets weirder," the Rancher said. He'd started off in the direction of the wreckage from the pod, and Skunk unconsciously fell into step behind him.

"She *waited*," JR went on. "Had coffee with that smoked-lens freak and waited for me to come back. Then the Executioner – the same one who broke my neck, thank you kindly – she and Dr. Gayle said something about us being 'on our own.' They didn't bring *any* supplies, Skunk. And no new fish. Well, there's that bald one, but he didn't come in the way those Board types do, did he?"

"Nope," Skunk Pussy agreed. "So… what did you do to the pod? Could you have done that whenever you *wanted* to?" Skunk seemed both impressed and slightly irritated.

"*I* didn't do a blasted thing," the Rancher answered. They'd drawn near enough to the debris field that they were traversing its outer rim, where burnt shreds of shielding, broken glass, and black, fire-twisted spars and bolts began to intermittently litter the lifeless soil. *A bumper crop of all the worthless shit we treat like the King's treasure*, he thought with a sense of glumness leavened by acerbic spite. JR stopped and turned to face Skunk. "They came, they strangled, they said their piece, and up they went. I was watching when the whole shebang blew, Skunk, and it was as pretty as a picture – but I didn't have anything to do with it."

"Whatever you say." Skunk sounded skeptical. "Bold move, JR. But you fucked with the Board. It's about to start raining shit on *all* of us."

"Actually, SOCV-A101, I doubt that it's going to rain *anything* – at least, not for a while."

The voice was mild, almost amused, and distinctly female. Skunk Pussy was surprised to discover that he remembered "female" – at least in a vague, indistinct way. The interlocutor was clad in tight black fabric from the crown of her head to her fingertips and boots; the only visible part of her was her bored, shallow eyes. Here and there in places, her uniform still smoldered. Trailing just behind her was a figure that Skunk did recognize; namely, Dr. Gayle, celestial messenger of the Board.

"Well, *heck*!" bugled the Jolly Rancher, a grin splitting his face like a fault line filled with gleaming teeth. "Good to *see* you again, Executioner! Had a bit of a hitch, did you?"

"You could say that, B1," agreed Executioner Ketch. "I must admit, falling to my death was a novel experience."

"It gets old," said Skunk in a flat voice. "God *damn*, the two of you look spiffy. That looked like a lot of fire." He wasn't wrong, the Rancher noted. Neither the spectacular explosion nor the impact of falling hundreds of feet appeared to have left a smudge. "Came back to life pretty darned quick, too," the Rancher added. Ketch shot him a knowing glance at that, but said nothing more.

"It *was*," Dr. Gayle said tersely, "a *lot* of fire." What Gayle did not add was that their white jumpsuit, like Executioner Ketch's black uniform or, indeed, the garb of many representatives of the Kingdom, was a more complicated garment than appearances let on. In Ketch's funereal garb and Gayle's immaculate white suit, two layers of acrylonitrile butadiene styrene (one manufactured at a high temperature and one at a lower one) were woven into the lining, rendering them all but impervious to impact and temperature. The garments had survived the explosion and subsequent fall, even if their occupants had not.

"His Majesty's mandate shielded us," Ketch said, and though her face was hidden by the cowl, Skunk thought he could hear a sardonic smile. There was good news, as Ketch saw it; whatever restoration process resurrected Arson's prisoners had restored her cognitive implants' function just as it had rewoven her splintered skeleton and restarted her heart. Ketch suspected, though she'd have to ask Gayle to be sure, that her status as a person not incarcerated in Gayle's Pocket had helped hasten her revival and that of Dr. Gayle.

"*Say!*" the Jolly Rancher exclaimed. "What was that about it not raining, Executioner? I mean," he clarified, "it's never rained in Arson, I get that, but I think my associate here was referring to the fabled cavalry coming for the two of you." A charred bit of fuselage caught Skunk's eye and he bent to inspect it, wondering if he could make use of it somehow. It was not only blackened by flame, he saw, but had a strange series of distortions pounded into it, as though it had been liquified, struck by a loud sound, then frozen in mid-ripple.

"The fabled cavalry." Gayle's voice was steeped in a bitter cocktail of emotions that JR couldn't quite untangle. "I suspect the fabled *cavalry* is the reason I just suffered a painful death and disorienting resurrection."

"Yeah," Skunk said, dropping the twisted bit of wreckage. "Like I said, it gets old."

The Jolly Rancher gazed placidly up at the hole in everything. The gleaming, multidimensional cracks were receding more quickly in the morning light. As he watched, they finished their eerie self-repair. The jagged remnants met and vanished, leaving no evidence that such an unnatural breach had ever existed. He always enjoyed the sight in the same way that keeping his trailer in proper order offered him a modicum of peaceful contentment (the riot of his tools and chemicals were another matter entirely). The thought jarred something loose, and his oil-black eyes lit with the manic glitter of an obsessive hobbyist with a captive audience. Dr. Gayle, seeing this, sighed and their shoulders slumped slightly. Their eyes remained invisible behind the smoked-glass lenses in their odd goggles.

"Say, Executioner!" JR's toothy smile displayed a slice of sly dentition. "While y'all are here, would you like to visit my ranch? I would *love* to show you what Dr. Gayle and I have been horsing around with!"

Ketch cast an unreadable glance at Dr. Gayle and responded, "You and Dr. Gayle, you say?"

"Welcome," said the Jolly Rancher proudly, "to the Open O Ranch. Forgive me for the lack of a fancy wooden sign with a Latin motto burned into it, but we're a bit short on supplies 'round here."

It was difficult for Ketch to look upon the Jolly Rancher's works with outright revulsion. But her outrage was somewhat tainted by the grisly exertions required of a Royal Executioner. What she felt instead was a sense of professional curiosity and dawning revelation. Dr. Gayle and the Jolly Rancher had been busy in Arson, and JR's burning desire to hold forth on the literal pet project (of sorts) that had consumed his long, empty days was apparent. His rambling explanation lasted for the entirety of their walk from the pod's crash site to the perimeter of his property. Well, Ketch reminded herself, "his" property. There *was* no property in Arson by definition, since the property rights of each subject were derived from the mandate and allowance of the King.

The perimeter of the Open O was delineated by wire; virtually all the wire that made its way to Arson since the

Rancher first landed there. Shoulder-height shards of wood, plastic, and metal were driven into the worthless soil at regular intervals, and the strings and strands of wire were wound together to form a mutated, devolved species of fence. The fenced-off area was modest, but made up for what it lacked in acreage with sheer industry. JR's first act, he told Ketch, had been to dig out the evaporation ponds. "Those are key," he emphasized. Then, he'd started experimenting. It didn't rain in Arson, nor was there a steady supply of, well, anything, but things as they currently stood in Arson were not the way that things had always been. There had been primitive dwellings (one of which survived as the heart of the Woodpile, another in the Rancher's clutches), there had been proper beds (broken out of boredom, spite, or for materials), and there had been chemical toilets.

The chemical supplies meant to replenish these toilets (and the bodily waste of Arsonists, which should have gone into them) formed the toxic, odious foundations of the Open O operation. Using broad evaporation ponds and the various salts and substances that JR leached from the foreign soil of Arson, the Rancher had dabbled. He'd blended, concentrated, scraped, and collected the evaporate of these base components for years.

"Condensates," Ketch repeated mildly, "extracted from the soil. What sort of condensates?"

"Let me show you!" the Rancher said brightly. He fished a long, jagged scrap of corroded metal from a nearby pile of debris and scraped it carefully along the outermost ring of one of the evaporating pools. The vapor rising from the pool was potent enough that Ketch, Gayle, and Skunk all stayed well back from it. JR coughed and spat, but seemed otherwise unaffected. Soon he returned with a pile of vivid white crystals on a ragged shred of oilcloth.

"It looks like salt," Ketch said mildly, entering notes into her memory tape as quickly as she could conceive them. *Recovery sabotage. Undisclosed activity in ARSO:N. Collusion between ICON staff and subject SOPS-B1.*

"It's one of the many fine varieties of produce found at the Open O," JR beamed. He waved at Skunk, who tossed him a dully gleaming object. He deftly caught it and proffered it to the Executioner. She accepted a small glassine jar filled with a thin, oily, unpleasant-looking substance. Ketch unscrewed the lid, and even before she brought it nearer to her cowl (with its in-built toxin screens) she could catch the smell through its protective chemical filters. It was the most ungodly reek she had ever encountered, and Ketch took a moment to savor the novelty of the experience. The stench had both organic and industrial undertones, and left a strange, curdled-medicine aftertaste on her tongue. She screwed it closed and passed it back to the Jolly Rancher.

"And what," she asked, "is that?"

"Mule vinegar!" Skunk volunteered, his voice as gleeful as a crow's. "It'll get you bug-eyed!"

Novel intoxicant concocted on-site with ICON collaboration, tapenoted Ketch. *Possibly related to mention of novel elements.* She red-flagged the entry **UNDESIRABLE SOCIAL EFFECT DANGER.**

"No doubt you are noting transgressions. Irregularities."

Dr. Gayle's interjection bought them a pause, as well as an inquisitive look from Ketch and a squashed frown from Skunk. "I may as well add to them," Gayle continued. They brought their fingertips up and massaged the skin around their tight eggshell goggles. "Forgive me. The light here is truly abominable. I designed it that way."

Ketch waited, her eyes soft and unblinking. Gayle sighed, then went on.

"I take it that you read 'The King's Pockets' in your moralpol education," Gayle said. Ketch didn't need to nod. "Of course you did. Forgive me, I forget how stringent… how much *progress* we've made. In the Kingdom. Well. The tailor in that story – the person who found the pockets in the garment of the Kingdom? That was me. Only, the truth is that we didn't discover the pockets. We made them."

"That's impossible," Ketch said. She sounded frustrated, bordering on irritable.

"Many thought so. But 'pocket' isn't really the right word for where we are, Executioner. An interstice isn't a pocket. It's a cyst. And we've filled the flesh of reality – of our reality; of *the* reality, locally speaking – with cysts. Places we can put poison and pus. But that's not a story for the Primary Youth Battalions, is it?"

"You *made* this place?" The Jolly Rancher's tone was strangely flat.

"Yes, I *did*, B1," Gayle insisted. "The substances you pull from the toxic dirt here…" They sighed the frustrated sigh of a short-tempered pedagogue. "The thing about interstitial engineering is that when you push something into nothing, or at least into the meat of the places between places, you start with the blankest slate imaginable. The cleanest start. You can't imagine. Did you *know*," Gayle asked, grabbing Ketch's arm in an uncharacteristic display of fierce pride, "that I've created new *elements*? New atomic structures? Given them new properties? Even the way things look here… the horizons, the sun, the painted mountains, the sky… I made it all. When I started working with B1 on moralpol and psychogrammar experiments here."

Ketch, still facing Gayle, reached behind her for the spar of half-melted scrap which the Jolly Rancher used to scrape his exotic condensates. In one smooth movement, she flung it forward with the graceful force of one schooled in the javelin. The spatulate end of the heavy spar had been tamped flat and scraped until its edge was sharp, all the better to collect JR's crystals. It flew as true as any missile lofted in an ancient war and Dr. Gayle dropped to the acrid ground, dead before they hit its surface. The metal spar had speared clean through one goggled eye socket, skewering the doctor's skull.

"Ah, *fuck yeah*!" Skunk Pussy cried ecstatically. He seemed on the verge of hugging the Executioner in his excited celebration of her kill. He caught a glance at her mostly-concealed visage and tepid eyes, however, and wisely held himself in check and shut his mouth. Blood soaked into the granular, semi-sandy soil beneath Gayle's head. The vapor-drifted ground behind Gayle's head was now adorned by a spray of brains and clotted red material. This seemed to please the Jolly Rancher.

"Oh, golly!" he exclaimed. "I can get some real good stuff from blood, you betcha, let alone *grey matter*. I gotta get to work before Gayle wakes back up. I think it might, you know…" He waved a hand. "…*offend* them if they found out that I harvested a little bit of this or that."

"I'm afraid not," Ketch said with genuine regret. JR's blood pulsed cold and, for a moment, he was certain he was about to die. Again. Sure, it didn't take, but that shit still hurt like a bastard. "What I need from you," Ketch went on, walking past him without so much as floating a glance his way, "is an introduction, of sorts. I've heard the word 'blumpkin' tossed around. I accessed prohibited colloquial scatology from the restricted moralpol archives. The description I found was noteworthy for both its vileness and its specificity. A perfect encapsulation of why the old order died such a syphilitic death."

The Jolly Rancher's mouth was as dry as Arson's miserable atmosphere. He tried to remember the last time he'd had a drink of water. Food and water were luxuries and analgesics in Arson, nothing more. After all, none of them could properly starve to death or wither from thirst. That was the *point* of the temporarily deceased Dr. Gayle's restoration algorithm. Suicidal ideation was a moralpol offense, and the King would hardly give those suffering at his pleasure such an easy and immoral means of egress.

"What," JR articulated with exquisite care, "may I do for you, Executioner?"

Ketch placed one black boot against Dr. Gayle's skull and yanked the spar free, drawing a satisfied "*Hah!*" from Skunk, and tossed it aside with a corrosion-muddled clatter.

"Take me to the blumpkins," Ketch said. "Explain what they are; in detail, for my record of this unconventional partnership and how you developed it with your slain collaborator." She stared down at the ICON researcher's mismatched gaze; one dark lens and one bloody socket. Dr. Gayle's dead face wore a dour, unchanged expression. Blood pooled beneath their pallid head, blood that the hungry hardpack of Arson would guzzle and never again relinquish. Ketch seemed to sense JR's reluctance to abandon the harvesting of Dr. Gayle before they reawakened.

"Don't worry about leaving Gayle," Executioner Ketch said, indicating that the Jolly Rancher should lead the way. "There's going to be a lot more blood for you to play with before I'm done here."

Hanging on a peg fixed to one fencepost was a collection of thick bundles, rags that Ketch had mistaken for hoarded trash. Trash they may have been, but these were now revealed to be crude, homemade respirators, of a sort. The bundles had been marinated in one of JR's mystery solutions, and as a result were laden with salts and compounds that he assured Ketch would provide at least a bit of protection for the journey. Ketch declined. Her cowl had served her well enough in worse environments.

It did rank high among the unwelcoming environments she'd visited. Both Skunk and JR were accustomed to the miasmic, burning hell of the Open O; the drifting curtains of toxic smoke and shimmering, transparent gas that boiled off of the chemical reaction pools. The burning fug was thick enough to occasionally obscure their path. After picking their way through the Rancher's open-air chemical processing plant, they reached the backmost corner of the Open O; the same section abutted by Skunk's crude shelter. And there, snug against the wires of the back fence and mired in six inches of simmering, smoking chemicals, was a crude hutch. It was a wire enclosure, with little in the way of amenities offered to its occupants besides a ratty tarp that half-covered the enclosure's roof, providing a generous wedge of shade over the chemical pool and the things that dwelled in it.

"I'm not sure what they are, to be perfectly honest," admitted the Jolly Rancher, dropping to his haunches at the edge of the wire enclosure. Its sharp, slender lines shone like polished silver, stripped clean of impurities by the potent toxicity of the bubbling stew. "Dr. Gayle brings pieces of them to me along with new prisoners, every so often. The first one got here..." He trailed off.

"I understand," said Ketch briskly. She did. Time in

the interstices was a strange thing which spooled and unspooled largely at the pleasure of the dear, deceptively departed Dr. Gayle. "Who decided to call them blumpkins?"

"Me," came a muffled chime from Skunk. When Ketch turned to face him, his squashed features were hidden behind the rag-mask of salts and extracts, but she could see the sneer in his streaming, close-set blue eyes.

"SOCV-A101, what does that word mean? To you?"

"Aw, heck, Executioner," said the Jolly Rancher, his oil-black eyes the only ones accustomed enough to the fumes that they remained untroubled – sparkling, even. "Let me *show* you what they are!" Lowering his rag-mask, JR placed two fingers in the front of his mouth and produced a shrill, penetrating whistle.

"What does the word 'blumpkin' mean to you, SOCV-A101?" Ketch asked Skunk again. Her peaceful brown eyes promised murder. In the caged hutch, mired in smoking, boiling, shin-deep fluid, something flopped and splashed.

Skunk Pussy had no fear of death – this was Arson, after all – but he didn't enjoy pain, nor did any spark of overt oppositional defiance remain in the version of him that had finally fetched up in Arson. "I don't know," Skunk answered honestly, and was surprised to hear how troubled by that fact he sounded. "It just seemed right."

"Good." Ketch immediately lost interest and turned to see what was lolloping out of the septic soup. For the first time since embarking on her journey to ICON, Executioner Jacqueline Ketch was lost for words.

The blumpkins each had a central, static mass; a ball of ruddy flesh about the size of a human head. The surface area of these orbs was made of stitched, scarred flesh that looked angry and inflamed where it wasn't split by orifices. At first, Ketch took these for wounds. On closer inspection, they were an assortment of openings, all of them from human bodies. Some of them held blistered, flapping tongues, while others were recognizably anuses or vaginas. This ball of tormented skin birthed a writhing, Medusan crop of fleshy appendages. These were decidedly *not* tentacles. It took it a moment to sink in, but eventually Ketch was forced to accept the evidence of her eyes. The blumpkins, blind, inflamed, and half-submerged in corrosive toxins, made their way through the world by each employing more than a dozen prehensile, grasping penises.

"What did I tell you?" asked the Jolly Rancher. He sounded like a child proudly showing off a new pet. "Aren't they *something*?"

```
ICON INTERNAL MEMO | INTERSTITIAL
ENGINEERING 112.24.01
DO NOT REPRODUCE | DO NOT TAPENOTE |
DO NOT KEEP
FROM: G. RUZICKA FREUND PhD MoralPolD ICON
Archdirector
TO: PHYNTIS Dr.
```

Dr. Phyntis,

Two matters. First, my most sincere thanks for your delivery on 112.16.01 of the items we discussed in our previous correspondence. The bonded tissue is beginning to take more readily with the addition of the compound, and the surgical instruments from Wolfaria are, need I say, not the type which would have been easily acquired without your help. With the inflammation reduced, the antihedon/hedon ratio is such that subjects' pain does not lessen over time.

Second. We were informed today that His Majesty has dispatched an Executioner – one of his pet Jacks or Jacquelines – to ICON. They will arrive here on the morning of the 31st. I made inquiries, and was reliably informed that the Executioner is unaware of our custody of Class 1, 2, 6, or 7 Offenders. What a stroke of luck. The plan is for my sister to demonstrate our research on one of our simpler subjects. I will then take Executioner Ketch to ARSO:N, where I will employ our most cooperative subject (SOPS-B1) to perform the death and resurrection show to Ketch's satisfaction.

I continue to hold true to our vision. If we continue, we should be able to extract exotic hormone antagonists and reagents in short order. The most exciting aspect remains the social-organic one. We've reduced humans, and combined humans, and then combined those combinations into a community. The blumpkins (quite disgustingly, but aptly, named by SOCV-A101) represent a new frontier in punitive carceral deterrence.

Besides. I'd love to hear my sister explain the Pit to His Majesty, and tell him how effective *she's* been. For all her stirring of the porridge inside these imprisoned skulls, nothing in her limited moral lexicon provides for the scouring agony true justice requires. Justice as understood in our Moral Foundations. Still, it's too soon to take our dispute – let alone our case – to the Crown. Certainly not until we get this Executioner out of our way. Our mission is paramount, Dr. Phyntis.

Most gratefully yours,
GRF

FW: PATRONS|NOTE ON METHODOLOGY William Blake once said; "Eternity is in love with the productions of time." He also said; "Without contraries, there is no progression. Attraction and repulsion, reason and energy, love and hate, are necessary to human existence." –Phyntis

5.
HOBOKEN

"Come on, now! Hurry!"

Even through a fog bank of disorientation, Uncle Funny recognized the voice with a shock that was bone-deep and electric cold. It was *his* voice, after a fashion.

"*Ri-ise,* and *shi-ine,* and *give God your glory-glory!*" the voice sang, so brightly! Of course the voice was bright. It belonged to a bright presence in many a child's life in the Kingdom. It was the voice of the Kindly King, a button-eyed puppet made of rich velvet and detailed stitching. The Kindly King was one of the motley crew of televised morality play performers voiced and given motive force by Uncle Funny. His Majesty should not have been perambulating by himself, without Funny's help. It seemed a little bit unnatural. Nonetheless the puppet advanced slowly, its marionette strings ascending from its bobbing head and limbs into darkness. It fixed Funny with its dead button eyes.

The sight knocked something loose inside of him, knowledge that came hurtling through the murk of his disorientation and crashed hard to the floorboards of his memory. Stimuli washed over him, inseparable from their associations. He could smell greasepaint and the burning tungsten filaments of hot electric lights; and as soon as he could, dim shapes began to coalesce from the gloom around him. He could feel the heat coming off of those lights, enough heat to melt a wax sculpture (which was why, Uncle Funny remembered joking, they didn't use wax sculptures as actors); and as soon as he could, the light itself came flooding forth as though spoken into yet-uncreated darkness.

Uncle Funny could see a tessellation of confusing details; rigging and stage lights, painted props, and complicated cameras among them. Only he *wasn't* Uncle Funny, was he? His real name was Ed. Ed Hall. And this wasn't Arson. What exactly *was* Arson, anyway? It felt like a nightmare receding from the waking world. Layered over the must of makeup, he smelled the specific spicy tang of long-accumulated grease and ancient dust. He knew this smell, knew it like he knew his face in a mirror. It was the smell of…

"Hoboken," Ed breathed. "WAPB."

"That's *right!*" trumpeted the Kindly King. His flat blue button eyes twinkled, and the crumpled fabric moustache that formed his puppet mouth sniff-snuffed in the way that always made children laugh. Even in the bright WAPB lights, the strings that held the Kindly King aloft stretched upward into an unremitting void of shadows. "Come on, now, Edward" said the Kindly King, "come on, my friend! There's so much to do before our playtime ends!" The puppet shuffled off to one side of the set in the spindly walk that delighted (most) kids. It was enough to bring a smile to Ed's face.

He followed the ambling puppet around the edge of the set and suddenly he was in his old dressing room at WAPB. He could even tell the time of year: it was another wretched Hoboken winter, to judge by the chugging thump of the heating vent in the room's northwest corner, the one he'd had to mitigate with a taped-on chunk of cardboard. The aged heating system's vaguely gas-scented dragon's breath was hot enough to melt Ed's jars of makeup if he didn't. He saw the big, flat mirror just as he remembered it (grimy because who was going to clean it?), framed by a perimeter of taped fan letters from parents and children. The uppermost of these fluttered in the tempered puff of the heater's air, dry and crispy from years of winter desiccation. His own reflection in the smeared glass mesmerized him. Ed's hair was still a close-cropped fringe, but one with a healthy black luster that matched the shine of his fulsome handlebar mustache. Ed was unsurprised to see another old friend dangling on marionette strings in the greasy mirror. This one a woman-puppet with a friendly face and braided, bright red yarn for hair. *Judy*, thought Ed, *Judy Juicebox!* Like the Kindly King, Judy Juicebox was possessed of dead, gleaming button eyes. While the Kindly King's were as blue as a cloudless, cyanotic noonday sky, Judy Juicebox's were a merry lime green; a color which evoked popsicles more than any fruit produced by nature.

"Remember me, Eddie? We had so much fun! We taught the kids *everything* under the sun!" Judy Juicebox's voice was just as Ed remembered it, and as his protege, Bill Redding, had voiced her; sweet and soft and motherly, a warm presence in a chilly world.

The Kindly King high-stepped into view on his strings and corrected Judy Juicebox. "We didn't teach *everything*, Judy my dear; we never taught pain, exploitation, or fear." Memory washed across Ed like a warm tide. It was true. In his entire career, his entire life, Ed Hall had never consciously hurt a soul. Certainly not any children, not when he'd devoted his life to entertaining and educating them. His head throbbed. There was so much he couldn't remember clearly. It was there somewhere inside of him, but it swam just out of reach.

Two blue button eyes stared at him from the mirror. The Kindly King's funny, scrunchy mustache moved as he spoke. "Sweet to His Majesty, loyal to a T – why are you trapped there in Arson, not free?" Arson. No; ARSO:N. Jesus. How had Ed forgotten? The heat, the dismal squalor, and the deathless perpetuity attendant to the memory made him gag.

Judy Juicebox's voice now took on an unfamiliar, chiding quality. "Don't you remember, you poor, silly rat? The books and the movies they found in your flat?" One arm lifted on its wire and shook an accusatory felt finger at him. "Pornography isn't allowed, *and that's that!*"

A terrible new voice sounded from behind him, and Ed whirled. This puppet was not familiar from the show, but he recognized it all the same. The long brown yarn hair, the lifeless brown button eyes, even the little velvet sport coat. It was Bill Redding, his old friend and right-hand man on the set of "The Kindly King." Bill Redding, but incarnated in stitched fabric, felt, and wire.

"*They threw you away, Ed!*" the Bill Redding puppet screamed, its cry crow-loud and rich with contemptuous cruelty. "*Thrown right out the door! And straight through a hole in the world to the floor!*"

It advanced on him and Ed, suddenly filled with terrified loathing, backed up until he bumped his ass against the mirror table. "Remember me, Eddie? My name was Bill Redding! You did me a favor just before my wedding! You brought a fun film to my bachelor bash, where we all had a blast and were blasted and trashed!"

Ed could now remember it so vividly that he actually felt a minor resurgence of the hangover that long, drunken night of revelry had merited him. "A stag film," Redding had requested with a wink, and Ed Hall – a man of lonely nights, well-lubricated palms, and an illegal collection of material that violated moralpol law – had obliged.

When the Kindly King spoke again, it was in a voice that began as a whisper and ended as an outraged roar. "But what happened Monday, you sorry old Ed? *HE CALLED THE AUTHORITIES DOWN ON YOUR HEAD!*" Ed squeezed his eyes shut. Pain and shame bubbled through him in a sick, thick flood as a memory surfaced like something long dead dislodged from its resting place beneath swamp water. The knock in the middle of the night; not a subtle sound, that hard, official *BAM-BAM-BAM*. His head hung in shame and self-hatred as the King's Guard led him away in painful bite-cuffs. The Kindly King went on, voice denuded of any good humor it had once contained. Ed's flesh crawled with horripilation; it was still his voice, his Kindly King, but as he'd only imagined and expressed it in private. It was not a version of His Majesty that would ever see a television camera. "How the neighborhood *muttered* and *murmured* and *fed*, from your humiliation, as off you were led!"

There hadn't been a courtroom. There'd been an ugly little cell that smelled of fear and despair. In that windowless concrete box, the King's Prosecutor had entered wordlessly. Ed's hands were shackled tightly to a broad table. It and his small, uncomfortable chair were bolted to the floor. The Prosecutor was flanked by two whey-faced guards bearing big, black plastic trash sacks, and from them – one incriminating, shameful piece at a time – he had enumerated and elucidated Ed's sins, one sordid, well-thumbed issue of *Fuck O Matic*, *Hard Sex*, and *Cheri XXX Hardcore* at a time; noted each scuff-covered video copy of *Perverted Planet*, *Fuck Slaves 4*, and, ironically, since it was the one that had been so riotously well-received at Bill Redding's stag party, *Dirty Oral Cumshots 2*. Possession of even softcore pornography (as it had been known when such distinctions still existed) was enough to earn one the dreaded SOPS jacket on their file. Ed had had no idea what came next, but few illusions that it would be pleasant.

With a buzzing murmur and an arrhythmic series of clicks, the fluorescents in the claustrophobic cell died, plunging Ed Hall – lately known as Uncle Funny – into darkness as absolute as a mineshaft. Disorientation swam through him once more, and then a pale gleam began to dawn. It was light; a nacreous light that, dim as it was, showed him he was back at WAPB in his dressing room once more. Illumination crept through the cracks around the door, painting outlines subtly but with enough definition that Ed made his way out of the room, down a short hallway, and back toward the stage set without difficulty. The set, source of the glow, was floodlit in red and blue gels. Ed had never seen a gel effect that created such an unearthly, shifting violet glow.

Light suffused the set, which had been dressed with depleted-looking sand, and which now hosted a mâché version of the monstrous front of Frank Blank's truck. There, behind the wheel, was a velvet puppet version of Frank. In typical comedic puppet fashion, Frank didn't seem particularly concerned with safe driving habits. Indeed, his insouciant puppet-legs, encased in tiny boots, were propped up on the steering wheel, directing it lazily this way and that. Puppet-Frank was the first character in this eccentric vision whose eyes were invisible. Were there buttons beneath the brim of that big, cream-colored hat? Uncle Funny had a terrible feeling that, if there were, they were a color never seen by human eyes. Puppet-Frank's hat even had its decorative band, complete with a decoration made of minuscule, dying flower buds preserved in plastic. Behind the mâché truck and its passenger, the set's backdrop slowly rolled upward to create the illusion that Frank's pink truck was barreling down a desert highway. The puppet's voice was, naturally, the desert-stone rasp of Frank Blank himself.

"My name is Frank, and I dwell in the wastes. I showed up one fine day and offered you tastes of the pleasure His Majesty stole from your loins like a Puritan taxman purloining your coins! I brought you remembrances of long-lost scenes; of urges and surges now hid by a screen. A pair of old panties, some torn magazines; anything bordering on the… *obscene*." Puppet-Frank pronounced this last word with sarcastic loathing undershot by a prurience that Ed "Uncle Funny" Hall had never heard in Frank's voice before. *Puppets don't think like we do*, Ed thought in a dissociating drift; but the statement felt more like a plea than an assertion.

CLACK! The spot illuminating puppet Frank and his lazy, sick-light cruise through unending wastes evaporated, as did the other stage lights. Ed was plunged again into darkness, but one that felt different – palpably and literally – than it had before. The air was close and rich with the slick, sweet smell of saliva mixed with precum, undershot by the stale, bleached, animal stink of old semen. The atmosphere was more humid than the hot, dry studio. Ed knew where he was; knew by feel and smell, even in the dark. It had been the place he'd gone in his fear, his doubt… his shame. Above all, it had been where he'd gone in his lust.

Unmarried and rounding the dispiriting mid-race marker of his life, Ed Hall had lived alone and ensconced in a hopeless loneliness. He'd had but one love, and it had been a generalized, altruistic love utterly devoid of romantic delusions, predatory intent, or any sort of sexuality. He hadn't been a pedophile; indeed, he could imagine no viler crime. What he *had* been was an enthusiastic, unusually dedicated masturbator. That alone, could it have been proven, would have been enough to knock him from his perch at WAPB. The Kingdom's paranoid and self-policing populace had long ago internalized the peculiar psychology of the moralpol police state. He'd seen this for himself in the guilty, sweet relief he'd seen in the eyes of his neighbors as the King's Guard hauled him away. *Thank God they're taking him*, their eyes had said. *Thank God that this time it's the strange man who talks to children with his velvet friends*. Which was all a way to say: *thank God it's not me*.

A sudden radiance pierced the gloom, accompanied by a resounding *CLICK!* Ed wasn't at WAPB anymore. This time, the light fell in a sharp cone from a desk lamp in the tiny room where Ed had gone to satisfy himself, but more importantly, where he'd gone to *look*.

Not even Ed Hall's grandfather remembered a time when pornography had been freely available. Not in the Kingdom, which relentlessly pursued constant improvement, human perfection, and moral rectitude. Lust, slovenliness, sloth; all the vices which were said to have rotted out the old order and brought it crashing ruinously down had been expunged (or so the King said, and one could hardly dispute such assertions).

Pornography did not even *exist* anymore, they said, not even in the decadent world outside His Majesty's wise rule.

Ed knew this to be a lie. Pornography could still be had. Narcotics, too, and proscribed texts. Hoboken's black market was a strange constellation of things that shared one commonality: they all were banned. Quite stringently. And so, spending what meager extra funds he had, Ed visited an ever-shifting series of smoky apartments and basement storefronts hosting back room bazaars. He'd met men (it was *always* men) in parking lots to browse through open van doors and popped trunks for what he sought. Ed paid handsomely, kept his mouth shut (even after he'd been seized), and had, over time, accumulated quite a hoard. He hadn't even kept the *memory* of his sub rosa Athenium when he'd arrived in Arson. Here it was; his nonpareil comfort, his mottled pile of dragon's treasure. Every magazine was blessed with one or two *special* spreads or even individual photographs; the ones that excited the particularly potent, paraphilia-tickling neural nodes that were part of Ed Hall's sum total makeup.

He'd felt guilty each and every time he'd opened the locked spare room. There he kept his volumes in meticulously-indexed filing cabinets and black-covered binders. He'd felt guilty every time, yes, but hadn't that added piquancy to his ritual? A little something extra, something… *illicit?* And when he'd been forcefully waddled out of his sad little apartment by His Majesty's finest, hadn't it felt like the inevitable consummation of a fear he'd held inside himself his entire life? Hadn't it felt like he was, on a basic, bone-deep level, *sick?* That word. That unusable word, the sole linguistic taboo in the bright, blighted barrens of Arson.

Ed was oddly unsurprised to hear the dreamy voice of Morrison Spare behind him. "Do you want it all back, Ed Hall? You can still be Uncle Funny, if you want to. The Ed Hall that you were died when they sent you here. I can give them back, though. The memories. The things that made your gears turn."

Ed "Uncle Funny" Hall turned and immediately flinched, shielding his eyes. While Ed's cabinet of cum-soaked curiosities remained illuminated by a single cone of sunshine-yellow lamplight, the doorway no longer led to the dim recesses of his tiny apartment. Instead, it framed a searing rectangle of Arson's bleached sunlight; sunlight which, while bright and terrible, seemed neither to shine nor to cast shadows in the dark half of the room. Against this framed impossibility, Morrison Spare was a shadow cutout with a burning indigo halo.

"Frank Blank figured out how it all works. The machinery. The secrets. It's all up *here*, you see?" Spare tapped one of his radiant temples. His smile looked more than beatific; it looked drugged. "You might say it's a Mystery. So I can give it back, whatever name you want to use. But you've got to ask me, and you've got to mean it. That's how this works."

The puppeteer who loved pornography stared at Spare for a beat. He looked back at his randy reference library; his tacky treasure trove. Who had he hurt, he wondered, ever hurt in his life? The women in these pictures? Maybe. Yes, if he were being honest, maybe so. But moral calculus, like natural law, functioned differently once one had made the trip to Arson.

"Ed Hall died in Hoboken," Ed said at last. "Uncle Funny was born in Arson. I'll stay Uncle Funny. And Mr. Spare? I'd like it back. I'd like it *all* back." He looked up, and in the reflection of the gleaming brass cone of the lamp, he could make out the distorted, ghostly figure of the Kindly King, hanging on his spindly wires, waving one hand in a mocking goodbye.

"And *fuck* the King," Uncle Funny snarled through a savage smile.

Outside the indigo shed, in the deathly light of Arson's artificial sun, Frank Blank watched with unseen eyes as the ring of bleached bones surrounding its perimeter vanished in a brief and mellow drift of chalky dust.

Their first death, Dr. and Moral Philosopher G. Ruzicka Freund reflected, had been *much* worse. Torn from their trajectory and vanquished by velocity in mid-ascent, they and the Executioner had been pummeled by the detonation's vast concussion, then, aflame, had fallen like a pair of burning meteorites. Thanks to the exotic weave of their ICON uniform, Dr. Gayle had still been very much alive when their body had hit the Arson hardpack, and *that* had been a brief but memorable pain as well.

All of this would have made wonderful test notes, if I'd had the physical courage to terminate myself in Arson before now, Dr. Gayle reflected rather bitterly. Whatever they may have learned from the experience, it would likely remain here with them forever. Dr. Gayle had no illusions regarding what had transpired to bring about their first death, nor who was responsible. They should have expected this from Kinsey, that psychotic, manipulative coward. Kinsey lacked the courage of Gayle's convictions; she always had. That made Gayle's work – their progress in the realms of excruciation and penitence, the possibilities hitherto only dreamed of in infernal religious doctrines – too dangerous for Kinsey's liking. The "accident" had tied it all up nicely. Evidence, research results, and Dr. Gayle themself had been neatly sealed away in ARSO:N's interstice, a place accessible solely through arcane and esoteric science that only the perpetrator (aside from its inventor, Dr. Gayle) could operate. *A masterstroke*, the interstitial engineer grudgingly admitted.

Their second death, delivered by Jacqueline Ketch, had been an indignity piled atop a reprehensible betrayal: insult piled on injury, although the insult had been inarguably injurious. Dr. Gayle lifted a pale hand to their eye socket. They noted with interest that their skull had expelled the projectile while they'd been dead; a not-inconsiderable effort on the part of the repair algorithm. They lifted their fingers, pleased to see that the digits appeared in their vision. *Exceptional*, Dr. Gayle thought. The repair algorithm had always worked on the complex machinery of organic human flesh, as it had been designed to, but *this* was unexpected.

Dr. Gayle cast around, discomfited to have their eyes so exposed. To their annoyance, the dark glass goggles hadn't regenerated, and were ruined. One lens had burst as the Executioner had neatly skewered Gayle's cerebrum, and the impact had been enough to break apart the other. Their blinking, squinting eyes were now revealed to daylight (of a sort) for the first time in years. An observer may have been surprised by Dr. Gayle's eyes. They may have noted that the orbs were without evident pupil or iris, the entirety of each prosthetic instead inset with a swarm of lenses of various shapes and sizes. They were like the eyes of an enormous and technologically advanced insect, resized and transplanted into a human face. Sheltered behind a layer of high-impact plastic, the lenses dilated and contracted with a complicated series of adjustments. The eyes, and their attendant plastic covers, had regenerated, even if the lenses hadn't. They cycled through filters and algorithmic overlays as Dr. Gayle took stock. There was quite a bit that Dr. Gayle could take stock of with those eyes.

By the angle of the light, Gayle determined that they hadn't been dead long. They could only conceive of one place where the Executioner and the subjects would have gone, given the course that the conversation had taken before the doctor's untimely demise.

Gayle took a moment to knock the colorless hardpacked dust from their uniform, then began to trudge in the direction of the Open O Ranch. The Ranch was a place of ruination with which they were all too familiar. Dr. Gayle was not the timid violator of the King's prerogatives that their sibling was. Having defied His Majesty's parameters for the governance of ARSO:N so thoroughly, they hadn't seen the point of sticking to any royal mandates restricting their remit whatsoever. Gayle would readily admit it was their sister's sycophancy and interest in the more... call them *political* aspects of the project which had secured ICON's status and legacy. Those same traits regrettably made Kinsey morally weak, in Dr. Gayle's estimation; one who paid homage to the wrong virtues and was too quick to label a true virtue a vice.

For example; the ridiculous royal prohibition on cerebral enhancements. Archdirector Kinsey followed this law to the letter. Dr. Gayle, by contrast, found the idea that they weren't responsible enough to govern the improvement or renovation of their own mind deeply offensive. Thus, they'd simply disregarded the decree and taken careful steps to ensure that their enhancements weren't detectable to a casual observer. A visitor more focused on the workings of the Pockets, say, which was the only type of visitor that their remote, incomprehensible, top-secret facility tended to attract.

Among the least of Dr. Gayle's illicit endowments was a vanishingly tiny device, yet one which, in this situation, proved vital. It was simple enough; crude, really, since its sole function was as a text message relay. These messages had to contain so little information that they were transmitted in binary. Passe as binary may have seemed, this gadget would have been enough to earn a 20th- or 21st-century theorist-cum-technician several lifetimes' worth of laurels.

With the help of a few novel tweaks to long-shelved theories of anti-de Sitter space, Dr. Gayle could twitch a pair of photons caged in their temporal lobe, causing the particles' entangled twins in ICON to change positions simultaneously, no matter the distance. Those photons chained like Prometheus in the ICON Interstitial Laboratory would then, in turn, twitch another pair of particles. A pair located… *elsewhere*, was the best way to put it, and leave it at that. Dr. Gayle was confident that this trick would work, but passed a moment in palpitations nonetheless. After a delay of seconds, the crude communication node in Gayle's brain tickled out its reply from an existentially vast elsewhere. This drew a smile from Dr. Gayle, the often-dour Moral Philosopher.

PHYNTIS, they'd sent.

RECEIVING, came the reply.

They hadn't been *absolutely* sure the technology would work, and for good reason. This all-too-prosaic communique constituted the first successful transmission between discrete universes in humanity's history. Gayle smiled because they'd proved their design worked even after a generous portion of their brain and skull had been destroyed and then regenerated, *twice* now. If anything could be called a successful field test, this was it. They'd been wise, they concluded, to keep *this* trick to themselves. Despite their siblings' murderous designs and the royal pain in the ass that was Executioner Ketch, Dr. Gayle had an advantage. Soon, they'd have more than one, if their hopes were consummated.

KINSEY BLEW THE POD AND STRANDED ME IN ARSON WITH EXECUTIONER KETCH, they sent. *I'm practically a demigod of creation and destruction*, Dr. Gayle thought, amusement tinged with bile, *and I'm reduced to a cosmic telegraph. "SEND HELP STOP"*

There was a pause impregnated by more than a mere transmission delay. Then:

YOU ARE NOT ALONE

Dr. Gayle was slightly irritated while receiving this first line, and was about to transmit a confirmation that, yes, Executioner Ketch *was* in ARSO:N with them, when Dr. Phyntis continued.

ONE OF US IS IN THERE WITH YOU A pause. **SOMETHING LIKE US BUT WE DO NOT KNOW THEM** Another pause. **THIS OTHER ALSO BROUGHT ONE OF THE MYSTERIES**

Though the air was baking and the soil beneath them hot enough to scald, Dr. Gayle shivered as a palpable chill coagulated their guts. **ASSIST OR EXTRACT** they sent to Phyntis. "Demand" was too strong a word for the intent behind this transmission, but not by much.

STAND BY AND WAIT FOR ASSISTANCE sent Dr. Phyntis, twitching photons from beyond the veil of dream and nightmare. **DO NOT TRUST UNKNOWN INDIVIDUALS AND BE ON**

GUARD AGAINST PHYSICAL VIOLENCE TO YOUR PERSON

A little late for that *warning*, Dr. Gayle thought, and flicked a bloody bit of their brain from one shoulder of their white uniform.

When the beatific Morrison Spare escorted Uncle Funny from the indigo shed and into the ersatz-butter-yellow mid-morning of Arson, Funny reemerged awkwardly dragging three large suitcases. His fringe of hair had regained its jet-black luster, and he sported a distinguished handlebar mustache; one which he had not had when he'd entered. His rags – the uniform of a long confinement in Arson – were gone, replaced by a checked suit. Despite this garment and the miserable heat of Arson's days, Funny looked and felt as cool as an ice cream sundae. He could remember *those* now, too. Uncle Funny could remember *everything*.

Within half an hour of Funny's departure, a scrawny man with a toffee-toned complexion and an unkempt, patchy beard limped from the shadows onto Ardor Street to eye the sheds (and pointedly *not* eye Morrison or Frank). "Hello Balloonman," murmured Frank, and added in a low, jocular tone; "It's spring and the goat-footed Balloonman whistles far and wee, is that about the size of it?"

"Hush now, Frank," said Spare gently, and followed Balloonman as he somnambulated with glazing eyes toward the citrus-bright orange shed. By the time he halted before it, swaying as though in the grip of some narcotic haze, Morrison was crowned by a burning halo the color of the mythical citrus groves of long-lost Florida. "What's lost is never lost forever," began Morrison. The words he exchanged with Balloonman floated through the latter's mind in weightless, colorful profusion. Minutes passed. Of his own free will, Balloonman entered the shack. When his heels passed the threshold, he vanished like a gambler's lucky streak. Frank watched the shack's door swing shut behind the space the patchy-bearded man had recently occupied.

On Balloonman's journey beyond the boundaries of Arson and into the bright hues and dark shadows of his past, he discovered many things. The name he'd been born with, which, just like Uncle Funny, he chose to discard. Glimpses of dawn's pale, golden light as it had probed the festering wound of a remembered hangover. Jagged recollections of his "sprees," as he had called them; of waking in the switchgrass next to Rita and a sparkling charcuterie board of empty liquor bottles. The name – her name – blew through his long-stagnant mind with terrible, tempestuous force. *Rita!*

Rita, his love, his high-quality, platinum silicone companion. Balloonman remembered purchasing her; the most hazardous, adventurous excursion of his life. His voyage of infatuation had involved not one but *three* undocumented crossings of the Kingdom's fiercely-guarded borders. It had been worth each dram of gold and sweat expended. Balloonman now marveled at what had been stripped from him. Days of silent, happy companionship; dancing for his soft, compliant partner, singing: *"Immortal and life size, my breath is inside you."*

Then Balloonman remembered *that* morning. The terrible morning when he'd awakened in the switchgrass to dawn's lance limning the leering, lowering faces of the King's Guard. They held their weapons leveled at him like he and Rita posed them any harm. Like they posed *anybody* any harm. Then there'd been the grim room where a sour-faced man with beady eyes had lofted words like "public licentiousness," and "agalmatophilia," and "sexual offender." He felt a hand fall gently on his shoulder, and suddenly Morrison Spare was there. Spare told him that he could have it back, *all* of it. Including Rita. Like a dream brought flawlessly across the border of the waking world, Rita was suddenly there. Balloonman wept for the first time since his arrest and incarceration in Arson. Rita (and his memories) were all that he took from the orange shed; all he needed.

Frank Blank watched (perhaps with eyes) as, in the zenith of the deathly sky, the poison sun was challenged by a drifting scrim of cloud. This was the first cloud ever to inhabit Arson's atmosphere.

The next to find their way to Ardor Street were Prod and Pinetop, Arson's only couple, who'd arrived together one day in the murky past. Since their transportation, they'd clutched each other fervently, as though by cleaving unto one another they would wake one day to find their time in Arson was no more than some new, beastly species of shared nightmare. Morrison Spare trailed them as they drifted in a daze toward the sunlight-yellow shed. When Spare told them the bargain, they accepted, agreeing in one instant with one breath. Crowned by radiant yellow light, Spare opened up the shed for them, and Prod and Pinetop tumbled into memory.

And in that memory, too, they tumbled; tumbled to their sprawling bed with tangled limbs and languid sighs in satin sheets and nights of love. They'd loved each other, and *that* the Kingdom permitted – barely. A generation past, the King had re-decriminalized same-gender marriage, but such couples were subject to the same stringent adultery and divorce laws as their mixed-gender fellows. Prod and Pinetop were carefree life-lovers. They embraced their joys and passions without looking back, baptized in each other's sweat and cum and anointed by the sweet fluids of their other lovers; the ones they'd tossed into the throbbing tussle; the ones they'd brought home from nightclub, party, opera, or wherever their fancy took them. They lacked a paranoid's conception of how their King-sanctioned marriage enhanced with these new, exotic elements could bring such pain down on their heads.

They remembered the knock and the stone boxes in which they'd been interrogated separately. Each was judged by the gimlet eye of the same grim-faced young woman. *Surely she's too young,* Pinetop had thought, *to be the wielder of such terrible power*. She'd sneered the word "troilism." The words "criminal promiscuity." Then there'd only been the awful, lifeless dirt of Arson, and the lingering gratitude in each man for the other.

"You can keep this," said Spare, his features saintly in the lemon light, "if you want." For his part, Spare had his doubts. What had ICON's censors taken from this pair but pain? To Spare's surprise, Prod gladly told him *precisely* what it was they wished to keep.

"We've got to keep hold of the wrong done to us," Prod said in a trembling voice. "We've got to keep the memory. We can't forget, lest we forgive."

"And *fuck* the King," appended Pinetop with a flash of proud defiance in his shy and boyish grin. And so, all Prod and Pinetop took from their forbidden trysts were their sweet recollections and the wisdom born of pain. They exited the sunshine-yellow shed with straight backs and heads held high.

Frank Blank heard the distant, distorted thunderclap of

peaks collapsing on Arson's horizon. A mountain folded slowly, crumpling like felt before revealing emptiness past the hole in the scene. Frank smiled, and watched Arson's terrible sun crawl across a sky dappled by clouds. As the haloed Spare escorted an Arsonist named Pharaoh – a massive, coffee-colored slab of a man – into the indigo shed, the bloody yolk of sunset broke over the horizon. Frank slipped away from the row of colorful impossibilities on Ardor Street and back to his truck. He climbed the back steps to the trailer and twitched aside the heavy black cloth that sheltered its interior. All was as it should be.

"Perfect," Frank Blank murmured to himself. His lips curled at the corners in a manner reminiscent of a contented tortoise or a sun-warmed iguana. Such surface similarities were terribly misleading. Nothing in the cosmos in which Earth spun, nor in Arson, bore a family resemblance to Frank in full, unfettered bloom.

A strange place, Frank reflected as he looked on Arson's sparsity. *Where wolves, dogs, and sheep are skinned so none of them can tell who's who.*

The sons of Arson's daylight had, by this point, made their way to Morrison Spare and gladly accepted his sacrament – or Frank's sacrament, to put it more accurately. Now that sunset lit the cloud-occluded sky, Frank took time to breathe the vague scent of dusk in the dead and cooling air. *Soon it will be dark*, he thought with uncharacteristic eagerness. A thing of the desert, he loved the sun more than the night, and loved the brutalizing light of untroubled wasteland skies best of all. *This evening and its attendant darkness*, he reflected, *will be a rare night. One to savor.*

Come nightfall, Ardor Street would see a more refined assortment of visitors; those who sought to reclaim thorny joys and sharp desires. These were among the minds Frank Blank sought most avidly to grapple with. These were strutting archetypes of the Pit; those forged by a special, poisoned flame produced by burning circumstances and the infinitely evolving innovations of human libido. They'd come, and he had no doubt they'd take what Spare offered them. What Frank Blank *wished* for them. Nighttime congregants would differ from the others in subtle ways, but in all else, they were kin. Night or day, each would choose the moment to cross the proper threshold.

Unlike daylight's visitors, however, those who came at night would all enter the black shed.

**ROYAL STANDARD ENGLISH DICTIONARY,
3rd Edition
PUBLISHED BY HARVARD ROYAL COLLEGE,
CAMBRIDGE (MA)**

trans·por·ta·tion
/+tran(t)spər+tāSHən/

noun

1. the action of transporting someone or something or the process of being transported
"the era of interstitial matter transportation"

2. the action or practice of transporting convicts to a penal colony
"for crimes against the Crown, the poacher was sentenced to transportation."

**MORALPOL PUBLICATION CONTROL
NOTE: Previous editions of the RSED
[editions ONE and TWO] are to be
recalled and pulped. The distinction
between "penal colony" and
"interstitial transportation" was a
poor choice from a moralpol and Crown
standpoint. Mistakes have been made.
Mistakes will be made.**

6.
CLOSER TO 12°

"Pedagogy in your King's utopia is a curious thing," said the monster in the darkness. He smiled. He knew his keeper was nearby. He went on.

"By many measures, I'm sure the graduates of your Youth Battalions are much brighter than the children prior civilizations used to mass produce." Shrouded in the deep black of his cell, he perched atop the edge of his clean and spartan bed. "Still, I'm left saddened by the gaps; the fascinating and extraordinary things that are left on the cutting-room floor."

He rose to his feet and began to slowly pace the length of the room. It was not the only room in his small and winding suite within which he was kept. He navigated unerringly in the darkness. Every inch and corner of the experimental environment had been committed to his memory long ago. "You needn't hide behind your veils, Kinsey. I know you're up there." He paused, and stared up into the unlit gallery where he knew she stood and watched him from some veiled panoptical perch.

His hands had thick, strong fingers, but their calloused tips were surprisingly sensitive. He lifted them to the crown of his head. Just above the circumference of his

124

eyebrows, no hair, scalp, or skull remained to provide their fragile shelter to the meat of his brain. Instead, it was enclosed by a brushed steel dome embossed with reinforced antennae and compact, unbreakable plastic bubbles. During interface experiments, these bubbles came alive with coruscating, multicolored lights. He'd seen their colors reflected on the polished walls; could, in fact, see winking yellow standby lights as he addressed the smooth dome overhead. Despite the quaint appearance of such nodules, this was no whimsical robotic thinking cap from some musty antique comic book. The implant's incision into his skull had been brutally wrought, and the flesh there was left permanently red and rageful.

"I can't *not* know when you're about now, can I? Not with all of these… *exciting renovations* you've made to my fucking skull." He caught himself and offered the unseen observer a sigh. "Ah, pardon me. I forget the Kingdom's distaste for obscenity. Goodness, I just committed, what, a Class Four violation? 'Behavior in Activity Proscribed for Undesirable Social Effect, Minor?' That's enough right there to net me an alphanumeric string, yes? One with 'PS' in it?" The darkness in the gallery did not reply to his queries, unlike the darkness inside of him. *His* darkness was often quite talkative. It had the same corpse-lively sense of humor he did, and they'd had some good laughs together, he and his darkness. He had no doubt they'd have a great many good laughs yet.

"But, despite your high place in the King's good graces," he said thoughtfully, "you don't seem to mind my filthy mouth that much. Maybe you just don't *care* quite as much as your abominable peers, Kinsey." He began to stretch his arms above his head in the first of his calisthenic exercises that day; and it *was* day. Mid-morning, if his natural biological rhythm was anything to go by. He trusted it more than he trusted his zookeepers' intentionally disorienting statements about time of day; after all, his chronoception had always been unusually precise. "If you were encumbered by a distaste for obscenity, I wouldn't *be* here. I *am* an obscenity, Kinsey. And you keep me warm and well-fed."

He caught his breath at an all-but-imperceptible whisper of air from the gallery above. "Ah. Fed, that's right. You feed *all* of my hungers, too. But I diverge from my point. Apologies." Each joint in the monster's knees and elbows and each knuckle in his fingers and his toes, popped softly as he finished stretching. He began to rapidly do pushups, first with both arms, then each arm alone.

He went on, his breathing untroubled by these exertions. "Getting back to the sorry state of education in the King's Battalions, let's take *you* as a case in point. You are the best-educated and most esteemed psychoscientist in all the land, if I'm not ill-informed. And yet, I'd bet the top of my skull – *wherever* it is," he added with a gruesome chuckle, "that you are unacquainted with John Lubbock or Willard Small. They built mazes, too, but they did it with rats. Mice. Hymenopterans, in some cases. Furthermore, Kinsey, they built their little mazes to study *learning*. They didn't realize they had discovered the field of metapedagogy, and, indeed, that field's 'pioneers' never mention anything so crude or uncivilized as putting frightened rats in labyrinths like a review board called by King Minos."

He wondered if he should explain who Minos was, then discarded the notion and kept on with his lecture. "Or ponder the Children's Crusade of the poor, beleaguered monkeys. Strapped down with their lustrous, veiny brains exposed. Imagine their *terror*. Barbaric. Too terrible to teach, even to teachers. Even to those who'd train your Kingdom's budding psychoscientists." His shiver of delighted repulsion as he fingered the antennae and connections of his own brushed-steel crown was not feigned. "And so… here we are again, Kinsey. Me, an animal in a maze. You, a student of the mind."

Dr. Freund's calm, amplified voice washed over his environs like a soft breeze redolent of surgery. "We'll be running an experiment shortly, VSOSeSa-A01." Her affect wasn't icy; it betrayed nothing so pedestrian as disdain. As always, she strove to be the voice of Control. Control had different voices for the different minds it sought to wrangle. In the case of the subject she'd shown Executioner Ketch, the peeled husk of SOPS-E305, that meant soft, motherly command. In the case of other offenders, it meant playing the martinet.

This strict tack would have proven counterproductive with VSOSeSa-A01. His subject code was as good as a screaming red **WARNING: EXTREME TOXIC PERIL** sign to researchers who understood the categorization system, and it didn't even come close to describing who – or what – Sa-A01 was; the danger he posed, or the insights and innovations that could be gained by cracking his hard, black little heart and vivisecting his lively, vicious mind.

"Of course, Kinsey." *Now* the researcher could hear the smile in her subject's voice. He spoke with condescending good humor, rich and bitter as brandy steeped in wormwood. Archdirector Freund had seen that smile many times on the night-viz cameras: a terrible, toothy smile that would look perfectly at home fixed in the face of some ferally sadistic forest creature.

She drifted to the complex cell's command console, donned the haptic gloves, and activated the chromate-geometric psychogrammar terminal before her. It had considerably more keyboards, screens, and modules than the one she'd used to paint the mind of E305 for Executioner Ketch. She sank into sensation: the ripple of stroking clicks that ran across the flesh of her hands and the blossom of neutral, sea-green, holographic light that pulsed before her, waiting for her to make her wishes known. As the interface came online, a screen silently rose before the Archdirector's station. She could see the maze laid out below her with no difficulty, and could hear each breath that Sa-A01 drew through his wet gullet, but the portion of the gallery occupied by Dr. Freund was now completely sound- and light-proofed.

"*Red progression,*" the Archdirector murmured sotto voce into her collar-mounted microphone. "*Primary initiation. Test subject; Pox Class Offender VSOSeSa-A01.*" A low, dark red glow began to ooze from the baseboards of the walls, the rooms, the hallways, each mazy turn, and every blind dead end. The sullen, clotted light was just bright enough to illuminate the outline of a hole in the floor in the outermost of SeSa-A01's suite of rooms and passageways. At the center of this warren was SeSa-A01's bedroom: his nest.

Now, before the Archdirector's watchful eyes, a young man (ghost-pale with night-black curls and around twenty years of age, by the look of him) ascended on an elevating round of tile from this unlit lacuna. He rose straight-backed and proud; unarmed and clad in the vivid blue of a Royal Navy uniform. The square clicked home when it reached the level of its mates, sealing the man into SeSa-01's habitat. An attempted naval deserter, he'd been pressed into Dr. Freund's volunteer pool in lieu of execution. Though the volunteer did not know it, his naval uniform eliminated quite a bit of trouble on the Archdirector's part, being pre-wired to monitor the Petty Officer's vital signs.

The cells' diabolic glow was bright enough to sketch vague outlines, but far too dim to pencil in details. ICON had kept SeSa-A01 confined in low to no light since his acquisition, reflected Dr. Freund, and he'd had time to acclimate. That gave him a distinct advantage over the Petty Officer in what would soon transpire. Not that her prize subject needed any advantage to make use of this poor, inexperienced Navy youth. Only a fool would lay their money on the deserter to survive once SeSa-A01 was finished toying with him. She caught the drift of her thoughts and frowned. *This isn't a damned coliseum*, she reminded herself (and not for the first time); *this is a scientific experiment.*

SeSa-A01 was already gliding through the hallway just outside his nest with eerie elegance, silently sniffing the air and listening attentively. *It is*, thought Kinsey, *the way an apex predator would act*. In some ways, she supposed that this test subject *was* an apex predator, evolved to hunt his human prey in one of the King's most populous and policed cities.

The haptic gloves that Dr. Freund had donned for the session provided more than tactile feedback; thanks to minuscule, spiked electrodes, they transmitted a thrill of complex sensation up both arms to their elbows. She lowered her head until the chromatic geometric psychogrammar readout before her took on proper depth. The Archdirector gazed into a dancing desert dune-scape of carmine, beneath whose surface serpents of electric-blue excitement writhed.

The Archdirector pressed a thumb stud on the interface and a second ghostly hologram was painted over the shifting mass of shapes and colors. Now Dr. Freund saw the hallway through SeSa-A01's eyes. This feed arrived courtesy of the brushed-steel helmet she had fixed in place over the subject's rare and awful brain, as though to bang the lid back down atop Pandora's box. One thread in the braid of signals flowing from the metal fixture was a feed direct from Kinsey's subject's visual perception.

As the Archdirector looked down on the theater of her craft, she saw reality on three distinct levels, all juxtaposed. From a pedestrian perspective, Kinsey looked down at the arterial murk of the maze spread out beneath her shrouded perch. She could see the labyrinth's outlines clearly beneath the second layer: the pulsing, four-dimensional geometry of SeSa-A01's cognition, which in turn she saw through the faint haze of his direct optical feed. To a layperson, she knew it would seem muddled as a muck puddle. To her long-practiced eyes, it was an optimal maximization of her data-to-visual-capacity ratio. She felt that her unpleasant sibling would be almost proud of that last turn of phrase.

SeSa-A01 spoke again; conversationally, as though he and Archdirector Freund had been engaged in a diverting discussion that must, alas, be temporarily put aside. "Though we've been interrupted by a guest, Kinsey, we really must continue this some other time. I'm simply *dying* to know what it is you expect to learn from me. Maybe I could be of some help. If I *knew*, that is. For now…" Sa-A01 pulled a trick he'd picked up recently, one that Dr. Freund didn't care for. He lazily slid his left eye closed then opened it: a wink to the invisible rider watching through his eyes. "…enjoy the *show*."

By the time the Navy deserter's screams had gurgled to a stop along with his life, Dr. Freund had already discarded the haptic gloves and stormed away from her console. Rage burned inside of her, no doubt an

RGB 102,0,0 reaction with radiance spikes of 20°. She unclenched one shivering, white-knuckled fist and looked at her fingers curled like talons. Closer to 12°, she decided. Kinsey took her daisy-chain of shortcuts and secrets byways, and reached her private office within a handful of minutes where an unschooled visitor might only find their way in hours (if ever). Another handful of minutes later, a handful of pills were beginning to blunt the edges of her frustrated rage and bewilderment.

The Pit. The goddamned Pit, she thought. *Every time, and it makes no sense.* Dr. Freund's efforts had hit a dead end of such magnitude that she had recently resorted to a desperate, undreamed-of tactic: she had asked her sibling's advice. Ruzi had listened, as they always did, and had asked questions afterward. Incisive questions. So much so that before Kinsey realized what was happening, the Freund siblings were collaborating, in a proper sense, for the first time in an abyss of years. They'd swiftly hit an impasse, though, and to Kinsey's lasting sorrow, it had been a *philosophical* impasse – the hardest type to clear.

"We can use CGP effectively with other classes of offenders," Dr. Gayle had mused. "It's only, what, *one* category that trips this result?"

"It's even stranger than that," Dr. Freund had said after a swallow of wine. "It's not a category – it's a paraphilia, one that runs across a number of categories, but always in much smaller numbers. In whatever category they land in, the sexual sadists – SeSa's – account for a minute number of criminal transgressions, but those transgressions are by far the most..." She'd searched for a word and, without liking the taste, landed on, "*spectacular.*"

"Mmm," mused Dr. Gayle. Their begoggled eyes had

bored into Kinsey over the top of their own wineglass. While Kinsey Freund had, by her own estimation, a rather well-developed palate when it came to wine, the only bottles the sweet-toothed G. Ruzicka Freund would touch were atrocious German dessert wines, so sugary they made Kinsey's teeth hurt.

"*Mmm* is not particularly helpful," Dr. Freund had replied.

"What if the Pit – this total sensory negation effect you get from the CGP and haptic feedback – *isn't* a malfunction?"

"What?" Annoyance creased Kinsey's eyes, causing the crown and heart tattoos beneath her eye to dance.

"What if there's nothing there to create a representation of?" Dr. Gayle tapped one temple with a stolid finger. "Or what if the representation of negation *isn't* some sort of glitch? What if that *is* the psychogrammar's translation?"

"That doesn't make sense," Kinsey insisted. "That implies that there's no emotional or cognitive context for their behavior."

"Or," replied Dr. Gayle, "the emotional and cognitive context *are* represented by the Pit."

Dr. Freund sat back and absorbed that notion. "We've had irregular results before, Ruzi. They always create the Strobe. You remember; that intern discovered it. What was his name? It blinded him for three months. That was before we put in the photonic shutoff threshold."

Dr. Gayle chuckled at the memory. "Anyway," Dr. Freund continued, "we unraveled that what we were seeing was an emotional overload. White is all the colors, as we all learn in the Primary Youth Battalion."

"Yes," Dr. Gayle had said, and fixed Kinsey with their eyes hidden behind their tiny, smoked-glass lenses. "And black is the lack of any color at all."

Dr. Freund had thrown her hands up in frustration. "Well, if *that* were true, Ruzi, what in heaven's name are we even *doing* here?"

"Not punishing the guilty," had been Dr. Gayle's odd reply. "*That's* for sure." It had sent a chill cascading through Kinsey's blood like an infusion of cold saline. '*Punishing the guilty,*' she'd thought later that night, staring up at the colorful and gently pulsing nocturnal CGP prompt as it played across the ceiling of her personal quarters. *Our remit is containment, management, and study. What's going on in that head of yours, Ruzi?* What she wouldn't give to get her sibling into a CGP mapping unit; but that was a topic on which Gayle had proved utterly immovable.

That conversation had taken place before Dr. Freund learned of her sibling's… "improvements" to the original design of several of the King's Pockets. As always, as it turned out, the twins had been pursuing the same goal from opposite directions. Kinsey sought a Virgil to explore the infernal workings of hellish minds. Ruzi, ever the tinkerer of the two, had decided to design and build an inferno of their very own, complete with its own descending circles. Unlike the diabolist of Florence, however, Dr. Gayle Ruzicka Freund was bereft of even the paltry mercies encouraged by theology. Their hell had no deepest circle. It simply kept descending into madness forever.

During Skunk Pussy's frolic with the blumpkins that afternoon, a wiry, sunburned little man with a pronounced German accent joined Ketch's impromptu tour group. At the time, she was watching with a fascination that went well beyond the professional as Skunk, his filthy, uniform-clad legs drenched in an exotic stew of toxins that raised black blisters on his flesh, threaded several of the blumpkin's penises into its various orifices. This process delighted the troll-faced blonde, though it seemed clear to the Executioner that Skunk would have been hard pressed to explain precisely why. Those portions of who Skunk had been in his native universe were gone now; scoured away by Archdirector Freund's CGP erasure before he'd been deposited in Dr. Gayle's minuscule macrocosm.

"*Hah!*" Skunk honked out an unlovely laugh as he threaded a squirming, veiny rope of cock into an inflamed, puckered orifice that had likely been an asshole. "*This* one doesn't like this game much," he explained, dropping the flailing ball into the burning ammoniac bath. The word "cocktopus" squirmed through Executioner Ketch's mind, and she felt vaguely soiled.

"Does it, ah… have a name?" she asked.

The Jolly Rancher looked at her as though she had addressed them in some slobbering glossolalia. "Names? No, Miss… ah, *Executioner* Ketch. I thought Dr. Gayle went through all of this with you."

"Pretend she didn't." Ketch's tone was cold stone.

"Huh." JR rocked back on the heels of his decaying boots and surveyed the hutch full of writhing, acid-bathed monstrosities. "Well, from what I understand we're not the worst bunch in the King's Pockets. There are other pockets. Ah, *deeper* ones. At least, that's what Dr. Gayle said."

"That's true," Ketch confirmed carefully. It seemed that while Archdirector Freund had technically murdered and marooned the King's Executioner, her transgressions might pale in comparison to those of her sibling. Interfering with *one* Pocket was bad enough. Ketch had a feeling Gayle's ambitions were more grandiose than that.

"Gayle came to me a while back," JR said. His affability was strained by his plain discomfort at the presence of Arson's new, confrontational authority figure. He nudged the crystals at the edge of the blumpkins' toxic lagoon with the tip of one boot. The brittle rime crumbled into the liquid, where it dissolved with a wisp of noxious-looking vapor. "And Gayle said that they had an idea about the real bad guys – you know, the real violent kind. At least, that's what they *said* those folks were."

JR paused in his recitation. He looked on philosophically as the indomitable Skunk plucked another plaything from the burning pool, raising weeping wounds on his forearms and palms. With this blumpkin tucked beneath one arm, Skunk began to slide one of his fingers playfully in and out of a distinctly labial opening. "*STOP THAT!*" Ketch roared at him. Skunk did, dropping the blumpkin in shock. His face bore the surprised resentment of a schoolchild caught at a pleasurable but forbidden activity.

"Yeah, well," JR continued uncomfortably, alarmed at Ketch's reprimand of his fetid friend, "Dr. Gayle said that those Pockets had been packed up. Or were being used for something else. I forget. The blumpkins…how did Dr. Gayle put it?"

It was at this moment that a thin, Teutonic voice behind Ketch spoke up, every word carefully enunciated. "Dr. Gayle said 'I have reduced them to their essential nature and recombined them.'" Ketch whirled, surprised and furious at being crept up on. The Executioner almost killed the little German with a hammer palm to the bridge of his nose but caught herself as he flinched like an abused animal.

"Eichmann!" Skunk hailed him gaily. "We're showing Executioner Ketch the blumpkins!" By the time he'd finished his sentence, Ketch's shallow brown eyes had Eichmann's measure. Her inloaded cognitive roll of ARSO:N subjects had identified him.

"SeSa-C32," she greeted him. "Preferred appellation 'Eichmann.' You snuck up on me. That's quite an achievement. I wouldn't make a habit of it, though. Around me, it's a habit that will get you killed."

Eichmann, unlike the other penitents she'd encountered, quailed immediately. He seemed to comprehend (perhaps on a sub- or pre-conscious level) what Ketch's black cowl entailed. Or, perhaps, it was the name, since "Jack Ketch" had been a byword for the last argument of kings since before the Restoration. In days gone by, it had been the pseudonym adopted by hooded executioners, particularly those who'd worked the gallows. Eichmann backed away from Ketch two paces, his watery eyes flicking back and forth like those of a cornered vole seeking the salvation of a thicket. Alas, Arson was a place where no living thing grew. Dr. Gayle had designed it that way.

"Don't worry, C32," Ketch said to the sunburned little man, softening her tone. "I'm not here to hurt you."

This statement drew an amused, resentful cough and a subvocal grumble from the Jolly Rancher, but Ketch ignored him. "Do you remember anything else that Dr. Gayle said about the, ah, blumpkins?" she asked.

Eichmann relaxed marginally. He still wrung his soft little hands like a worried rodent. "I… I think I may have been a biologist? Back in the world?" Eichmann said hesitantly.

This, Ketch knew, was only true in the most macabre sense imaginable. Regardless, she nodded encouragingly to the diminutive German.

"I remember scraps," he said. "Bits of interesting nonsense. Sometimes I talk to Dr. Gayle, and they… I suppose they wanted someone to, ah, impress?"

If so, Ketch thought, her eyes unreadable as ever, *Gayle Ruzicka Freund might be the saddest soul to have ever visited the King's Pockets.* "Go on," she said.

Eichmann stared at the blumpkins in their mesh enclosure. Their gamboling garlands of grasping cocks churned the acrid bath. "Dr. Gayle mentioned something about 'an outside agency.' I assumed… I thought you might know about that, being representative of the King. As Dr. Gayle is." This last sentence wasn't *quite* pronounced as a question.

"Pretend I *don't* know," said the Executioner.

"Dr. Gayle and I spoke about inflammation and acute chemical burns. The mysteries of the flesh, if you will." Ketch's eyes were placid pools, but a careful observer may have noted a twitch of her lethal fingers.

"It was nice to talk," Eichmann went on. "Just speak of bodily things. And then…" He hesitated, guilty hands writhing like two pale spiders escaped from their exoskeletons.

"Please," said Ketch, "this is very helpful, C32."

"Dr. Gayle asked if I wanted to help them pick up a shipment of tissue samples. From this so-called 'outside agency.' I thought that might be why you were here."

Ketch's well-trained voice was mild as milk. "Why would I be here because of tissue samples?"

"Well…" Eichmann now looked vaguely confused. "This outside agency's representative didn't arrive in a Pocket Protector, the way that Dr. Gayle arrives with the new subjects and supplies and so forth."

Eichmann now had a rapt audience. Executioner Ketch, the Jolly Rancher, Skunk Pussy: they all stared at him. The little German blushed deeply enough that it filled in the patchy, pale portions of his sunburn.

"How did the tissue samples arrive, C32?" asked Ketch.

He blinked his watery eyes. "Princess Innocent brought them, Executioner."

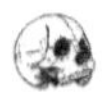

Not every multifaceted lens set into Dr. Gayle's eyes showed them what humans think of as "reality." They needn't have explained this to a mind devoted to interstitial engineering, had any such minds still existed. Actually, if Gayle were honest, their mentor hadn't understood them either. He had been a Royal Natural Philosopher named Hans Feynman, and had expressed ridiculous concerns in terms like "metastatic fracture" and "ultraterrestrials" and "dimensional leakage," which had badly disappointed the younger, less jaded G. Ruzicka Freund. By that point, they'd outstripped their mentor in knowledge, technical achievements, and Royal laurels. This trifecta ensured that the Crown had listened to the Doctors Freund when they'd set out their plans to radically expand ICON's scientific remit. The King had coolly disregarded Dr. Feynman's dire, booming warnings.

Dr. Gayle had heeded neither Feynman's warnings nor the dictates of the Crown, and had constructed their eyes with their own two hands before the orbs had been installed. Some of the gleaming facets of Dr. Gayle's ocular apparatuses were fashioned from exotic materials; in fact, "exotic" may have been an understatement. Their atomic structure was completely unlike anything found in the known universes.

How was this possible? Because the King's Pockets could perhaps best be understood not as pockets, moralpol Primary Education notwithstanding, but rather as cysts: bubbles filled with "reality" injected into the flesh of the cosmos. In such cysts, the reality which had been injected was painstakingly engineered by Dr. Gayle and composed of layers of interlocking rules and relationships, a page torn from the astronomic playbook, but marked up in red pen by their singular mind. Dr. Gayle had always been a lonely being. They'd toyed with the notion of godhood, considering that they'd created tiny universes and then peopled them with conscious organisms. In the end the idea held little savor for the thoroughly atheistic Gayle; not to mention that they were singularly uninterested in answering petitions (though, in time, this would change).

One day, Dr. Gayle's peacock solipsism was unexpectedly broken. They might have no peers in the flawed universe that spawned humans, but – first to their terror, then to their confusion, and ultimately to their delight – it turned out that they had peers in *other* universes. They'd discovered that when those peers made contact.

Personhood was a complicated concept in the brilliant, sideways mind of G. Ruzicka Freund. The former residents of the Area for Registered Sex Offenders: South, for example. Dr. Gayle had never considered them "people," not with a Criminal Violence (CV) suffix in each and every subject number. That was why they'd felt no guilt when they began to play with the parameters of ARSO:S, tweaking this or that linked substrate and crafting bespoke laws of physics, all to maximize the Pocket's...

unpleasantness might be the word. After toying with the laws of aerology and atmospheric physics, Dr. Gayle had forced the tortured sky to rain a mixture of fermented urine and sulfuric acid. This signal accomplishment had led to the first tentative transmission from Dr. Phyntis, who had contacted Dr. Gayle through a subroutine in the massive ICON engines that powered the King's Pockets.

Gayle liked to think of Dr. Phyntis as a "person," though Dr. Gayle had no illusions that the entity so named was human, humanoid, or, indeed, of any equivalent makeup, biological or otherwise. Phyntis seemed to know all there was to know about the universe inhabited by the hominid race that had birthed Gayle, a fact they readily and quickly proved. Hominid or no, Gayle's modifications of and alterations to the ICON systems and the King's Pockets had attracted Phyntis' notice. To Gayle's slowly-thawing delight, Dr. Phyntis offered to collaborate. To report such contact and such an offer to the dullards and courtiers of the Crown was unthinkable. What would follow such a revelation? Execution and the dynamiting of Mount Elbert, in the best case. War in the worst. Unless, that is, Gayle and Phyntis could reform humanity. Those who had no interest in improving or helping improve would make delightful scientific playthings, Phyntis assured them.

Tentatively at first blush, and then with waxing zeal, a working partnership had been developed between two discrete realities. This partnership, Phyntis assured Gayle, would only take place in the interstices that belonged to neither world.

Dr. Gayle traveled to ARSO:N regularly, and at Phyntis' suggestion they'd moved the residents of ARSO:S there. Well, *portions* of them. The relevant portions, in Gayle's opinion, recombined into a more efficient, manageably excruciated form. A half-bright ARSO:N subject, SOPS-B1 (preferred appellation: the Jolly Rancher), proved happy to take custody of these obscenities. B1 even volunteered to collaborate with Gayle on these deconstructed subjects' care and tending. Once the tumbling, turgid things had been re-transported, Gayle collapsed ARSO:S. The interstitial engineer (and Moral Philosopher) fed the surplus power generated by this astronomically ruinous act back into the reification engines generating ARSO:N. The power Gayle possessed at that point would, indeed, qualify them for godhood – albeit only in absentia, shaping ARSO:N from the *real* reality.

They developed quite a scientific fondness for ARSO:N. Its bubble of turbulent reality became the playground in which Gayle and Phyntis carried out experiments. These were still ongoing, and Dr. Gayle noted with grim satisfaction that the local realism still seemed undisturbed, despite their sister's ill-advised assassination-cum-imprisonment attempt. It rankled them to no end that Kinsey, knowingly or not, had exploited a key weakness and wryly underlined an irony in one pyrotechnic blow.

Outside of ARSO:N, Dr. Gayle had nigh-unlimited power over it and its occupants. While they were in the Area, however, they had no such might. In fact, should Kinsey ever figure out how to operate the reification engines as creatively as they had (unlikely but not impossible), Gayle would be worse off than an insect in their sister's palm. By this point they were concerned, but hardly on the point of panic. After all, they had a wild card up their sleeve. A wild, *alien* card.

Gayle had volumes of unanswered questions about their colleague Phyntis and the separate reality they hailed from. The vast majority of their communication after that initial tendril in the reification engines had been by quantum binary. Gayle had asked more than a few of these unanswered questions, of course, but Phyntis had been coy and slow to answer. Why was Phyntis unable to travel to ARSO:N or ARSO:S personally? Why the need for proxies? I AM MORE COMPLICATED THAN YOU. Fair enough, was Gayle's reaction. What were things like where Dr. Phyntis hailed from? SIDEWAYS, they had said, and SOFT, and, finally, disquietingly, SHARP. Gayle was not known for their squeamishness, but something in the sibilant simplicity of those responses had caused them pause. They'd momentarily reconsidered their collaboration. This discomfiture had only spanned a moment, true, but it had been… disgustingly psychological. Like something their sister would equivocate about or craft apologetics for.

Perhaps Dr. Phyntis had detected this response on some level, because they had sent a Pocket Protector of their own to ARSO:N the next day while Gayle was there. It was exotic and bewildering, like something iron-hard made from sunlight and black silk. When it evaporated, it left the sweet taste of lead on Gayle's lips. Left behind were eight tiny chips of a substance whose composition ruthlessly mocked natural law. ARSO:N or Gayle's universe; jurisdiction was no help. Shortly afterward, Phyntis transmitted instructions for their use and, after a frustrating and exhilarating process of meticulous adaptation, Gayle had made the lenses; for that, in so many words, was what they were.

What the lenses did was complex and, if Gayle was honest, not something they fully understood. They independently discovered new properties the secretive lenses possessed on a regular basis. One of the exotic devices' basic functions was to make visible to Gayle's optical-neural interface phenomenon not ordinarily detectable by four-dimensional apparatuses. For example, they rendered the transmission of interstitial signals visible in ways that defied ordinary human perception. With their exotic lens display engaged, Gayle could see faint shadows of the past movements of people and objects, and to see split-second futures cluster in a centipede-wreath of arms and legs and stances. It also let them see the full, unfiltered horror of a breach between discrete realities (thus, Gayle theorized, the discomfort and – in some cases – outright horror caused in some subjects by the sight of, as one called it, "the hole in everything").

Dr. Phyntis' emissary called herself – and, oh, she *was* a she, she'd made no small deal out of *that* fact – Princess Innocent. Gayle detested Innocent's name with a depth of feeling usually reserved for plotting acts of murder, and had complained to Dr. Phyntis on more than one occasion. There was, it seemed, no way around it. Princess Innocent had been the name that Phyntis' creation had picked for herself, and, therefore, Princess Innocent it was.

Dr. Gayle was wary of her, and with ample reason. Consider: subject SeSa-C32 – "Eichmann," by preferred appellation – was one of the vanishingly few subjects in ARSO:N who retained useful (if, in his case, hideously-gotten) skills. Skill enough to help her work, so he had been allowed to trundle after Dr. Gayle to one of their infrequent meetings with Princess Innocent. Eichmann had held both his tongue and his gorge for the duration of the encounter, but once Phyntis' factotum had departed, Eichmann vomited profusely and explosively. He'd also (much more irritatingly) refused to cease weeping and wailing until Dr. Gayle, both bored and busy, executed him with one shot from the pistol that they carried on each visit. He'd seemed well enough the next time that they'd seen him, fully healed by Arson's repair algorithm and even willing to explain what had upset him so.

It seemed the exotic material technology which had preceded Princess Innocent's first visit had been given out of more than simple generosity. Lenses, Gayle knew, could do much more than merely magnify; some of them filtered out as much as they revealed. In the case of Phyntis' familiar, the filtered view of Innocent was, well, innocent enough. When Gayle asked Eichmann to elaborate on what he'd seen, he'd been reluctant. In the end, he'd only said that what he'd seen was "a mannequin" or "a puppet."

That didn't sound so frightening to Gayle, but they were a brilliant scientific theoretician and engineer, not some half-bright, half-mad butcher. Eichmann had been lucky not to land in ARSO:S in the first place. There, he'd have been made into a portion of a blumpkin. Even so, the man's reaction to an unfiltered view of Innocent made Dr. Gayle reluctant to look at her without the strange, eightfold lens array. Dr. Gayle suspected their artificial eyes would have saved them the worst of the debilitating vision which had so unmoored C32's reason. Gayle's research suggested a strong correlation between organic tissue and the strange effects of interstitial dynamics. Just another reason to be glad they'd shed their fleshy eyes and made some very special modifications to their brain, His Majesty's royal edict be damned.

Not long after hailing Phyntis for aid in the wake of their second death, Dr. Gayle's special anti-puppet lenses (as she drily thought of them) began to pick up the first signs of an incursion into ARSO:N's local reality. Hair-thin networks of intricate, crystalline beauty began to knit themselves out of nothing in the empty air, the patterns a bit like frost climbing a winter window. These were no crystals, though; they had infinitely more dimensions than that. As their vectors, gradients, and ephemeral lines began to double and redouble, Gayle's ape-brain (as they thought of their more atavistic impulses) attempted to rebel. They crushed this budding panic with the titanic weight of their persistent scientific fascination.

These lines – or webs, depending on the angle one approached them from – twisted around a terrestrial spindle, a rapidly-congealing shape that wrapped itself out of the very material of air and desert scenery. It was like watching a person walk straight through a bedsheet hung from a clothesline, wearing it in their continued perambulation. The distorted spindle-human quickly took on three-dimensional solidity, climbing down from whatever state they normally existed in.

Princess Innocent took four reifying steps and stood before Dr. Gayle. She was short; shorter than Gayle by at least a head. Innocent was, to Gayle's eyes, a blonde girl of perhaps fourteen or fifteen. She was winsome, with sparkling and slightly outsized blue eyes. She wore the same clothes every time Gayle saw her, though Gayle reasoned that the "clothes" were as much a part of the organism as her skin, hair, or anything else. Innocent wore a stylized, one might even say *fetishized*, short red checked skirt and brief white button-up blouse. A uniform of the type that pre-Restoration private tuition students wore, if Gayle weren't mistaken; a classic SOPS/SOCV erotic misplacement object.

"*Hey*, you!" the thing which called herself Princess Innocent piped in a pure, clear girl's voice, bright as a field of daffodils. "Dr. Phyntis sends their regards! My *gosh*, have we got a mess on our hands or *what*, Dr. G?"

WAPB PROGRAMMING SCHEDULE, SATURDAY 2/20

APPROVED: ALL AUDIENCES
4:00 – 5:00 AM: Understanding Our Kingdom's Faith with Dr. Monson Hansen, ThD, Brigham Young University. "Today is the day our Heavenly Father made! Learn about the wonders of our Kingdom's role in these latter days."

APPROVED: CITIZENS 18+ IN GOOD STANDING
5:00 – 6:00 AM: Royal News – Morning Edition. "News for Saturday, 2/20"

APPROVED: ALL AUDIENCES
6:00 – 7:00 AM: Essential Oils, Essential Knowledge. "Today's program will focus on the medicinal uses of Oil of Bergamot, with special guest Elma Christiansen, author of 'Healthsome Herbs!'"

APPROVED: ALL AUDIENCES
7:00 – 8:00 AM: State Street: "Kind Youth Battalion Mother: Bill, Johnny, and Josh are disappointed when their Youth Battalion Mother is sick and cannot read them moralpol stories. They decide to pass the time by painting pictures of all the kind things their Youth Battalion Mother does for King Cleon."

APPROVED: ALL AUDIENCES
8:00 – 9:00 AM: The Kindly King: "Judy's Zoo Day: Judy Juicebox takes the kids to the Hoboken Royal Zoo, and guess who they run into? The Kindly King helps Judy find Buckles, who gets off his leash!"

7.
THE BORDERS OF REALITY

Time, like space, was more a playful means of torture than a constant in Arson. It was hard to say how long each of Arson's residents had been there in terms of pedestrian, terrestrial years, let alone the ersatz chronological flow of the King's Pockets. By any standard, an age had passed since the penal reality's subjects knew an evening of such delights. Rebellion and the flames of lust had been rekindled, roaring and resuscitated by the outcast angel sideshow on Ardor Street's crumbling macadam. The schemes of would-be gods had come unstitched and the lives of prisoners were once more sweet and sharp.

The twilight overture was provided by a newly-resplendent Uncle Funny. Earlier that day, he'd assumed a post inside the Woodpile, accompanied by three mysterious suitcases. Funny swilled mule vinegar like a desert drifter gorging at a sweet and longed-for oasis. When the mule's mad teeth bit deeply, his newly-whitened corneas rolled and glowed like silver moons. At last, the time was right; Funny volubly declaimed that he had something to share with his fellow Arsonists; something they would simply *love*.

Novelty was a barter good in Arson, and this act of

generosity on the part of Uncle Funny drew a gaggle quickly. When Funny brought the puppets out, Salty nearly killed him out of hand. The scar-faced man was furious that the evening's promised entertainment seemed, at best, a joke at their expense. Employing the loquacious coruscation which had plucked his nuts from self-lit fire more than once, Uncle Funny implored the skeptical patrons of the Woodpile to have a jar or two of the mule and then see what he had in store. While Salty and the others did so, Funny clambered up the rickety, porch-like entrance to the tumbledown public house. He dangled down his marionettes, and without preamble, the show began.

And by damn, in short order the dust-choked rut before the Woodpile rang and roared with the laughter of long-simmering resentment's fierce release. Funny found that, far from losing his knack with the wire and voice work, he seemed to have absorbed every voice his old partner Bill "Ratfucking Son of a Bitch" Redding had managed. In fact, his Judy Juicebox was a broader-palate performance than Redding had ever managed. Admittedly, his new act wasn't aimed at kids, but Funny's improvised material was killing. It wasn't hard to understand why. *Good satire*, he reflected sagely, *is difficult, but in the hands of an artist it can be a thing of subtlety and incisive wit.*

"...and *UP* we go!" cried Judy Juicebox, thrusting one skinny puppet arm shoulder-deep into the puppet posterior of the Kindly King. Uncle Funny was amazed at his own skill; neither he nor his felt creations had possessed anything like this sort of dexterity before.

"DEEPER!" squealed the Kindly King, wriggling his plush buttocks. "TRY TO FIND MY BALLS, I'M SURE I LEFT THEM UP THERE *SOMEWHERE!*"

The small crowd of well-vinegared men howled with laughter. At Mount Elbert, deep beneath the rock that held ICON's massive reification engines, something gave a deep, tectonic shudder.

Prod, Balloonman, and Pinetop were near enough the Woodpile that they heard hilarity erupt there, but none of them paid it any mind. They were preoccupied. All three, having rediscovered facets of the human experience long-occluded from them in their life as Arsonists, found that their recovered joys meshed perfectly: or perfectly enough, at any rate. Balloonman sank his member into Rita's soft-walled silicon interior and stared into her dead doll's face, the unmoving lips and uncanny glass eyes just as he remembered them. As he did, Prod's own meaty member was buried tonsil-deep in Pinetop's throat. Balloonman's performance thrilled both men like an erotically condensed static charge. As he serviced Prod with unashamed abandon, Pinetop engaged in Arson's inaugural act of onanism, pumping away with one eager, spit-greased fist as his lover's slick, thick cock throbbed beneath the ministrations of his lips and tongue.

The three Arsonists climaxed in quick succession like a string of firecrackers going off, the first orgasms to ever rock the Area, and a neural pattern completely out of line with the baseline reality of Dr. Gayle's penitential Pocket. This time the engines at ICON's mountain fastness did much more than shudder. They gave a lurch that wrested sheets of stone from the cliffside shielding them. These thundered to the valley floor below, leveling a swath of forest.

As riotous, mocking laughter rang and loins quivered, the sky of Arson fluoresced with a carmine effulgence that shimmered the rich color of cheap, corner-store wine. After this display, the daylight fled, never to exert its grip upon the penal world again. Deep as desire, endless night took Arson in its arms.

The wine-bright shimmer of the sky did more than signal the arrival of the dark, sacred night. Every Arsonist, without exception, felt something shift beneath their feet and in their hearts. The air first throbbed with a painful, unreleased tension, then relaxed in silken shivers sensuously through each spine.

At the Open O Ranch, Ketch had tired of the blumpkins quickly. She'd seen enough before that point to condemn the Freunds thrice over. Morbid curiosity, alas, could only be indulged for so long, and she lacked the resources to deal with such a perverse moralpol crime on her own. The best that Ketch could do for now was shoo Skunk Pussy from the simmering, miserable hutches so the unlikely tour group could make their rag-masked way back to the fence line. The twilight glistened like a film of chum on the surfaces of reeking pools of toxic piss and soil-leached, freakish compounds. They wove through smoke-cloaked craters where the Jolly Rancher brewed his potent, stimulating poisons, and Ketch was just reaching the shabby wire fence when the sky lit like a neon sign tasting a humid Friday night.

The flashing sky did not have the strange, sensual effect on Executioner Ketch that it did on the Area's CGP-affected denizens, but she felt *something* when she saw the momentary blink. Magnetic polarity? Gravity? Both? Whatever force it was, it tilted something fundamental in an alarming way. The sensation made Ketch painfully remember, for the first time in a long time, that she was a fragile, existentially tiny mortal treading in a universe made not by the mathematic inevitability of her native cosmos, but by human artifice. Highly imperfect human artifice. (Not that the uncaring cosmos was such great shakes either, in her opinion.)

"What was *that*?" the Executioner barked, staggering a bit as her center of gravity wobbled wildly and the ground beneath her seemed to simultaneously tip and stretch in some uncannily perceived way.

None of her companions replied. Skunk, JR, and Eichmann all stopped dead in their tracks, heads cocked as though hearkening to a bewitching sound; one which they could hear but she could not. After a moment they turned as one, heads jerking as though at the ring of a gunshot. Their slackened, sleepy faces pointed back in the direction of Arson's main clutch of structures; an area she'd heard them refer to with unconscious (if any) irony as Ardor Street. Eichmann, Skunk, and JR began a slow somnambulation, unhurriedly but unerringly proceeding toward their goal in a tightknit trio. Jacqueline Ketch – appointed for scrupulous lack of remorse and keen instinct alike – did not attempt to rouse them from their strange trance. She dropped back and began to follow them. She had a hunch that whatever the hell had just happened to local reality, their sudden, silent, tarantula-like migration was related.

Their little band didn't have far to go. Before her journey to ICON's fastness atop Mount Elbert, Executioner Ketch had accessed the files laying out the basic physical properties of ARSO:N (if any such exoticism could be considered "basic"). She knew they wouldn't have had much of a walk, no matter *where* they were bound. As far as Ketch could ascertain from the bewildering files of the Doctors Freund, the Pocket was less than ten kilometers in circumference. The flash which seemed to have unseated the reason of the subjects she was trailing didn't alarm her the way such an event back in the real world would. While Ketch didn't pretend to understand interstitial engineering, she knew a little. She knew that much of the sky – that toxic, awful "sun," for instance – was an illusion, not to mention much of what appeared to exist beyond Arson's manufactured walls.

She didn't know as much as she thought. When she caught sight of Ardor Street, the Executioner was stunned (though she suppressed her surprise with professional aplomb). The crumbling terminus of a blacktop road stood where it had no right to. Worse than that, a long, straight string of asphalt highway snaked away to a strange ring of bones and, beyond that, to the illusory, mountainous horizon. A horizon that, now that she inspected it, seemed to be a bit more gap-toothed than she remembered.

Worse still, something that *absolutely* had no business in Arson crouched atop the mysterious blacktop. The closest descriptor Ketch could attach to it was "truck," but that was entirely inadequate. It was an unrelenting bubblegum hue, from its spotless tires to its stacked, misshapen exhaust pipes. The object measured nearly ten meters in height and more than 75 meters in length. Her profession had not inclined the Executioner toward anthropomorphism, but she had an unshakable feeling that the ugly, fleshy truck was leering at her.

The position of King's Executioner was not an easy job. She knew that in some regimes, the position of Executioner was a sadist's sinecure; a gory performance in which captive prey was dispatched for His Majesty's amusement. That was *part* of her job, yes, but the Kingdom's Executioners were drawn from the ranks of the Royal Army and Royal Navy's most elite special combat officers for a reason. Jacqueline Ketch had been trained to a razor's honed edge well before she donned the cowl and took her nameless name. She was surprised, but trained to let surprise roll through and over her without impacting her. Her heart rate did not elevate, nor did her breath catch, when she saw the loathsome pink truck. Her eyes' static irises, of course, did not dilate or pucker as she saw the row of brightly varicolored sheds behind the truck.

One sight did elicit a well-trained reaction. Courage had always been compatible with caution in her book. The Executioner slid behind the rolling rise of lifeless hill she'd topped. There she contemplated the impossible presence of intruders, and what the implications of that were. Had this been the Royal Court or a battlefield, the first thing she would have been on guard for was an infiltration. In Arson, she had let her guard down. Sneaking through the Kingdom's border was no mean feat, but it could be done. The borders of reality were quite another thing entirely, and she'd allowed herself to trust in their security. *Ridiculous*, she chided herself as she counted for long minutes. When no voices or weapons were raised, she tentatively let herself think she might still be unseen.

Ketch slowly rose until just her mild brown eyes crested the rise. This crocodilian vantage gave her a clear view as she tried to make sense of the situation. Had some foreign power with technology comparable to ICON's engines penetrated Arson? She discarded the notion. Royal Executioners were nearly as well-briefed as His Majesty himself, and there had been no inkling that the Kingdom's foes had engineered a means of interstitial injection. Another gambit by one of the Doctors Freund, one which – like the blumpkins – she hadn't been meant to discover? It was possible, Ketch decided.

She catalogued the intruders. Two men; one with a bald head and onyx skin, clad in the uniform of an ICON subject, and one whose provenance was harder to determine. He was a bleached, tanned, desert-colored thing, from the crown of his preposterous cream-colored cowboy hat to the soles of his well-worn leather boots. While Ketch hung back to spy, the Jolly Rancher, Skunk, and Eichmann slowly made their silent way down to the patch of decomposing road. As they reached its edge, the man in the cream-colored hat greeted each with evident cordiality. Some degree of the mesmeric daze induced in the Arsonists by the sky's flicker-flash seemed to have worn off, and Ketch could hear the indistinct syllables of the hat-man's words, spoken in a dry voice as he conversed briefly with JR and Skunk. As the three chatted, the sunburned little man with the pronounced German accent (*SeSa-C32, preferred name the quite distasteful "Eichmann,"* she recollected) wandered toward the bald man, who spoke to him in a soft voice. He led Eichmann to the black shed, the last one in the line. It stood at the far end of its jolly brethren like a grim diagnosis delivered at the end of a long, lovely summer.

While Ketch did not enjoy the full suite of active-combat augmentations she'd possessed back in the King's Army, before His Majesty cremated her name, she *did* have many. These included an inset zoom lens in one eye, an inload of her files of ICON personnel, and rudimentary facial recognition memetics. From her supine stance she had a clear and unobstructed view of one invader's face. The hat-man's eyes and brow were concealed beneath his ostentatious chapeau, but there was enough of his face showing to grab a basic read from the jawline, nose, and mouth.

For hat-man, Ketch received no matches. That alone was strange enough to damn the man. No matter that the Doctors Freund had gone rogue and may have invited him; the project was well beyond classified, and access to ICON was to be determined by His Majesty, not the Freunds. A stranger with a lurid, experimental-looking machine in the heart of the Kingdom's deepest secret was beyond bad. To Ketch's dismay, it turned out not to be the most alarming thing about the pair. That honor belonged to Mystery Morrison Spare.

The Executioner didn't have the proper scientific or moralpol theoretical backgrounds to understand some aspects of ICON's programs, and the Mysteries had been second only to the reification-engines in complexity of function. The engines were a project of machinery; a collision of exotic fields fed by a ruinous amount of power poured into a carefully arranged collection of elaborately manufactured plates of rare material. The Mysteries, by contrast, were a *human* project. Unlike the engines, which fell firmly under the jurisdiction of Dr. Gayle, the Mysteries were one of Archdirector Kinsey Freund's discontinued projects. No shame there, for Dr. Gayle had many failures to their name as well.

What, precisely, went into creating Kinsey's Mysteries was gibberish to Ketch, but the practical applications had been quite comprehensible to one who'd studied political ideoplasty (as Ketch once had). The Mysteries were reality reconfiguration experts; technicians of perception, magnetic fields of social metaphor, and generators of quantum un/shared frameworks. Where it might take moralpol instructors and CGP technicians decades to manipulate a major change in socially processed cognition, the Mysteries – it was claimed –

could do it in a year. Less, perhaps. How they did this wasn't clear, but based on what material had not already been destroyed, Ketch thought it safe to say the Mysteries did more than recite pretty speeches.

They were, in essence, psychogrammarians. Reports said they'd been capable of writing new rules of baseline human psychology. They wrought these effects through the application and maintenance of concentrated will, channeled through experimental and highly classified cerebral enhancements. When she'd read the notes before reaching Mount Elbert and the stranger points beyond, the Executioner had thought this smacked suspiciously of magick. At one point, the Mysteries' role in the future of the King's Pockets had been bright. Had been, in fact, the meat of the most fruitful and longest period of direct collaboration between the siblings Freund.

But it hadn't worked out, and even the project notes had been expunged. *Why* they'd been expunged had, naturally, been expunged as well. One was left to wonder what was failure (or success?) enough to evidently make them rethink things so radically. One was also left to wonder, Ketch thought with a chill, why a canceled project's test subject was not just wandering Arson – he was somehow listed in the personnel file she had inloaded.

Ketch was suddenly, achingly aware that she had lost herself in thought, and lost her lensed-in focus on Mystery Morrison Spare. When she found him again, his hairless cranium was ringed by a reverse sun disk; a halo of darkness so total that it had an inside-out, pitchy radiance. The black shed's door was open, and, as she watched, Eichmann vanished into the shed's lightless innards and the door swung smoothly shut. *Known quantities*, she tapenoted grimly. *Unsanctioned presences in ARSO:N, including the deployment of a Mystery named Morrison Spare to the Pocket. Some sort of experimental psychogrammar reprogramming possible…* Her note trailed off, and the cognitive implant helpfully stopped recording on its own a few moments later.

Executioner Ketch stared up at a form looming over her, silent as a cavern's heart. It was the man in the silly cream-colored cowboy hat. He had either scuttled as quickly and silently as a desert spider on the hunt or simply appeared nearby mere seconds after he'd been at the blacktop's edge. His outline was a tall black silhouette, darker than the deepening hue of the evening.

"Royal Executioner Jacqueline Ketch," said the black man-shape in a dry, smoked voice. It was a voice that spoke of tombs where heat-cured mummies gently gnawed each other's ancient flesh in serpent-nest communion. He reached one hand down what seemed like an abyssal distance, blunt fingers spread like a grasping cosmic claw. The hand hovered before Ketch's unshockable, shallow brown eyes, and after a moment she accepted the hand up, rising from her supine pose behind the hardpack hillock.

Now that she was level with him, Ketch beheld a broad, unsmiling face. tanned by sun and time and miles. A checked western shirt. Worn jeans, scuffed boots. Atop it all, that broad, soft-looking, vaguely fungal hat, with its leather hatband and strange floral fetish.

"I'm Frank Blank." He smiled, presenting an even row of harmless, blunted pearls for inspection. He made a big show of inspecting his unadorned wrist as though consulting an imaginary wristwatch. "And you are right on time, Executioner!"

Dr. Gayle was making their way toward the Open O Ranch when the sculpted sky of ARSO:N incandesced with wine-bright fervor and the world-engines of ICON shuddered. They were trailed in their trudge at a distance of several yards by Princess Innocent. Dr. Phyntis' factotum skipped in circles as she followed the Moral Philosopher. Actually *skipped*; Gayle was marveling with a sense of loathing bright as a stripped wire. Occasionally, Innocent gave voice to sing-song nonsense as she flitted back and forth. *I really must talk to Phyntis about this messenger*, Gayle reflected. *It's not* just *that she irritates me, though that hardly contributes to my…!*

Pain and ecstasy blew through Dr. G. Ruzicka Freund's brain like a sword of sugar hammered home by lightning. Their close-cropped skull, with its illicit, buried mechanisms, sprayed a pyrotechnic spectacle of vivid green and violet sparks. Gayle dropped to the lifeless dirt, their mind completely blank for endless fractions of a second.

"Hey, Doc!" Princess Innocent exclaimed. She sounded muffled to the still-recovering Dr. Gayle, as though her voice were being sucked away, and out, and *up*. "What's your deal? Are you, like, *okay*?"

Gayle could not respond at first. They managed to exhale a withered handful of words.

"Engines. Accessed. Parameter… negation."

A rapid scuttling sound achieved a brief, violent crescendo, and Princess Innocent was on Gayle like a jackal on a guineafowl. Innocent's pale, smiling face, trailing a blonde comet's tail of cornsilk hair, swam large in Gayle's unsteady vision. *This is apocalyptic*, they thought, with slightly more emotive subtext than usual.

Whatever the nature of the interstitial event that had just ripped through ARSO:N, it had coursed through the mechanisms buried in the meat of Gayle's brain. These were the very systems that linked them to the vast machinery entombed in the core of Mount Elbert, and the surge had fried the majority of their prosthetic eyes' many lenses. *Temporarily*, they desperately hoped as their basic cognitive implants began to reset and power back up. Gayle struggled to their hands and knees and glanced up.

Princess Innocent looked different. She bore no resemblance to whatever puppet-nightmare Eichmann had imagined. Rather, this version of Princess Innocent was painted in translucent light and fantasy, a figure both cartoonish and unreal. *The exotic lenses,* realized Dr. Gayle. *They're not linked to my reification array. They're still functioning. The other lens arrays – those that show* reality *– are still rebooting. What I'm seeing is the illusion draped over Phyntis' factotum, not the substance. Just the wrapping paper.*

Gayle realized with a start that there was something they couldn't quite see wrapped around their throat, squeezing with inhuman strength; a waxy thing like an oversized artist's manikin hand, but one boasting a proud surfeit of fingers, each with far too many knuckles.

"*WHO*," groaned Princess Innocent through her glowing smile, which stayed as joyful as a robin's song. "*HOW*." There was nothing human in the voice, though its cuckoo creak was still concealed amongst the fragile eggs of human sounds and human words.

"Don't... know... get... *off*," Gayle choked out. The clicking appendage grasping their throat tightened instead. The cartoon face, composed of light and color, beamed with murderous good cheer. Having died and risen twice that day already, Dr. Gayle did not intellectually fear a third death. Nonetheless, they were awash in mortal fear's adrenal bath. *As far as I've advanced*, they reflected, their breath restricted to hot, hard spurts, *I'm still a prisoner of a ridiculous genetic imperative to survive at any cost.*

As quickly as the flicker of a candle's flame, Princess Innocent became more real. The hand around Gayle's neck still felt as hard as steel, but now they felt no supernumerary joints or digits. *The implants*, Gayle realized, *have rebooted.* Their first act, on this realization, was to tapenote a research observation that Phyntis' abomination had a physical form shaped, in part, by an onlooker's perception. This fact was, scientifically speaking, fascinating.

Dr. Gayle's second act upon their implants' reboot was to access the ARSO:N reification engine. At the speed of thought, they accessed certain subroutines and made a few adjustments to Princess Innocent's mass and axis of gravitational effect. This should have thrown the otherworldly emissary back like they'd been hit by a freight car. It *did* knock Innocent away, but with no more force than a hearty shove. She traveled briefly through the dry air, falling to the hardpack with a heavy *THOMP*.

Princess Innocent hit the dead dirt with an undignified and very human squawk of surprise. As she did, Dr. Gayle ran through the reification engine data logs in a high-speed hunt for any explanation for the intense interstitial event which had lit the sky and touched Gayle like a lick of luscious lightning. They discovered a furious litany of error reports, but no sign of what had caused them.

"Irksome," Gayle grunted as they clambered to their

feet, referring to both this distressing mystery and Innocent's display of pique. The surge through the Moral Philosopher's circuitry left them slightly dizzy but, it seemed, otherwise intact. Princess Innocent, too, seemed unharmed, though *that* was hardly Gayle's concern. Innocent, for her part, seemed embarrassed by the altercation, and even let her bright-eyed girl mask blush a bit to show as much. "Gosh, Doc," she mumbled, "I'm awful sorry about that. Sorta lost my temper."

"Think nothing of it," rasped Gayle through a contused throat. *I will discover if your kind knows pain and, if you don't, I will teach you*, they thought, sealing off their fury until it could find release. "And no. I checked the data logs and engine outputs. What just transpired is, at present, undetermined. Perhaps some sort of Λ hyperon bombardment…" Gayle trailed off. Innocent's eyes had fixed on something over Gayle's left shoulder. A beatific smile of happy welcome limned her face. Gayle turned, beheld a hellishly familiar figure, and froze. *Howling Andy*, her numb mind reported unnecessarily.

Dr. Gayle believed in strict control but readily acknowledged happy accident and random chance's roles in technological progress. They had thus encouraged the Jolly Rancher to branch out into "experiments" of his own. One of JR's innovations had been the highly toxic intoxicant the residents of the Pocket called "mule vinegar," and it had proved as fascinating as it was frustrating. Mass spectrometry of a sample had proved bewildering. Decoding what, precisely, "mule vinegar" *was* remained an ongoing ICON project. The Rancher also, much to Gayle's delight, took it upon himself to test the limits of the Area's regeneration algorithm.

Finding a test subject wasn't difficult. ARSO:N was a bleak and dismal place to live, and die, and live again. One subject in particular proved particularly and incurably despondent. His designation was SOPS-A07; a man, like all of ARSO:N's prisoners, cleft from his past and passions and committed to the untender mercies of the Moral Philosopher. A07 had been sentenced to transportation for the moralpol violation "Prostitution: Solicitation by a Patron" with the aggravating circumstance of CGP-verified odaxelagnia.

In the ever-practical parlance of prostitution, A07 was what was called "a biter;" albeit one who'd been up front about his picadillo, and who'd been happy to pay extra for the privilege. In more explicit terms, he'd paid to sink his blunt teeth into vulnerable female flesh while his loins came aflame and his bony hips pumped passionately in the idiot rhythm of the paraphiliac's Pachanga. While A07 couldn't even reliably recall his own name after the shriving of his memories, he somehow still retained a sense of outraged injustice; a sense that he'd been wronged by his consignment to the unforgiving King's Pocket of ARSO:N.

All that A07 (first preferred appellation "Sad Andy") wanted was to die.

The residents of ARSO:N believed that there was one way out of their predicament. Each of them could speak with Dr. Gayle about "Parole," which Gayle assured them meant a final execution with no chance of restoration to their misery. This release, they told the prisoners, was granted by a Parole Board, of which they were the chairperson. None of this was true. "Parole," in truth, meant that the unfortunate applicant became a fragment of a blumpkin. Though Sad Andy applied for "Parole" countless times, he always was denied. Dr. Gayle had a notion that A07 had a larger role to play.

A07 wished to die? Gayle had been inclined to grant

his wish. Not out of any misguided sympathy for Sad Andy: no one could credibly level the charge of Criminal Compassion at a soul as desiccated as G. Ruzicka Freund's. Gayle had simply been curious, in a scientific sense. When they'd turned Sad Andy over to her proxy JR, Gayle desired answers to specific questions. What would it take to bypass the regenerative algorithm built into the Pocket? Was there such a thing as irreparable damage in the dry, self-winding hourglass of ARSO:N?

The answer to the first question turned out to be "quite a bit," and the answer to the second a qualified "yes." While Sad Andy lived on (and on, and on), irreparable damage had, indeed, been done to him. Dr. Gayle had witnessed much of it, though the actual disassembly had been carried out by the Jolly Rancher. The exotic elements which Dr. Gayle had, with the help of Dr. Phyntis, introduced into the warp and weft of ARSO:N produced a canker crop of novel compounds whose effects had supplemented JR's eager wet-work. Whistling above Sad Andy's screams as he worked, the Rancher made a series of thorough renovations to the prisoner's physique. He'd worked with blades, hammers, clamps, and flame, all provided by Gayle and used beneath their watchful, smoked-lens gaze. Some of JR's work regenerated, healed by the reification-engines, but some had not. Andy had discontinued his participation, in no small part because he had been driven mad. He'd learned to shun the sun, and creep forth only when the poison light relinquished its dead tyrant's grip. In the lightless night, he filled the air of ARSO:N with the sound of his inchoate grief and pain. Sad Andy became Howling Andy.

Though naked, he was clad in tatters. Andy hadn't bothered with clothing since his degeneration at the Rancher's hands, and so the scale and variety of his unhealing wounds were displayed with neither shame nor ostentation. His scalp was bare to bone in broad swaths. The bleeding scraps of flesh still clinging to his face didn't lend themselves to recognizable expressions. Shorn of eyelids, his bulging eyeballs stared. Divorced from lips, his cracked and broken teeth grinned unceasingly. Though bipedal when he chose to be, Howling Andy's preference was to hunch on all fours. As he stared at Dr. Gayle and Princess Innocent, Andy clenched his ever-bloody fists in the stinging dirt. With detached fascination, Gayle realized that they could see Andy's heart pumping fitfully but steadily through a broad, bone-bypassing rent in the mottled meat of his flank.

A07 HAS SEEN MY REPRESENTATIVE

Dr. Gayle was startled out of their inspection by the unmistakable photonic twitch of a communique from Dr. Phyntis. As the message arrived, Princess Innocent walked slowly toward Howling Andy. Andy's peeled eyes were fixed on the approaching figure. The partially-disassembled man began to shake so violently that his tremors dislodged bits and scraps of defiled flesh from his scalded bones. Gayle remembered Eichmann's reaction to Princess Innocent, and the mercy-killing which had subsequently been required. *If I were to deactivate Benway's exotic lenses,* they mused, *what would I see?*

DO NOT DISABLE YOUR TRANSLATION LENSES

Gayle froze. They hadn't sent that message to Phyntis, merely thought it. They hadn't even *deliberately* thought it; it had merely been a fleeting flight of speculation. Innocent continued to approach Howling Andy, her manner as nonthreatening as that of a bighearted girl approaching a wary, feral dog. The simultaneous accuracy and total alienness of this comparison sent a rare thrill of existential discomfort through Gayle.

WE CAN CONTINUE THIS DISCUSSION MOMENTARILY, sent Phyntis through an infinitesimal pinprick of caged light. RIGHT NOW I WANT YOU TO WATCH

That sounds like something Prod and Pinetop might have said, once upon a time, Gayle thought inanely, then hoped that *that* gem hadn't gotten through. There was no use pretending: clearly, Phyntis had no difficulty picking up their thoughts. *Why the business with the quantum telegraph, if it wasn't necessary?* This time Gayle hoped Phyntis *would* reply, but there was no transmission in response. *Maybe it's a one-way street,* thought Gayle, but she suspected not. She suspected other motives. If Phyntis had shown up in their head, instead of making fumbling contact, would Gayle have been as welcoming? Would they have thought they'd lost their mind? Would they have reported it to Kinsey and brainstormed... something? Honestly, Gayle wasn't sure. And if they weren't sure, why would some extraplanar intelligence take that chance?

At least the full array of lenses functioned once more. Phyntis' factotum once again looked human and not like a low-tech hologram. Howling Andy's shivering intensified with every step the strange, girlish ambassador took toward him. "Shh," she said gently. Andy threw back his head and voiced the chilling, inhuman ululation of outraged grief and agony that had earned him his second sobriquet.

"Shh," said Princess Innocent again, and laid one hand upon the ragged revenant's bleeding brow. "It's over now. It's all over now."

Her touch *unmade* him. Dr. Gayle was stymied for a better word. One moment, Howling Andy stared at whatever visage Innocent showed those not wearing Phyntis' exotic lenses, his raw face as expressionless as ground beef but, nonetheless, a face. The next, a loose conglomeration of poisonous, half-Earthly dirt – the base substrate of ARSO:N's terrible terroir – stood in Andy's place. It held his shape for a long, eerie moment. The moment passed and it swooned into gravity's embrace and joined the surface of the Pocket. Dr. Gayle, transfixed, tapenoted this experimental result; the first true death in ARSO:N. Howling Andy – whomever he had been, whatever he had dreamed in his degeneracy – would not pollute the Kingdom with his corpse. He wouldn't even pollute the *universe* in which the Kingdom sat. The Moral Philosopher made a second tapenote; a new concept to pitch to His Majesty, should Gayle surface from this ordeal in good standing. A small graveyard universe, one in which to bury the unwanted, unclean, *unworthy* dead of His Majesty's carceral wroth. That would appeal to him, if Gayle was any judge of royal inclinations.

Princess Innocent dusted off her hands and turned to Dr. Gayle, smiling as she did. Gayle at first mistook the hand-brushing as a bit of theater, a humanism meant to put Gayle more at ease, but this was not the case. A bit of Andy – the bit of him which Princess' hand contacted, most likely – had adhered to her palm, and the last of Andy exited her brisk claps as a dun-colored dust cloud.

"Well!" said Princess brightly. "That's *one* mess taken care of!"

"Mmm." Dr. Gayle approached the pile of granules which comprised the remnants of longsuffering Andy, cycling through their optical analyses. "I suppose it is, at that. That was remarkable, what you just did." Gayle bent, took a pinch of dust between two fingers, and inspected it more closely. The grit fell from their fingers, and they turned their compound eyes to the darkening heavens, then round at the stillness of the wastes around them.

"Where in God's name did the excess energy go?" Gayle spat at Innocent. "I'm not picking up any heat, no fission fragments or alpha particles." They began to feel a creeping sense of uncanny unease. It was one thing, they discovered, to create a universe and assume a rightful place as deity; it was quite another to learn that there were things much *bigger* than a god. And, if Princess Innocent was simply an ambassador, things more monstrous yet.

Though Dr. Gayle directed their question and their ire at Innocent, it was Dr. Phyntis who replied. They did so via twitching, temporal lobe-tickling photon semaphore.

I AM SLIGHTLY DISAPPOINTED BY THAT QUESTION DR. GAYLE, transmitted Phyntis. *Point taken*, Gayle thought with a hollow feeling. Changing atomic structures with little evident effort was, in the grand scheme of Gayle's understanding of Phyntis' people, small potatoes indeed. She decided to ignore the reprimand, and directed a different statement at the skipping thing in the schoolgirl skirt.

"The Mystery. The Executioner. And whatever else Phyntis said was here. We've got to fix them. Quickly. The Crown will have already dispatched another agent – probably a whole damned team of them. We should expect visitors. And whatever…" They searched for words in a poorly-stocked storehouse largely bereft of poetic flourish. "I felt something. Something wrong with the engines, and with ARSO:N. I've never felt anything like it. It was like we didn't stand on solid ground."

Princess Innocent's giggle was as gentle as a riding

crop, a thing of puerile malice. "That's what we're trying to *teach* you, silly. You don't. You never will. You never did."

SECONDARY EDUCATION MANUAL | MORALPOL
IDEOLOGOGRAM B02.02
For distribution to all first year secondary
education students. It is advised that you
employ the provided educational aids (see
HAND PUPPETS A03.01).

The Moral Foundations of our Kingdom

The politics of mobs and chaos cannot be constrained except by the dominant will of a sovereign, who in his person embodies, represents, and protects the interests of his people. To place limits on the power of our King is a contradiction of our fundamental rights as subjects. As the king is – in his reason, in his actions, even in his temperament – his people, to constrain him is to constrain his people. To give him sovereign freedom is to give that freedom, through him, to his subjects.

A weak King cannot exercise his will on behalf of his people. He is impotent; shackled or hamstrung by the limited understanding and power of the very nation which he seeks to elevate. A mighty King, unrestrained by limits on his power, will inevitably feed the bounty of that power to his councilors, his agents, and his representatives throughout the land. They, in turn, grant that freedom and power as they see fit to those beneath them. Thus, the power and will of the sovereign drive the productivity and happiness of an ordered land.

The first, inalienable rights, as conceived by the failed thinkers of the past, were forms of self-perpetuation or self-fulfillment, expressed (most often) as the right to self-defense. This thinking is an invitation to the bleakest anarchy if extended to the paltry, immoral, and weak individual. When extended to the Kingdom as a whole (and as expressed in the person of the King), self-perpetuation is a right, as is self-defense. And from the rights extended to the Kingdom come the liberties permitted to us all by our stations; our proper places in the great body of governance.

MORALPOL|APPEND.633
Disruptive pupils will receive this presentation again during a CGP evaluation session. Watch for radiance spikes of <55° in RGB 255,245,3 and flag for further monitoring and possible rendition to carceral authorities.

8.
FRANK ON BLAKE

"Presenting," rang the shrill rasp of the herald on the conference screen, "His Royal Majesty Cleon, Third of His Name!"

Archdirector Kinsey Freund faced the screen on one uncomfortable knee, eyes to the floor. It was, as Executioner Ketch would have noted, marble, and it hurt.

"You may rise," emerged from King Cleon in a bored, let's-get-this-over-with voice. Once Kinsey lifted her eyes to meet the King's, his anger flared. Evidently he wanted to stare into the Archdirector's eyes for this one.

His Majesty had never been a handsome man, not even in a cruel way and not even in his prime. Kinsey, like all subjects of His Majesty, had been bombarded by portraits of the King when he'd been a serious, unsmiling youth, and age had soured seriousness into a bilious, reptilian bad humor as predictable as it was unleavenable. His wrinkled, liver-spotted boulder of a head perched atop a wrinkled buzzard neck, and the coronet of pale gold he wore served only to emphasize the growing pallor of his skin. It was easy to be lulled by appearances, though, as Kinsey knew full well. King

Cleon had looked terrible for decades, and while each year brought no improvement, his visible age seemed to have frozen solid somewhere on the middle slope of his ninth decade.

"Kinsey," spat Cleon, narrowing his eyes behind enormous rimless spectacles. His voice was low but clear, a slow and dour sound. He spoke, the Doctors Freund had always agreed, with a venom that was only matched by the brutal brevity of his audiences.

"Your Majesty," answered the Archdirector.

"You've really done it this time, haven't you?" Cleon sneered.

She was wise enough not to answer this question. After blinking at her for a moment, the King went on. "Did you kill my Executioner, Kinsey? I'll find out if you did, you know. If you're up to something. You and that… *unusual* twin of yours." *He doesn't know about the regeneration effect in Arson*, Kinsey thought. The notion was vaguely reassuring; she had at least one card up her sleeve, it seemed.

"We don't currently know the disposition of my sibling or Executioner Ketch, Your Majesty. Translation sheaths are being poured right now, and I plan to lead a-"

"No," the King interrupted her.

The Archdirector's words withered on her tongue. She swallowed, then ventured: "Beg pardon, Highness?"

"No, you won't do anything to recover the victims of this regrettable accident. What you *will* do, Archdirector Freund, is wait for my special envoy. He'll be there at dawn, along with a squad of his best. Very competent people, Kinsey. Not accident prone, as your twin evidently was."

Dr. Freund felt like some chemical injection had set her blood to literally boil, starting in the center of her gut. It was a hot, physical sensation, not the least bit metaphorical or poetic. "I see, Highness."

His smile was a thing of almost charmingly childish nastiness. "I'm sure you do, Kinsey. When my envoy arrives tomorrow, you will do the following. These are commands, Archdirector, not *suggestions*. You will deliver a full report on the disposition of every soul in ICON custody. *Every* one of them, Kinsey. In that report you will include a full diagnostic of the reification engines so that *my* technicians can examine them. I've heard alarming rumors about instability in ICON's output." He paused just long enough for Kinsey to wonder which ICON employee was His Majesty's royal rat. The King went on.

"At dawn, you will escort my team into the Area for Registered Sex Offenders: North. You will ascertain the status of Dr. Gayle and Executioner Jacqueline Ketch. Lastly, you will extract them. Alive, preferably. If one or both are dead, extract what remains can be recovered. My team will take charge of these latter procedures. You are to answer my people's questions and assist them however you can. And Kinsey? If you know what's good for you, you won't hide a sainted thing from them. That will save us all a lot of dreary melodrama."

"Highness," Dr. Freund struggled. "We..."

"File your report," King Cleon said. "Then enjoy your evening, Doctor. I look forward to comprehending the entirety of this matter. And believe me, Kinsey; I *will*."

The screen went dead.

Kinsey strode to her chair and perched, rigid, on its edge. She forced herself to breathe slowly and steadily. Her brittle composure had been shattered by the King's goading words, and the jagged edges of it scored her self-control. Black, boiling hatred surged – and something else. Something deeper, redder; an unfamiliar lust marbled with throbs of an uncanny hunger. A quiet, creaking pop brought the Archdirector back to herself and she glanced down, fascinated, to see that her fists were clenched so tightly that the entirety of their taut flesh had gone shock white. With effort, she relaxed them. Her hands tingled gently as the blood returned to them. She stroked one tingling fingertip across the nearby intercom switch, cleared her throat, and spoke. "Bob?"

That was the only summons necessary. Robert Flanagan, the green-eyed aide with whom the Archdirector had recently struck up an inadvisable (but enjoyable) sexual relationship, appeared as if conjured from the air itself. When he entered Kinsey's private study, the dome overhead displayed an unsettling CGP pattern of dark, striated reds and purples. The squirming colors' texture was like the skin of an alarmed cephalopod, rising in thornlike spines and spikes. "Dr. Freund?" Bob inquired gently. A chill crept over his shaved skull, a strange sensation like a breath of cold air from an open window. But there were no windows, open or otherwise, atop Mount Elbert's 4.5 kilometer-high summit.

This was a delicious thrill of dread, though; one which made Flanagan's cock stir in his tight-fitting uniform trousers. The Archdirector's dominance in their on-and-off dalliance was complete and often cruel. That was the way, he had discovered, that they *both* liked it. His soft tongue tried to wet his lips, but Flanagan discovered that his mouth had gone as dry as driftwood. A low glow the color of organ meat played unceasingly across the silhouetted shapes of Kinsey's quarters, but Bob couldn't locate her in the half-light. "Archdirector?"

"Bob."

Her breath was a silken whisper blown into the soft, pink conch of his ear. Gooseflesh rippled up and down Flanagan's back. A combination of primal terror and erotic delight flooded his veins. He'd started to realize that this cocktail was more powerful (and more addictive) than he'd first suspected. Kinsey's stalking him in the throbbing semidarkness was a new game, but not at all out of character for the woman he had come to know. Or thought he'd come to know.

Bob felt Kinsey's cold hand slide along the taut front of his uniform breeches. Her chilly digits gave his cock a gentle, teasing squeeze. At the same instant, Kinsey's teeth snipped neatly through his earlobe.

The combined sensations hit the unsuspecting aide like a sugary thunderbolt, fusing the pleasurable sweetness in his limbs and freezing him in place. He climaxed, and not for the last time that memorable evening. Flanagan considered himself as tough as any person in his orbit, but having his earlobe severed was beyond the pale. Blood sheeted down his neck. A scream would have escaped him (in spite of himself) had Kinsey not clamped the hand that wasn't otherwise occupied over his lips. He heard his lover's lips smack and her throat gulp, and realized she had swallowed part of him. Not much, in the grand scheme of things. A little bit, a bite, a nibble now part of her forever. That quieted his cry, although his ear still hurt like hell.

"Bob," whispered Kinsey through blood-wet lips. "You would do anything to help the work we do here, right?" The question confused him, but he nodded. She did not remove her hand from his lips, perhaps sensing his lack of comprehension. On the other hand, she didn't move her hand away from his crotch either, instead continuing to palpate his tender manhood. "I mean, you'd do anything for *me*, right? For us?" That much, he could nod his agreement to. Kinsey removed the hand over his lips, but not the one still tormenting his post-orgasmic member. "That's good," she said, and turned him so they could meet each other's eyes. She could smell terror and arousal washing off of him in waves almost as potent as the scent of his ejaculate.

"Bob," she said, sliding down the zipper that ran down one flank of his uniform, "I'm going to fuck you. Then, I'm going to kill you."

Later, in the drudgery of cleaning up her excesses and varnishing her sins, the Archdirector found herself meditating on two moments during that long night of love, sex, pain, and death. Two moments, each of which illuminated decades of research and, in their own way, chopped the Gordian Knot of her life's work.

The first moment had been no *single* moment at all, and that was what fascinated her. On one side of a line, Flanagan resisted (albeit weakly) her decision to kill him. It hadn't been a painless death, not by a long yard of shrieking guts, but it hadn't been bereft of pleasure, either. It had, in fact, been such a blend of bittersweet toxins that, on the other side of that line; in his agonized, sex-drunk eyes; with red lips, slit tongue, and broken teeth; Flanagan had embraced the ecstasy of his dissolution. It was easy enough to choose isolated moments clearly one side or another. The way he'd first resisted the stiletto, making his protests known with feral grunts of pain and straining muscles, and then, at the end, had reached his own trembling, bloody hands up to pull the handle as she pushed, helping drive the final strike into his heart. A third party observing this most intimate of moments might have suggested to the Archdirector that, by that point, Flanagan simply wanted it all to be over. She knew better. She knew what she'd seen and felt. Condemnation of this consummation came from blinkered thinking.

And what were you guilty of, whispered the disembodied voice of VSOSeSa-A01 in Kinsey's mind, *if not blinkered thinking? The* old *you, anyway. Tonight you've joined the ranks of the enlightened. Breathe it in, Kinsey.* That was the rub, wasn't it? The thing that kept the Archdirector awake that night, even after her surroundings had been cleansed from abattoir to anodyne and every soul atop Mount Elbert was asleep.

There had been another point in her indulgence, a more distinct one in which much had been made clear. She'd found the Pit, and it had been inside of her. She'd watched the CGP feedback play across the dome of her lair. The rolling coruscation was no recorded pattern, as Flanagan had thought, but was instead a real-time display of her own chromatic-geometric psychogrammatic output. In her sanctum, Kinsey liked to watch the workings of her mind the way a master watchmaker might admire the mechanisms of a finished piece.

Archdirector Freund had felt something inside of her mind give way about halfway through the bloody crux of the affair. She'd driven the stiletto into Flanagan again and again, his blood smeared over Kinsey's eyeballs, lips, and teeth. Had she seen her own face then, perhaps she would have wished to stop, although it was already far too late. Something at the limits of rationality cracked like a tooth atop an abscess. Instead of infection pouring forth, a clear, cold calm had caught her in its dreadful stillness. Her heart rate, she observed, slowed, as did her respiration. The texture of horripilation that had stippled the activating-emotion reds and purples of the display deepened, darkened, and became a black and freezing vacancy.

It was, she thought later, like footage she had seen of space shuttles leaving Earth's atmosphere. First, the burning sky the pilots saw would lighten, thinning as the air grew more disperse. Then, the night. The stars. The crystal clarity and frigid darkness of *true* space, revealed at last. Or… perhaps it was like being born? Yes, maybe that was it. Bob Flanagan had died so Kinsey Freund might be born again, rebaptized in lust and blood.

Happy birthday, Kinsey, whispered the smiling voice of VSOSeSa-A01. She slept.

The next morning, she decided to confront the King's envoy directly. The evening's activities had, at first, left her blissfully unconcerned with minutiae like the tantrums of a tyrant. The sunrise brought her fluttering nerves back to life. *This won't do*, she thought as she dressed for the day.

Archdirector Freund had waited for the arrival of the Royal Envoy in the ICON lobby, preferring not to traverse the freezing, windswept walkway to the ICON landing pad, and she saw no need to behave any differently with this new… *special envoy*. She hated the taste of the words, the way they felt in her mind, like an already-indefensible accusation.

A small craft sailed in from the east at the exact moment of dawn, a level of punctuality which Kinsey couldn't help but admire. It was a spectacle she enjoyed, whatever the circumstances. The incoming craft was only large enough to hold the Envoy, their pilot, and their team, and the starburst of silver against the peach glow of a mountaintop sunrise was quite beautiful. Kinsey savored the scene from the lobby, watching on the display there. She well aware that, as lovely as the scene might look, the environment outside of ICON's sealed and atmosphere-controlled doors was, to put it mildly, inhospitable. She watched the figures make their way from the craft and along the ice-strewn metal walkway that connected the pad to the facility. Kinsey had, at that point, passed through dread and entered the shadowlands of grim acceptance. She hadn't even bothered to modify the output reports or cover her tracks. While she hardly planned to confess, she was aware that the evidence against her was damning.

The front doors of ICON, behind their sealed layers, opened, and the King's Envoy entered. Head held high and shoulders stiff, he was accompanied by a squad of five blandly lethal-looking special operatives. The Archdirector stared at the Envoy's face, unable to believe her eyes. The Envoy grinned, stainless steel veneers on his teeth flashing in the amber light of ICON's lobby. It was an affectation Kinsey knew well.

"Go secure the other staff for interviews," the Envoy said to his team, removing a fur-lined ushanka from his head. "We'll start at once." He watched with lively blue eyes as the team – three men and two women – made haste to obey. When they'd left the room, he turned back to the Archdirector and shared a milder, less predatory smile. "Good to see you, Kinsey," said Honorable Justice Dr. Kerik Goetz, the King's Eastern Prosecutor and the Archdirector's surreptitious collaborator.

"God damn," Kinsey Freund said, relief nearly stealing her breath. "Not even a tenth as good as it is to see *you*, Kerry."

The moment Executioner Ketch saw the stranger up close, she knew that something at ICON had gone indescribably, apocalyptically wrong. Ketch's ex-military implants and augmentations went far beyond a zoom lens or a tapenote apparatus. She looked up from her prone position at the man in his cream-colored hat, examined his proffered hand, and kept her eyes on him as she took it. Using the sensors beneath the thin faux-flesh of her leather glove, and triggering the temperature and biometric measures in her eye implants, it took Ketch less than six seconds to determine that the stranger wasn't biologically human. Hell, she couldn't even tell if he was an organic or inorganic object. He did not breathe, except to speak. No heart beat in his chest, and no blood flowed in his veins. Spectroscopic analysis pinged him with an absurd level of lanthanoid elements, chemically pure praseodymium in particular; a thing which should not have been possible, given how reactive the element was. Ketch thought that, all things considered, it was best to treat him – it? – with caution.

He'd said his name was Frank, who- or whatever he was. After helping Ketch up, he turned and took a few steps down the rise. He stopped and glanced back over his shoulder. Or, at least, she thought he did. She had yet to see eyes beneath the low, broad rim of that creamy, off-white hat. Ketch continued to clock him with her unreadable, silt-colored eyes, but she followed. As the two descended to the row of sheds and the monstrous truck, Frank spoke in a sandy, husky murmur.

"Glad you made it, Executioner. You came here to have a look at what Dr. Gayle's been up to, I take it. I imagine their petting zoo wasn't exactly what you were expecting. I thought I'd have a word with you; clear the air on behalf of the powers I represent. That Open O mess showed you *exactly* what the powers Gayle's been working with are all about, even if they weren't up front with you that they were, ah… 'consorting,' I think would be the word? ... with outside interests. So to speak."

Ketch revised her opinion. This was evidence that something had gone so wrong there wasn't a proper word for it. Something an order of magnitude greater than "apocalypse." *'The powers I represent?'* Ketch thought, following in Frank's footsteps. *'Consorting?'* *'Outside interests?'*

"Mr. Blank?" she inquired mildly. That made him laugh, an unsettlingly humanizing touch that sounded entirely authentic.

"Frank," he chuckled. "Please, just Frank."

"Frank, then. Pleased to meet you." She paused, weighing the value of a tentative approach, then quickly discarded such notions. "Who.. or *what*, I guess, are you, Frank? And what are you doing here?"

"Me?" Frank touched the brim of his creamy hat and lowered it a few centimeters, as if his eyes weren't already hidden. The wilted blooms frozen in the buckle of his hat brim shimmered softly. "I'm just a passing fancy, Executioner. A whisper in the warm summer night. A little bit of midnight mambo, if you catch my drift."

"I don't, Frank. Not at all," Ketch said. Their stroll had taken them near the handful of Arsonists muttering to one another at the derelict blacktop's frangible edge. She thought about the wine-bright sky, the sudden somnambulism of the Jolly Rancher, Skunk, and Eichmann. She wasn't quite sure how to phrase her question, but made a good faith effort.

"Are you doing something to me, Frank? To my mind?" She hesitated and remembered the "accident" -- the exploding transport pod, the boiling liquid flames, and the long, burning fall to the Pocket's toxic dirt. "Am I... are we really having this conversation?"

Frank nodded. "You're here. I'm here. And no, I'm not

fiddling with your mind. As of yet."

"Would you tell me if you were?"

They'd reached the others. Skunk and JR were discussing blumpkin husbandry in the muted tones of two enthusiastic conspirators. Frank clapped a big, blunt hand on Skunk's greasy shoulder. "Skunk, my man. Am I fucking with your head?"

"Oh, absolutely," Skunk said brightly. "Got my eggs real scrambled, boss."

Frank turned to the Rancher. "JR?"

"You bet!" piped the Jolly Rancher. "Honestly I'd rather not be here, Frank; that black shed has me scared shitless. Can I go, please?"

"No. And you're right to be scared of that shed," Frank said with weary wisdom.

"You got it," JR smiled back, and returned to the topic of irritated stitches and proper blumpkin tooth enamel and colorectal maintenance.

Frank turned back to Ketch. "See? I'm not going to lie to you and say I wouldn't suggest a thing or two if I had to, but I *don't* have to, do I, Executioner?"

She took a moment to answer. "I suppose not. I need to know what's happening in Arson. The King will want to make sure this is an isolated incident." She gazed up at the Pocket's night sky, as artificial and convincing as a trompe l'œil. "*Is* it an isolated incident, Frank?"

He shrugged. "As far as I know, sure. But I can't speak for Phyntis. Hell, I can't speak *to* Phyntis."

Ketch's tapenote clicked, recording the name's phonemes. "Phyntis?"

"Phyntis," Frank mused, his low, slow voice turning the name into a meditation. "I can't speak for Phyntis." He led Ketch past JR and Skunk and onto the impossible blacktop. Though its existence ran counter to the architecture of the Pocket, it persisted in existing and felt soft and solid underneath her boots. It even *smelled* like blacktop, Ketch observed, and wondered if it had its origins in some mundane ICON manufacturing facility or if it had, instead, come from the same wherever which had coughed out Frank Blank and his hideous pink truck.

There was another stranger standing beside the black shed. A man with lovely ebon skin and the depilated cranium that marked one as an ICON initiate. The depilation, Ketch knew, was to better ease and fine-tune intracranial-to-sensor communication. In Ketch's pre-trip review of the exploits of the Doctors Freund, the Executioner had watched countless videos of CGP-trained ICON personnel, occluded from the neck up by a head cage of sensor panels and interface cables as they processed stimuli, adding to chromatic-geometric psychogrammar lexicon one mental morpheme at a time. Looking at the second stranger, Ketch thought: *At least he's from the right species and cosmos.*

This human stranger's face was placid, bordering on vacant, and he had one palm pressed flat against the black shed's closed door. Ketch's cognitive implants cycled through ICON's files, scanning for the man's identity. The result was so jarring that she halted in her tracks, causing Frank to glance back over his shoulder.

The King's Executioner had access to nearly every information resource in the Kingdom; but "nearly all" meant "not every." In her service to the King, Ketch had been denied access only once. Certain the denial must have been an error, Ketch had inadvisably investigated things herself. Her subsequent inquiries revealed that the classified file had contained, among other things, a recent medical report. The report tried hard to dance around its central fact: that King Cleon the Third had contracted a virulent (the term the King's Physician actually used was "roaring") case of gonorrhea. This was a fact Ketch had wisely kept to herself. Keeping the royal clap under wraps made sense to Ketch, who understood the art of propaganda and had no illusions about the King's personal adherence to the Kingdom's strict moralpol standards.

When her scan of the ICON man's face triggered an INQUIRY DENIED impulse, Ketch consulted a mental list of those who had the authority to place the man's identity beyond her reach. It was a remarkably short list, and neither Doctor Freund was on it. Picking up on Ketch's confusion, Frank gently placed a warm and stony hand on her elbow and led her closer to the black shed and its keeper. His touch sent a physical shudder through the Executioner's body, from toes to crown. There was something unnatural in Frank's animation, subtly transmitted by his touch. *It is*, Ketch thought, *as though a scarecrow has come to life and taken me by the arm.*

"Executioner Ketch," said Frank, "this is Mystery Morrison Spare. Morrison, this is Royal Executioner Jacqueline Ketch."

"Ketch me if you can," Morrison replied in a sleep-talker's pleasant, vacant tone. When Ketch had first approached, she hadn't been able to make it out against the night, but this close to the baldheaded man she could see a black halo; an anti-radiance that crowned Spare's gleaming pate.

Frank chuckled. "You'll have to excuse Mystery Spare," he confided, "his mind is elsewhere."

In her time as Executioner, Ketch had chased a few strange rabbits down some curious holes, but this trip to ARSO:N had become the most peculiar puzzle of her life. Life in the Kingdom was replete with mysteries; for example, the nature of the technology that underlay the Kingdom and made it function smoothly. That was wisdom seldom shared, and never without ample cause. However, the Kingdom hadn't been a place of capital-m Mysteries for quite some time. The records on the project were sparse and scattered. Ketch had a fairly good idea why. When King Cleon axed the project, calling it "too dangerous and disruptive to the Kingdom's stable, happy way of life," facilities had been burned to their foundations, and every Mystery had been summarily executed. Ketch amended that: reports said they had all been slain. Contrary evidence was standing before her, smiling like a drugged initiate to a cult of chemical enlightenment.

"Mystery Morrison Spare," she said carefully. "That's a title I haven't heard in a while."

Frank responded for the haloed man, pacing in a lazy semicircle at the black shed's entrance. "I can imagine. Your species is quite good at killing things, when you put your minds to it."

Ketch found her own calm vaguely disturbing. She was conversing with an intelligence from elsewhere, most likely somewhere a *hell* of a lot further away than another star system. She felt no crawling horror, though; no screaming, xenophobic panic. She supposed it helped that Frank looked and sounded more or less human; even unexceptionally so. Except for that strange, bulbous cowboy hat of his. There was something about it that Ketch irrationally disliked.

"Are you *sure* you're not screwing with my head?" she asked. "I... am taking all of this remarkably well."

Frank lifted one desert-browned hand and snapped

his fingers. Immediately, Skunk Pussy and the Jolly Rancher broke into an eerie, almost mechanically choreographed soft shoe, whistling "Chattanooga Choo-Choo" in perfect harmony as they did. It was an awful sight; enough to make Ketch feel slightly ill (she, who had publicly executed no fewer than three dissidents by impalement in the Winter Palace courtyard not two months previously). Frank snapped his fingers a second time and the awful, jerky puppet show ceased. Both men gagged and gasped for breath.

"God *damn* it, Frank," Skunk Pussy snarled when he caught his breath, "I told you not to *do* that again. That shit fucking hurts, man."

"Sorry, Skunk," Frank said with breezy insincerity, then to Ketch: "If I were screwing with your head, you'd probably know it. And I certainly wouldn't deny it."

"He wouldn't," murmured Morrison. "It was one of the very first things he said to me. 'Morrison,' he said, 'you're going to have to let me drive the bus for a while.'"

"That's right," said Frank, patting the man on his arm. He turned back to Ketch. "What did your last census of this place tell you, population-wise?"

"Eighteen souls in this specific Area."

"How many do you see here, answering the call of the wild? Or the call of the Frank, as it were."

"Not many," she said, and looked again at who had paid heed to the wine-bright flashing of the sky. "Two. Only two, not counting Morrison."

"Three, actually," Frank said, "not counting Morrison. Eichmann is in the black shed right now."

"I see." She didn't; literally or figuratively. "And what is Eichmann doing in the shed?"

"Eichmann is being weighed."

That was an odd turn of phrase. "Weighed by whom?"

"Himself, of course," Frank said, then raised a finger and declaimed: "'If the doors of perception were cleansed every thing would appear to man as it is, Infinite. For man has closed himself up, till he sees all things thro' narrow chinks of his cavern.'"

Ketch stared, mouth open beneath her cowl. "Is that… Did you just quote William Blake to me?"

"Hey, how about that!" Frank said affably. "We've got something in common! Blake's a pretty big deal where I come from. We're big fans."

"You and these 'interests.' You're 'big fans.' Of William Blake."

"Oh yes," Frank assured her. The Executioner believed him. Some things, in her experience, were too weird to be lies.

Ketch contemplated the abyssal void of Arson's night sky. The gesture felt appropriate, though it was symbolic at best. There was no space out there in Arson's "sky," no frozen gulf specked here and there with motes of cosmic dust. The universes of the Doctors Freund were all small and very crowded ones. Arson, unlike the universe where Ketch hung her cowl, was not expanding, and it never would. Wherever Frank Blank – and this Phyntis entity – had come from, it was no place in that ersatz sky. If Ketch had to guess, she'd say Frank's home was as distant as it was near; all around them, touching skin-to-skin with this pustule of the Kingdom. Ketch was no student of interstitial engineering, but she knew enough to guess that much. Frank may just as well have crawled out of the sand or landed in a glowing UFO. Ketch glanced back over at the truck, its bulging pipes and strange, half-organic shapes. That, in fact, looked like *exactly* the type of vehicle that might --

"Nope," Frank said, startling her and interrupting her

train of thought. "Let me nip that notion in the bud. The rig's a different deal. Maybe I'll explain later, but we've only got so long before things get much more complicated, and there's lots to do. Your King has contacted Kinsey Freund and sent a team to accompany her here. And although not even Kinsey knows it yet, His Majesty is planning a surprise inspection. A *personal* inspection."

"*What?*"

"I'm excited too!" Frank sounded genuinely thrilled at the prospect of King Cleon the Third dropping in on whatever the Freunds had unleashed with their reification-engines and Mysteries. "But, like I said, lots to do, Executioner. To start with, I'd like you to think over what Morrison is about to say."

Spare turned his smooth, mesmerized face to Ketch and treated her to a beautiful, broad smile, a thing of warmth and easygoing cheer. "Hello Executioner Ketch-me-if-you-can," he said. "Would you like to see into Eichmann's darkest, most secret places? Think about what that means. Has the dime dropped yet, Executioner? Can you tell me why these *specific* men are here – the Jolly Rancher, Eichmann, and Skunk?"

Actually, it had occurred to Ketch fairly quickly. With her implants, she had access to each subject's files. "They're the only offenders in this Area who have a CV on their jacket."

"CV. *Seeee veeee*," Spare repeated, turning it into a musing mantra.

"They're all sexual offenders whose transgressions involved criminal violence."

"That's right," said Spare. "That's why they've all come to the black shed to be weighed."

"And what does that entail, exactly, Mystery Spare?"

Frank's voice behind her was quiet; a tumbleweed husk

of a whisper. "Would you like to see, Executioner Ketch? Not some blobby color crap CGP display. To *really* see?"

Morrison held out one hand, sleepy eyes back-shadowed by his negative halo. "They get it all back inside these tiny spaces, Ketch-me-if-you-can, every bit. The good. The bad. The things that went on that nobody ever, *ever* saw. And if you want to, you can watch. No charge. No obligation."

"I doubt there's anything edifying inside of some degenerate's head," Ketch said too casually.

"Who said it would be how Eichmann saw it at the time?" Frank asked, his voice snakeskin dry and dusty soft. "We stand on the threshold of revelation, Executioner. 'If the doors of perception were cleansed every thing would appear to man as it is.'"

Ketch hesitated, but she didn't hesitate long. "Show me," she said, and placed her hand in Spare's hand. The world of Arson vanished like a dream on waking, or the waking world when slipping into dreams.

**ROYAL LIBRARY DISTRICTWIDE MEMO |
111.13.05
FOR GENERAL DISTRIBUTION TO LIBRARY
STAFF | URGENCY: HIGH**
FROM: MAYA LOVE MoralPolD Royal Library
District Director
TO: FRANCIS WU MFA MLIS Subdistrict 5 Head
Librarian

Ms. Wu,

Please find below the most recent updates to our Proscribed Title Index. These changes are a supplement until the PTI's new 4th Edition is released. We remain hopeful that the compilation of the PTI 4 will happen in short time and good order. Until then, this PTI Update (PTIU 5.2.A) shall go into effect immediately. As you're aware, if any titles listed in the PTI are found in a library, either on public shelves, behind the desk, or in a library employee or volunteer's possession during a routine or random, plainclothes inspection, both yourself and the offending party may face consequences up to and including public execution.

If you have questions regarding why titles may or may not have been selected, please submit your inquiry in writing to the Proscribed Text Index Department of the Censor's Office.* The PTIDCO is always willing to answer reasonable inquiries.

PTIU 5.2.1

Baldwin, James <u>Notes of a Native Son</u>
Blake, William <u>Songs of Experience</u>
Feinberg, Leslie <u>Stone Butch Blues</u>
Paine, Thomas <u>The Rights of Man</u>
Scarry, Richard <u>What Do People Do All Day?</u>

Please stay vigilant for any further updates to the PTI, and thank you for your compliance.

Have a blessed day,
ML

Please allow between 42 and 75 weeks for a response to your query.

9.
I'm Anywhere Tonight

Announcements from the Royal Broadcast Corporation and the handful of "independent" publications in the Kingdom concurred. Life had never been better. Never mind the number of jobless subjects quietly grown desperate in their crowded tenements; never mind the breadlines or the fistfights over day labor jobs that paid a pittance; never mind the hunger of the children. Hunger was less evident in adults, whose faces might grow gaunt and whose eyes may be deep-socketed, but who maintained the grizzly stoicism expected of the King's loyal subjects. The children, on the other hand? They didn't know enough to (or simply couldn't) hide the strain of deprivation, and often they would cry.

Before his name was Eichmann and before the poison desert, Friedrich "Fritz" Harmon had loved the little ones. While much of Hanover (and, indeed, the territory once known as "New Jersey") slumped into financial ruin, Harmon's bakery prospered. He shared that prosperity whenever he could. He supported hungry families with his day-old loaves, and shared his cookies with the children who would swarm his stoop. He specialized in gingerbread and crafted little Kings with yellow icing crowns to celebrate His Majesty. Fritz Harmon: caring neighbor, big-hearted pillar of his neighborhood, loyal subject of the Crown.

That had been the Harmon who the world had known. It had been the face he'd worn in public, his pate balding and his hands almost as soft as the dough they kneaded every day. But there had been another Fritz; a septic, predatory thing that lived, lusted, and hungered just behind his watery eyes. *That* Harmon watched the children who'd come begging for his sweets very carefully. He'd sifted them with monstrous connoisseurship for the telltale signs of those who might, hypothetically, disappear without causing a stir. Orphans, runaways, neglected products of unhappy unions: Friedrich plied them all. His sweet gingerbread Kings led them to the bakery basement where, Harmon assured them, he'd constructed such a wonderland of ginger-dwellings that the child could pick their own and take the *whole* thing with them.

Half of this was true. He *did* keep gingerbread houses there, for the cool, moist air preserved them. His guests would never bear their prize away, however. When a child turned their back on him to look, when their eyes were filled with sustenance and their stomachs growled in sweet anticipation, he would strike. And strike. And do some other things besides, once any cries had been extinguished. Some of these lost boys and girls were not as lost as they looked, however, and whispers became murmurs, which became (in one or two cases) calls to the authorities. But clever Fritz had *many* secrets, not just one, and some secrets kept watch over other, darker, and more private ones.

Everyone in Hanover knew the Royal Police – everyone in *every* city, every town, every hamlet in the Kingdom.

They weren't well-loved, those cruel men in their death's head officer's caps, stiff blue uniforms, and polished jackboots, but they were well-feared. And one of clever Fritz's secrets was that for many years he'd been a paid police informant. Well-paid, too. He'd worked his way up from snitching on his cellmates and co-conspirators to living a reformed life in which few knew of his past. In this new life he also placed weekly calls to update his RP handlers with the mumbled grievances of those who'd complained about the price of bread, or whom he knew to be involved in the city's black market.

Eventually, missing children multiplied, as did complaints about Harmon. The Royal Police were forced to search his bakery and the apartment he kept above it. They'd found enough to execute Harmon many times over, in many different and unpleasant ways (in fact, he'd later learn with a sick, secret thrill, a convocation of Executioners had been called to discuss how to properly excruciate him). Ultimately, it was decided that, though only dogs and traitors would repeat such filthy lies, some might say the Royal Police played a role in Fritz's late apprehension. When numbers were tossed to and fro regarding the monster's toll of victims – some put it as low as 27, some as high as 43 – conversations tended to drift toward how many of those might have been prevented, had the Crown been more responsive to its citizens and less to its informant. Only dogs and traitors said those things, agreed the Executioners, but in the end it was decided that a public trial and execution would just feed these scurrilous slanders. Mightn't it be better if the monster were placed in the custody of ICON, there to be dissected or disposed of as the Freunds saw fit? Thus did Friedrich "Fritz" Harmon become Eichmann, secret monster (secret even to himself) of Arson's wastes.

This fetid overflow of knowledge washed over Executioner Ketch in a slippery and nauseating wave. Ketch's memory felt sullied. All the secret time that Fritz spent in his hot, close basement, hacking, hacking, *hacking* with his heavy cleaver, separating joint from hip and head from neck. Ketch wondered with a migraine-ache of briskly processed horrors what Archdirector Kinsey Freund would make of such a bloody scene; what specific paraphilic whispers in the dead of night drove Eichmann-Fritz to these unspeakable extremes.

Executioner Ketch hadn't always been Executioner Ketch. Her path had led her from her former name and life through winding combat grinder-gardens irrigated with hot blood. Finally, she'd knelt atop a mountain of the dead and donned the black cowl. The way had been hard. Mild eyes notwithstanding, it had left her hard, as well. That hardness did not crack beneath the weight of Eichmann's spectacle, but it did creak. Wallow, Ketch reflected absently, wouldn't be too strong a word for the sight that greeted her inside the black shed: a view she saw through the medium of Morrison. Except, inside the black shed wasn't the dank space she had imagined. Inside it was the Hanover bakery's bleak basement.

The meek-seeming little man whom she had met in Arson, and who had charmed the hungry children of downtrodden Hanover, was nowhere to be seen. Here in his *profanus profanum*, Friedrich Harmon was a grotesque from the darkest depths of human nightmare. Blood plastered his pallid form and clotted in his thinning hair. This gory pomade made it stand out like the red wig of a charnel clown. Naked, Harmon writhed with bloody jaws and flashing eyes amidst a jumble-tumble bundle of severed limbs and glistening intestines; the harvest of a clutch of recent kills. Harmon's angular erection, as blood-drenched as the rest of him, jutted from his thatch of pubic hair like a dull, uncircumcised knife. Harmon was a vision of monster-as-glutton, of one who simply couldn't get enough of that which brought him pleasure. Woe to the hungry children of Hanover that it had been these acts of butchery and blood that tasted sweetest on his tongue. *In a better world*, Ketch thought, *he'd just have drunk himself to death.*

Mystery Morrison Spare responded to her thought: "Maybe it's a better world than you think."

The Executioner experienced a dreamlike condensation of proprioception; a sudden sense that she was *there* where she had not been there before, that she had form and cheap tile floor beneath her. She looked down at her black-gloved hands, her midnight boots, and back up at the hacked-off limbs, at Harmon's floor with its deep, inset drain. She realized that she could smell the stifling basement air. *Cinnamon*, she thought, *and blood*. It smelled like gingerbread and offal.

"I've seen a lot, Spare," Ketch said, "and I doubt it." His Majesty's murderer sounded quite forlorn. "I don't understand very much of what's going on. We're, what. Seeing the inside of his head?"

"You don't understand," Spare repeated, and nodded placidly. "Your kind killed my kind, you know. Of *course* you don't understand."

"I... what?"

"It wasn't you personally – I don't think so, anyway. You don't seem old enough. Me, though... I'm older than I look. I remember the night His Majesty sent his Executioners to slaughter us. The Mysteries. It wasn't enough to scratch the program, you see." He watched with icy and appraising eyes as Hanover's voracious monster writhed in his red effluent. "We were too dangerous to His Majesty's plans, and the control he had to have over what he wanted to build. On the backs of others, of course. The Doctors. The Mysteries. The scientists who developed the first interstitial fields."

"I don't know anything about that mission," Ketch said honestly. "But if it had been me… if I'd been the one they called, I would have done the job right. There wouldn't have been any survivors, Morrison. You'd be dead."

He smiled at that. "What do you think our friend Fritz would make of that sentiment?" he asked. "I think he would have made an excellent Royal Executioner. He worked well with the Royal Police, after all. For all those long, long years."

"*Fuck* you, you *mutant*, mind-reading *asshole*," she snapped.

Morrison Spare's sleepy smile slipped a stitch. "Now, Jacqueline Ketch," he chided. "That's not good moralpol. Not when you're on duty." He sighed. "I suppose the best thing would be to show you that we're on the same side here. At least when it comes to the fate of Herr Harmon."

"His fate," Ketch said carefully, thinking *I could kill Morrison Spare with just my bare hands and still make it appropriately painful.* "His fate was decided by the King, and hasn't been countermanded that I know of. He's going back to Arson. If we've *left* Arson, that is." She added this last with a ringing sense that they weren't in Arson anymore; that where they were was no particular place at all.

"He might or might not be going back to Arson," Spare said. "But that's not Eichmann on the floor. That's Fritz Harmon. Isn't that right, Eichmann?"

A rush of sound, as though her ears had to equalize their pressure, and suddenly the Executioner could hear a pitiful and nearby presence. The sniveling, whimpering mantra of misery came from just behind her left shoulder. Ketch whirled, and there hunched Eichmann, just as she remembered him; skinnier than the robust baker he had been, with sunburned skin, less hair, and eyes brimful of shocked, uncomprehending horror.

"I didn't *know*," he wept. "What I *did*. I didn't *know*. They took it from me, the Pit, and now all I see is *lamb chops through a god-damned sheep's eyes!*" This last began as a lament and rose until it wrung the air, shrieked like a dying curse.

"On reflection, I would very much like to kill him now." As soon as the words were out of her mouth, Ketch was shocked that she'd spoken the thought aloud and outright horrified at its simplistic, brutal honesty.

"I don't doubt it," said Morrison Spare agreeably. "But the question, Executioner Ketch, is this; which of these men would you kill?"

Ketch found the question difficult to answer, and she wasn't sure why. *This is turning into quite the day for unwelcome revelations*, she thought bitterly, *including a few about myself.*

The Mystery turned his back on Harmon, glutton at the feast of innocents, and looked down from his black halo at Eichmann, recipient of His Majesty's inconstant mercy. "It's your choice," Spare said to the cowering man. "You can keep the Pit, but that means you've got to pay the ferryman. Or, if you prefer, you can go back to Arson, safe as houses. Here's the tricky bit; if you leave this place, you leave it with the memories they took. I think they'll be enough to make you sick for centuries, now that you… how did you put it, 'see lamb chops through a sheep's eyes?'" He turned and looked impassively at Ketch. "Some people would call that a major psychoscientific breakthrough. Do you realize what it means?"

Ketch did, and it gave her pause. She was human, and, therefore, a being of reactions and emotional conflagrations. The Kingdom made her more than human. She was part of the great Body of the King. That larger part of her realized all too well what Morrison Spare meant. "You've… forced him to feel empathy," she said, tasting the notion as she pronounced it. "You've trained him or taught him – I don't know which."

"There's a blank spot in the heart of some. Frank calls it a 'hole in the bottom of the sea.' When psychoscientists explore it, they see nothing but a concrete darkness. Call it the Pit. 'Without form, and void, and darkness was upon the face of the deep,' if you like. And what good is a formless hole in things?"

"Ask Dr. Gayle," responded Ketch, and that earned her a sunny smile from Spare.

"When a Mystery sees that same phenomenon, we see a blank canvas. Darkness as a base upon which to paint shades of light. Migraine sunrise sickness, if it fits the bill."

"That sounds like it's about to have an 'or' tacked onto it."

"*Or* whatever His Majesty requires, Executioner. And His Majesty requires killers, doesn't he?" She couldn't very well argue with that. "The King's plan led to quite an impasse, I'm afraid, among the Mysteries. We split into three factions. One group of us approached the Crown with their idea; to use the canvas of the Pit to paint him new assassins. Another faction swore to fight against such efforts to their dying breath. I believe the word they used repeatedly was 'perverse.' They probably used that word because the Royalist faction found the warp and weft of paraphilias particularly useful in driving murder to new heights; sexual sadism turned to the King's purposes. The Antimonarchist Mysteries resisted vigorously, and even threatened regicide. That was a mistake. The midnight when the Executioners came calling at my barracks was the final word. The King had had enough. We were frightening enough already, and then to learn that some among the Mysteries were plotting against him?" Spare shook his bald head sadly. "*Every* Mystery was doomed."

"You mentioned a third faction," Ketch said.

Spare turned away from the cowering, weeping Eichmann to stare directly into Ketch's eyes, but he may as well have tried to discern meaning in a pile of dead, dry leaves. "The third faction," he said, "Yes. I guess we weren't *all* doomed, were we? The third faction – my faction – we'd had enough of the entire affair. We were desperate. We'd seen some of ICON's horror show and we didn't want to see any more. We'd had enough of the Royalists and the Antimonarchists. So, Executioner Ketch, we called for help."

Ketch snorted. "Called *who* for help?"

The Mystery's eyes were still so somnolent he could have been asleep atop his legs. Asleep and dreaming; and when his kind dreamed, if she understood the complex explanations correctly, they dreamed things into being. Usually, these were subtle changes wrought without the dreamer's knowledge. On occasion, a few documents had said in a vague and threatening tone, one of them woke up within the dream, a phenomenon called "lucid reification."

"We cried havoc." Spare's voice was low, but hot as kindled fire with the joy of the memory. "We cried havoc, and a place or thing named Pandemonium answered. The last Mysteries all took this journey and faced our darkness. All of us were weighed according to our nature, and thus apportioned our reward. We didn't get a choice, because we were the first." He looked back at Harmon, who'd spent his frenzy and lay panting in his carrion wallow tucked beneath his bakery's bland and anodyne façade. Then, Spare turned at looked at Eichmann, the peeling, mad-eyed wretch who'd spent untold days both dying and undying in the toxic sandbox kept by Dr. Gayle. The little man stared back, his mind unhinged and hanging by one stripped and slipping screw.

"You can have it all back, if you want," said Mystery Spare. "Or you can have the Pit."

"Give me back the Pit." Eichmann – *no*, Ketch thought, *Friedrich Harmon once again and always* – Harmon gasped the words out, any sense of shame or pride collapsing under the weight of his remembered horrors and his unremembered relish in them. It was the voice of one succumbing to damnation; succumbing to destruction when resolution fails beneath the dire weight of self-knowledge; succumbing with the first drink after abstinence, the first reestablished trust betrayed for want of self-restraint.

Ketch's well-trained guts roiled. It wasn't just the broken self-abandonment in Harmon's voice; it was also the way the words left his lips as puffs of black and roiling smoke. Denser with each passing moment, the darkness spilled from Harmon's choice began to spill from him in earnest. Rivulets of black exited his tear ducts, nostrils, ears, lips, and pores. The vapor and the tumbling spill of inky dream-stuff recombined on the floor where the younger version of Harmon no longer made sport. The vision of the hellish basement in Hanover dissolved into an abyssal hurricane, brick by brick and board by board, until a great, lightless void filled the space just beyond where Harmon teetered.

Ketch's mind cleft itself from bodily perception again, and she took in the sight of a lightless vista stretching from where the sky should be, through the nonexistent horizon, and into reason-defying depths below. The Executioner saw death in that void, but not the sort of death *she* dealt. This was a dissolution of the information making up what one was and had always been.

Friedrich "Fritz" "Eichmann" Harmon didn't give Ketch the satisfaction of shrieking as he toppled into everlasting darkness, an ocean of unending night where vast, black shapes roiled and writhed, forever and ever, death without end. The vast scale and power of those corpse-coils and their endless, peristaltic slither reached for Jacqueline Ketch's mind with uncountable and many-jointed fingers. The abyss was greedy to pluck reason from her like a toothsome piece of meat. Ketch, however, had been hammered out of sterner stuff than Morrison Spare expected, and she looked on with all her shrieking horror trapped behind her nonreactive eyes and black-cowled face.

She turned to call him on the stunt; to ask him what, precisely, he had meant by such visions of an endless, hideously populous abyss, but Spare was nowhere to be seen. Ketch experienced a flush of lightheaded disorientation, and the remaining shreds of the remembered butcher's bakery dissolved, leaving her in Arson's night again, standing before a black-painted shed.

Throughout the long day preceding the night of the black shed, Frank Blank called each soul to their specific wonderland and reawakened the banked coals of their divergent drives. He'd also left a gift for each of them, placed inside an ancient-looking steamer trunk. The trunk sat before the lurid grill of his truck like a last kiss on a sleeping lover's lips at dawn. The trunk was the antique kind, crafted from heavy wood, reinforced with struts, and sealed with leather strips. The bright brass latches on the front popped open with a *SNAP-CHAK* that the awakened Arsonists found inexplicably delightful (and which Archdirector Freund would have recognized at once as a haptic-neurological trigger, or, in her blinkered lexicon of acronyms, an HNT).

A trove of titillation, the trunk held objects tailored to whomever opened it. On his many sojourns to the sunbaked soil of Arson, Frank had tried to reawaken those imprisoned hungers. He'd brought the Arsonists so many totems, signs, and tokens, all of which had been received with greedy and frustrated longing. The prisoners were like starving animals too long-deprived to remember how to eat once food was finally put before them. It had taken a Mystery to un-solve the dismal answer that was Arson, but the floodgates were, at last, wide open.

Pharoah found a squeeze bottle of oil nested in a folded pile of rags and towels. Quicker than one could say "convicted of solicitation, file coded 'sthenolagnia,'" his eager, nut-brown hands had stripped the ragged uniform from Box Spring's massive, muscled frame, the better to stroke fingers over hard-yet-yielding abdominal ridges and the sensual, downward slipstream where his obliques met his transversus abdominus.

A tall, skeletal fellow who bore the *nom de damné* of Noodles (SOPS-B17) was delighted to find a red rubber hot water bag accompanied by an enema attachment, a four-foot, nozzle-tipped hose, and an unmarked gallon jug of lukewarm liquid. Taste-testing the contents with a fingertip, Noodles ascertained that it was a simple saline solution. No stickler for privacy in his most buttoned-up moments, Noodles dropped his tattered uniform trousers less than a stone's throw from the trunk and set about giving himself an enema. The process was accompanied by guttural sounds of satisfaction and, eventually, an unexpected and intense ejaculation.

In the same spirit as Pharoah and Box Spring, a pair of miscreants named Chili Dog (convicted of gross indecency, file coded "salirophilia" and "narratophilia") and Tearaway (convicted of sexual propaganda counteractive to moralpol, file coded "urolagnia") discovered that their specific pleasures were delightfully and specifically complementary. Without removing his uniform, Tearaway lay flat in Arson's dusty, beaten rut of a main trail while Chili Dog rained blasphemous obscenities and a stream of hot, mule-vinegar-tainted piss upon him. Cherubic in their bliss, the two disheveled men both giggled like a pair of rainy-day ragamuffins.

Some tended to the gardens of their regrown lust in more secluded bowers. Others still gave vent to lurid self-expressions as artistic (by their own warped yardsticks) as they were obscene. A big, potbellied man with shoulder-length white hair, known as Sharpy, had found a very special gift from Frank inside the antique trunk. He'd waited for nightfall to emerge from his dugout, where he'd consumed a pint of mule. When he crept out he was naked but for rhinestone-crusted cowboy boots, two bandoliers bustling with bullets, and a pair of holstered six-shooters slung low on his bony hips.

Sharpy stage-stalked up and down the rutted street

and sordid shanty shadows. He chased the Arsonists whom he scared up into the dark and gully-laden night, shooting down those he caught (and, to turn a phrase, shooting *over* those he killed in arcing, pearly parabolas of jism). It was all in good, friendly fun, he figured; after all, his prey would reawaken to the world again in hours. As he chased whatever quarry crossed his path, erect cock waggling before him like a murderous dowsing rod, Sharpy sang a song whose lyrics had returned to him. The words burned so brightly in him that black and joyous night that they may as well have been inscribed upon a mountainside in molten silver.

"Tropical hot dog night!" Sharpy yelped and sang. *"Like two flamingos in a FRUIT fight! I don't want to KNOW… 'bout wrong or right! Yeah, I don't want to know; I'm anywhere tonight!"*

Every shot that popped from Sharpy's revolver seemed to split the claustrophobic Arson night and send aloft a burning sonic flare. It did more than that, too. With every hammer-fall upon a cartridge and with every gout of torso-shredding flame, Sharpy added to the carnival of disassembly. With every impossible breach of the barriers and limits woven into Arson's very fabric, and with every violation of the logic binding world to world, the engines in the ICON stronghold high atop Mount Elbert in a universe both near and distant groaned. They gave up subtle shivers as their logic started to combust. It was slow poison, this introduction of such license into space so tightly governed, but it would do its work.

Havoc had been wreaked by Arson's reawakening of dead and eunuched Eros, too. The summoning of all the myriad perversities, potent pleasures, and specific, resonant displacements; of all that served as lust's most arcane handmaidens, sent shivers just as potent as those sent by Sharpy shedding blood and cum. There were no avalanches overnight at ICON other than those taking place within the mind of Archdirector Kinsey Freund; the damage dealt was subtler now, a thing of low, slow-smoldering fires deep in stacked and isolated server farms. Energy-deflecting and -focusing systems rearranged themselves. In half a day, the seeds planted by these changes to the arrays would fruit and, in doing so, break the reification-engine controls completely.

After he'd escorted her down the nearby hill, Frank Blank left Ketch with Mystery Morrison Spare and Eichmann in the shed, and wandered to the rutted, feral thoroughfare that ran the length of Arson's central section. His nose was sensitive as any Komodo dragon's flicking, ochre tongue, and Frank paused for a moment to inhale the desert's evening smells and hear the echoes of the nighttime celebrants' raw exultations. He smelled blood. He smelled the similarly human, similarly organic perfumes of a dozen acts of passion, any of which would be seen as a capital crime against the Kingdom's moralpol.

His creamy, fungal cowboy hat was pulled low over his unseen eyes, but Frank could see the desert night as well as any shroud-winged owl, or any southwest whip-poor-will peering down the pass from its arboreal remove. He could see more than that, too. He saw the liberation of bent souls and celebrated in the howling, madcap freedom of the newborn night – the reborn Arson. Not reborn as Phyntis would prefer it, either. Nor Wolfaria, Phyntis' grim, all-conquering world.

Spores are circulating, Frank thought and, at the same time and in reverse, *last calm night before the trip begins to take shape.* He was of half a mind to give Wolfaria the kingling's world, and maybe one day he would do just that. Should Pandemonium concur, of course. Frank Blank was, first and foremost, an agent of that great and primal confluence of clowns and murderers, seditious liars and unbending saints of great resolve, slipped wheels, bad cogs, saboteurs, and black-eyed poets marching in invisible ranks from world to world. It was a never-ending reel of dissolution, chaos, and – above all – liberation. So long as Wolfaria trawled the naïve realms for meat to feed their titanic machinery of penitence and torment, Pandemonium would never sleep. They loosened bolts. They unlocked cell doors in the dead of night. They slit the throats of slavers and of priests of punishment. Their methods, like their agents, varied. They could be apocalyptic visitations or could be subtle as a slide of sand on sand upon the downslope of a dune.

Pandemonium's games always started with the importation of contraband, whatever that contraband might be at any given time or place. Smuggling was so ingrained to Pandemonium's mythic architecture that the question of why such a simple method proved so endlessly effective was no longer even asked. When he imported contraband, the substance of the cargo was immaterial to Frank Blank (but for this last, precious load; the Mystery named Morrison Spare). It only mattered that the freight was something people wanted and which those who held knives to their necks did not want them to have. In some of the King's Pockets that meant drugs, the more exotic, strange, and alien the better. In others, it meant other things.

In Arson it meant sex; naturally. Arson could reject sex at the outset, thanks to the editing and retuning CGP deprogramming allowed. So: Frank brought bits and ends, paraphilic bric-a-brac that tantalized the minds of

Arsonists and filled their hearts and loins with familiar and unquenchable hungers. Psychologically, the puppets dancing here for Dr. Gayle had been gelded (or, to use CGP's language, "shriven of paraphilic residue and attendant traces"). Despite that, there was something in the things which Frank brought from the places he liked best; the alleyways and truck stops, basement bazaars, and criminal symposia. He brought shreds and tatters of the Arsonist's lost lusts. He didn't do it to trade for ridiculous, impoverished baubles, though he'd accepted them gladly enough. He did it simply to excite and keep alive the dormant desires and contrary inclinations in these hapless hominids.

Frank strolled back to the cab of his truck and clambered up the welded ladder rungs on the driver's side. He popped the door with a *CHUNK* and set one boot upon the cab's floor, standing upright for a better view. This vantage was the highest one in Arson's denuded huddle of half-shanties, nearly twice the height of the shambolic Woodpile, where Uncle Funny's puppet show went on and on to wild acclaim. Arsonists had dragged scrap wood from their meager shelters and piled it in the street before the Woodpile and its crooked porch, and someone clever had coaxed forth a flame. Now, the night scene was lit by the protean golden light of the Area's inaugural bonfire. Appreciative audience members fed Funny a steady stream of mule vinegar all night, and his performance ascended from mere satire to a rarified plateau of partially-coherent coprolalia directed at King Cleon III. The gathered derelicts roared their appreciation, and even Frank gave up an unseen half-smile at Uncle Funny's antics and the misadventures of his marionettes.

Balancing his weight on the toe of one boot, Frank

Blank planted one broad hand and took in the tableau of Arson's partial liberation (*more*, he promised himself, *will come in short order*). With his other hand, he gently grasped the crown of his cream-colored cowboy hat. With an expansive sweep, he lifted it away.

One of Arson's never-lonely onanists was a lean, antisocial fellow who went by Billy Burlap (convicted of possession of pornography, file coded "acrotomophilia"). Billy was on his evening's second round of spit-lubed, pumping masturbation when he happened to glance up from the treasure trove of amputee pornography he'd withdrawn from Frank's steamer trunk. What he saw was enough to arrest his vigorous self-grappling for a moment as he stared at yet another unexpected miracle. Though Billy Burlap didn't know it, he was the only one to see Frank Blank take the evening air.

Neither a pillar of cloud by day nor a pillar of smoke by night, the Pandemoniumite was both at once. He rose to touch the grand drape of the night sky's curtain in his native form: a column of boiling, noctilucent smoke, its rounded turbulations shining with a rainbow-spray of light and color. Nor did the sentient, slender cumulus tower rise merely to expand and stretch his proverbial legs; Frank bore yet another gift for Arson on that night of many gifts.

Since its conception as a set of initial parameters in an ICON simulation, Arson's night sky was intended to be a thing of total, all-encompassing darkness. No moon made steady courses as it waxed and waned; no passing satellites blinked down like watchful angels; most of all, there were no stars.

This changed when Frank Blank's luminescent cloud boiled high enough that his tendril reached the zenith of the interstice. A tiny portion of the smoke boiled off and slid across the black sky, gaining mass as it progressed across the Pocket's parallax. The effect was like a rippling aurora, and that exquisite sight was not just seen by Billy Burlap. Frank's boiling tentacle of smoke retreated and descended to his vessel, vanishing as quickly as it had appeared. Arson's first aurora was both brief and beautiful. What it left behind was something else entirely, and caused the whole carceral colony to cease its sybaritic frenzy for at least a moment as, one by one, the Arsonists beheld the change their revelry had wrought.

There were now strange stars and unknown constellations in the sky.

```
The New Amsterdammer INTERNAL MEMO |
110.01.08
ARTICLE SUBMISSION | 110 Issue #1
FROM: JACOBSON, KENT MoralPolD, MFA
TITLE: "Degeneracy for Degeneracy's Sake:
The Music of Erick Zinn"
```

Degeneracy for Degeneracy's Sake: The Music of Erick Zinn

By Kent Jacobson

Perhaps it is a problem attendant to age (and taste), but this humble author remembers a time when degenerate art was given greater license. Predictably, the subversive works that emerged from this period of laxity were not only offensive to moralpol, they were just plain offensive. Sensually speaking, there is more to be gained from a single glimpse of Piotr Veley's *Majesty* or Cindy Bulgar's *Rex* than from an entire glum afternoon contemplating a now-proscribed work like James Chauncey's *The Harrowing of Harlem*. Good art, as I wrote to Chauncey at the time, never mixes well with propaganda, particularly such a revisionist version of the past (if you don't believe me, consult your Royal History regarding the demolition of unsafe structures in the now-redeveloped neighborhood in question, and tell me Chauncey's views amount to more than petty whining by a displaced radical).

It's in this spirit that I resoundingly condemn the music of neomodernist Erick Zinn. Why Zinn has a following in the first place is questionable. I do not think it old-fashioned to expect music to have melody and resolution. Zinn's noise – I hesitate to even think of it as music – is made up of dull, atonal drones and lamentations from a choir of faultfinders. Am I mad to think that music in this Kingdom should invoke a sense of purpose and grand, glorious progress? Not according to Zinn.

My readers know I do not take this stance often, but I would go so far as to label Zinn's most recent work, *No Absolutes in Reality, Absolute Fantasy*, a potential candidate for condemnation as Degenerate Art. I only hope that, among my readers, one of His Majesty's censors takes it upon themselves to evaluate Zinn's work and charge him with Public Indecency. Perhaps a trip to the King's Pockets will persuade Mister Zinn that life in the Kingdom he "subtly" disparages is not as bad as he thinks.

MORALPOL|APPEND.23
Remove reference to proscribed artist James Chauncey and any of his artwork. Although used in a positive way (i.e., to condemn it), this still violates Censor Code 5.1.3 by referring to him directly. Perhaps allude without mentioning directly?

10.
SECRETS ONLY KNOWN BY THE ELECT

Dr. G. Ruzicka Freund began to experience severe doubts about Princess Innocent by the time a strange nocturnal flare brought unexpected, dappled light to Arson's vacant skies. This unauthorized change to the tiny cosmos Dr. Gayle had wrought had an unexpected and unpleasant side effect: it broke the few remaining strands of contact linking Gayle's cognitive implants to ICON's reification-engines. That such a thing could happen meant that Phyntis' "other" was more powerful and resourceful than either she or Gayle had guessed.

It was more than Arson's newborn starlight. The stars themselves should have made the Arsonists easier to find and unmake, but the converse was the case. Gayle and Princess heard the revelry easily enough; given the volume of the degenerate festivities and the small size of the Pocket, it would have been hard not to. Each time they chased the sound of grunting and ecstatic cries, or sought what sounded like a roaring audience, they found only rolling, empty hardpacked dirt as far as they could see.

Most unsettling of all, however, was Princess

Innocent's increasing rage. Gayle knew all too well that Innocent was just a construct, a purpose-built thing made specifically to interact with humans. But it was when Phyntis' factotum demonstrated such degenerate and *human* emotiveness that Gayle loathed her the most. There was something both in- and human about such messy feelings, and the way they crossed the schoolgirl's face was far too knowing, far too adult, and far too *alien*. If Gayle was being honest, they now thought slightly less of Phyntis just for sending such a thing. Given how unbreakably they'd hitched their fate to that strange outsider's star, this was an unfortunate realization.

"*Where the fuck are they*?" shrieked Innocent. She stood, straining with rage, at the crest of a low, rolling hill and stared into the empty wastes before her and at the distant, nonexistent mountains. Dr. Gayle winced, and not just at the cry's inhuman volume. Such outbursts scraped their nerves. They knew that Phyntis didn't consider moralpol the ideological cornerstone that decent humans did, but Phyntis shared Gayle's bone-deep hatred of the oversexed and monstrous monkey-nature of humanity's indecent present state. Up to this point, that shared hate had been enough. Princess Innocent wheeled on Gayle with furious eyes that had no place in such a young and unlined face, and Gayle realized that the girl-shaped thing actually expected an answer to her question.

"Whatever made those stars," panted Dr. Gayle, winded from their stagger up and down the rutted, meaningless terrain, "it severed my connection to the reification-engines. I'd put my money on the same thing unfixing the terrain. If I can reboot my implants, maybe I can reestablish some control."

This was a simple lie. The truth was, the force of

every bent strut and revised tautology flowing from this unknown point of anarchy had far surpassed the great Moral Philosopher's control. The structural revision flowing through the fabric of the Area had ripped through Dr. Gayle's cognitive implants and, to judge by the blood now leaking from their eyes and ears, the meat of portions of their brain had hemorrhaged if not burst outright. Princess Innocent noted Dr. Gayle's bleeding eyes and, in her brightest, most cheery voice, asked:

"Say, Doc! If that melon of yours goes, y'know, *POW*! Well... Does this whole place go *POW* too?"

"No," Gayle managed as they staggered forward. "Just... my control array. All of the King's Pockets are... anchored in Mount Elbert." Some sort of field distortion nearby was playing hell the lenses of their multifaceted eyes: more specifically, the lenses of exotic matter gifted them by Phyntis. The damn things stung. They more than stung; the pain grew more intense until it felt like tiny flecks of burning soot or superheated ash were nestled in the nerveless plastic corneas, burning them like vulnerable human meat. This was particularly distracting because, strictly speaking, Dr. Gayle had no flesh left in their eyes; not one scrap. Their eyes were totally synthetic, and not equipped with pain receptors anywhere in their entire structure.

"We've got to be close, right?" Gayle added, and took the opportunity to catch their breath. "Something is interfering with my visual input."

Innocent stopped stalking back and forth in search of Arson's residents and stood stock still facing them. At first, there was an unsettling shutter-click of something in the way she looked; in her carriage, angles, and the makeup of her strange regard. It was only a glimpse, but it was enough to churn Gayle's guts. Then, they realized that Innocent wasn't staring at *them* at all. She was staring intently over the doctor's shoulder. In the direction they'd just come from, and there'd been nothing noteworthy in that grim loop of dirt.

Dr. Gayle turned to glance back and froze as they beheld an arresting and exotic landscape. Alternating views shifted in and out of frontal focus in their muddled, many-lensed perception. The ICON electronics in their eyes revealed one world, and the octet of exotic lenses quite another.

The crumbling blacktop underlaid both visions. Seen one way, the strip was occupied by a pink monstrosity of a truck, behind which stood a line of tiny, brightly colored sheds. Before them stood a quintet of people, some of whom were prisoners and one of whom was Executioner Ketch. *Blink.* Seen the other way, the truck became an object with no clear conceptual parallel; it looked organic, veined (or roped) with cables, and breathed great clouds of shimmering smoke from upright metal tubes implanted in its fleshy back. Though these metallic vents seemed planted straight up in Gayle's vision, they simultaneously leaned at angles that made a ramshackle mockery of comprehensible geometry. In this altered vision, there were no sheds. The dirt behind the mollusk-like mechanical-organic slab was home to eight slender, silent cyclones. They rose from the hardpack like the slender legs of ghostly, oceanic waterspouts. Each bore within its gyrating ascension sparking, varicolored lightning; a different vibrant shade for each ascending whirlwind.

Blink. Gayle saw a stranger, a dusty-looking, sun-browned man sporting an oversized and bulbous cowboy hat. "Dr. G. Ruzicka Freund," the man said, his voice scale-on-stone soft and sagebrush smoky, "I didn't

think you were going to make it. I'm glad you did."
Blink. Seen through Phyntis' exotic lenses, he was no man at all. Instead, Gayle saw a coiled cumulus in which capricious humor and a vast, chaotic intelligence lurked, playing peek-a-boo in modes of perception too foreign to penetrate.

Blink-CRACK! A shower of white, phosphorescent sparks erupted from the back of Dr. Gayle's heavily-modified skull, briefly gifting the Moral Philosopher a blinding halo. Gayle took a drunken, staggering step to their left. Their eyes burned like two red-hot coals lodged in their skull. They lifted their hands to their artificial orbs and rubbed, as though the gesture could soothe fleshy organs now long gone. When Dr. Gayle removed their hands from their eyes the pain was gone, replaced by waves of sweet relief. They detected a faint glint in their cupped palms, and saw that Phyntis' exotic lenses had been wrested free.

"GAaayyyylee. AAaRre YoUUUU OokAaaayY?!"
The awful sound was not a voice, not in any way a human could recognize. The sound was paralyzing; a groaning, creaking ape of natural tones which, in their proximity to human sapience, revealed the utter, fundamental *otherness* of that which vomited such a foul and rubbery facsimile. *Those weren't just lenses*, Dr. Gayle realized belatedly. They remembered Eichmann, how the little man had simply unraveled at the sight of Innocent. They remembered Eichmann's file, the details of Friedrich "Fritz" Harmon's life. The Jersey Werewolf, many in the Kingdom called him. Gayle thought about Harmon's atrocities, the things he'd seen and done, and what it must have taken to lethally unseat his reason. It was far too late by then, but Dr. G. Ruzicka Freund's prodigious brain (or what was left of its sparking and

malfunctioning amalgam) finally connected the dots.

What have I allied myself with? they wondered. A researcher down to their bones, Gayle first activated their tapenote system, then engaged their full optical array (minus one specific filter, that was). Finally, they lifted their eyes, open wide, to see.

Their inspection lasted .75 seconds, and felt like an eternity trapped in some exotic hell; one even fouler than those that Dr. Gayle had wrought. After this appraisal, they fell to the toxic dirt of Arson, struck dead by their mind's exhaustive violation. Dead by means never even dreamed of by the Jolly Rancher or the suicidal Howling Andy; dead in the *true* death of an unrecoverable thing. *This* time, the doctor's death blew out the last controls of reification-engine 23. In violation of the laws they'd carefully constructed, Dr. Gayle was permanently dead.

At the blacktop's crumbling edge, Pandemonium's ambassador looked up the slope and watched with unseen eyes as two figures approached. "Mystery Spare," Frank said calmly as the two forms started to descend the hill, "could you blind Skunk and JR for a second? Might be best if they just take a little nap." Spare didn't even have to speak; at his mere thought, the two Arsonists folded to the hardpack like laundry unclipped from a clothesline. "Ketch," Frank continued, "if I'm not mistaken, you won't have the same problem with our visitor those fellows would have." He flashed a brief and joyless slice of pearly teeth. "All that exotic cognitive screening, I assume. The safest people here are me and you. Dr. Gayle's not really built for defense operations."

He wasn't wrong. Ketch watched the scene with the

same placid, plastic brown eyes through which she had watched events transpire since her ascension to Royal Executioner. Despite some basic similarities, her own synthetic eyes were not at all like Dr. Gayle's. While Ketch's eyes weren't as advanced in gleaning scientific data, they were *much* more advanced in other ways. Ways that, inasmuch as they were products of highly classified military technology, would have been above even the Freunds' impressive clearance levels. The Freunds were scientists, philosophers, and engineers. They weren't armorers, despite what they may have believed.

As the starlit shapes came closer, Ketch saw by the uniform that one was Dr. Gayle. Figuring that Gayle, having been assassinated once, might wish to repay the kindness, Ketch glanced quickly to and fro for any makeshift weapon near to hand. Before she had time to look far, Frank Blank gave a casual wave, stepped to his truck, clambered up, and came back with an axe with a flared, semicircular head and a long, wooden handle. He tossed it lightly to Ketch, who caught it with cognitively- and physically-enhanced ease.

"Gayle's pal calls herself Princess Innocent," Frank added mildly. "She's a nasty piece of work."

As the good doctor and her still-murky comrade halved the distance, a curious thing transpired. Gayle stopped their drunken, shambolic descent, swayed, and without further preamble began to spray brilliant white sparks. Two heartbeats later, Gayle fell to the ground unmoving. *One down*, Ketch thought with wry superiority. She had a hard time conceiving of an adversary who could match her one-on-one; even two allied against her would have been a paltry exercise, given her training. "This shouldn't take long," she said with a neutrality that was, in fact, her at her cockiest.

Her confidence evaporated the instant that the dark thing hurrying down the hill in disjointed, jaunty strides shambled into view in Arson's newborn starlight.

In her murky prehistory, when Royal Executioner Jacqueline Ketch had been Lance Corporal Ophelia Singh, she'd fought in the trench wars on the Western Front of the Kingdom's advance against the cyberdelic shock troops of the Network Society. The NS front lines had been outfitted in uniforms lined with textural light projectors and piercing, mask-mounted strobe stilettos which had transformed their goggled eyes into burning, stutter-stop stars. In previous engagements, the effect on unprepared Royal Army regiments had been ruinous. The sense-shocked, blinded Royals had been carved to bits by the nontoxic, biodegradable shredder rounds of the Society's high-pressure air rifles.

What the Society hadn't known was that, by the next engagement, Lance Corporal Singh and her fellow front-line killers had become the first generation of Royal Army cadets to give their eyes to the King. Those jellied fallibilities had been replaced by new eyes, synched to cognitive enhancements and well-baffled against the optical projections of the Network Society shock troops. Generations of refinements had followed, and as Royal Executioner, Singh – now Ketch – possessed the finest pair the Kingdom offered. Given that they'd conquered and absorbed the technology of the Network Society, they were very fine eyes indeed.

Some things, sages tell humanity, were not meant for mortal eyes to see. Dr. Gayle may have heartily agreed with that sentiment, were they capable of speech. Instead, they kept the secrets of the dead as Princess Innocent launched herself at Executioner Ketch. She gave no war cry as she scuttled forward. Her only herald was the rapid hiss and hush of an indeterminate number of feet striking the dirt.

Wolfaria's ambassador was inhumanity incarnate. Innocent revealed was a myriapod puppet-thing of tangled corpse limbs; pallid, ghastly, and lifelessly animated counter to all reason. The limbs themselves were ever-changing, cracked and bent with newly-forged joints. They swiveled in whatever manner took the monstrous thing most swiftly to its prey. Her mismatched eyes were brimful of a noisome species of delight which, as much as anything, marked her not as inhuman, but unhuman. Phyntis' proxy wore a face of slackened, wax-museum pallor pulled this way and that by rapidly-cycling, aped emotions. She was a rancid near-impression of a human being, a damaged child's primitive crayon drawing of a bogey brought to wrenching, multijointed life. It was an effigy of *homo sapiens* constructed by a strange intelligence which hadn't even tasted of the frozen and outlying wastes of its portrait subject's universe, let alone the air of humankind's birth-world.

Princess Innocent was on Ketch with nightmarish speed. She brought one awful, false-meat limb down in a brutal, clubbing blow. The Executioner was quick enough to bring the arm not holding Frank's axe up to intercept it with her forearm. Innocent's long, corpse-meat limb struck like a falling steel beam. Once, the force behind the thing's attack might have shattered Ketch's arm. The Executioner, however, had given more than just her eyes to the King. The frame she hid beneath her black garb had been built or modified to purpose, and that purpose was to visit wroth upon the Kingdom's foes.

Ketch absorbed the hammer-blow with only a soft grunt of effort. There was strength enough behind Innocent's limb that Ketch's boots sank several centimeters into Arson's lifeless soil. *Now I know what it's like to be a nail*, Ketch thought inanely, and before the Executioner could give the matter much more thought, she struck out with Frank's axe. And then again. And then again.

As terrifying and inimical as her aspect was, the construct known as Princess Innocent had not been built for combat. Combat as conceived of by humanity was, in fact, not *quite* a thing which she could grasp. She had been machined into existence as a go-between, a messenger: a creature who, amphibious, could clumsily exist in both Wolfaria's vast, grinding, crowded anti-space and in Arson's ersatz microcosmos. Innocent was an exotic piece of bespoke toymaking. Ketch, by contrast, was born to a combative species which bore a legacy of red and hungry murder older than the time it left the seas, let alone the trees. A standard human – warlike enough – had then ascended through the ranks of one of humankind's most brutally efficient militaries. She had stepped into the role which, in her private thoughts, she worried she'd been born for. Ketch was the King's will to death made manifest. In that capacity, she'd been reshaped; given form to match her function.

Innocent was strong, and quick, and possessed of an unspeakable puppet-vitality, but Ketch's placid plastic eyes were unamazed by the vile corpse-thing's contortions. The Executioner's arms were strong, her aim as true as any predator's. The work took less than two full minutes. When it was accomplished, Wolfaria's envoy to the late Dr. Gayle lay scattered over Arson's thirsty hardpack in hacked-up lengths. The frenzy at an end, Ketch stood, barely even short of breath, and looked upon her work. She nodded. Ketch then turned her eyes to the distinctive shape of the axe she held, and then back up to Frank Blank.

"Really?" She sounded both amused and tired. "An actual executioner's axe?"

He shrugged. Behind him, Morrison Spare began to reawaken Skunk and the Jolly Rancher. "I improvised," Frank said. "Could've grabbed anything, really. I've got quite the collection."

"Next time," Ketch said, "toss me a damn shotgun."

"Shotguns? Do you really think that's necessary?"

Archdirector Kinsey Freund's paltry attempt at detached nonchalance did nothing to hide her unease. A special envoy, she had assumed, meant an inspection team. King's Prosecutor Kerik Goetz, however, had shown up with what looked more like an assault team. The five anonymous soldiers were indistinguishable beneath their matte black body armor and obscuring masks, possessed of neither gender nor nationality, merely lethal function.

"Merely a precaution, my dear Kinsey," said Goetz in his ever-jolly way. "Better safe, as they say." He was a soft man, wormlike in his pallor and the clammy feel of his smooth palms. He tapped one pseudopod-like fingertip against his full lower lip. Goetz's lips were the only part of his face that displayed any lifelike coloration, and were a repellant shade of cyanotic bluish-red. Not for the first time, Kinsey wondered if His Honor Justice Goetz had been tested for hypoxia. Something in the lurid shade of Goetz's lower lip triggered a cascade of memory in Archdirector Freund, followed quickly by opportunistic inspiration. She cleared her throat and spoke softly, so that only Goetz could hear.

"Speaking purely hypothetically, Honorable Justice," Kinsey murmured, "if we were to encounter any sort of trouble today, it may provide an unexpected venue to gather data on a prototype we both may or may not be familiar with."

Goetz stared at her appraisingly with his moist, fishy eyes. They were, Kinsey thought, the exact shade of Baby's Breath blossoms. "For God's sake, woman," he quietly spat, "just *say* it, whatever you're trying to say."

Kinsey hid a wince. *One might as well expect subtlety from a machine gun*, she thought.

"Abyssus," she said, lowering her already-hushed words to near inaudibility. "Wouldn't this be a propitious time for a field test?"

Bright blue irises in fishy cradles, Goetz's eyes bored into her. "Is the subject… *ready* for that?"

"I think so, yes. And suppose he isn't? We can subdue him or scratch him. One of the King's Pockets would provide ideal deniability."

He mulled this over, rolling his tongue against his teeth behind his pursed lips in a way that made them (and her) squirm.

Dr. Freund could tell the ranking jurist was tempted. Hadn't the entire Abyssus Project been conceived and brought into its infancy in secret? Goetz's remit, as he'd already told her, was to ascertain if one or both Freund siblings had murdered Executioner Ketch. Ketch herself had originally been sent to ICON, it turned out, after whispers reached King Cleon's court regarding Dr. Gayle's rather unconventional penal philosophy. Kinsey would have given a majority of her substantial net worth to know where *those* whispers originated, but Goetz told her he had tried to solve that very riddle and had met with no success.

"How many people does one of your insertion pods hold," Justice Goetz asked slowly, "and do you have trained security armed with lethal force?" He caught her flash of irritation and chuckled softly. "Forgive my stupidity, Kinsey. Sometimes I forget that, while your sibling has the keys to His Majesty's celestial dungeons, *you* are the zookeeper who tends the most dangerous and fascinating animals."

"Oh, stow the flattery," Archdirector Freund said dismissively, but she was quietly pleased. Ruzi *did* get all the attention from the Court. Why, just look at the fact that Executioner Ketch had perfunctorily participated in a single paltry CGP interface session. The black-clad brute could hardly wait to jet off to the Land of Nod to see what the brilliant interstitial engineer and Moral Philosopher had wrought. Justice Goetz had shown real interest in Kinsey's work from its inception and, more importantly, he saw the full potential of her theories. For all her innovative brilliance and well-earned accolades, Kinsey burned with the quiet conviction that her contributions to the Kingdom were overlooked in favor of that of her odd and brilliant sibling. An odd, brilliant sibling, she reminded herself, that was also quite insane. *Had* been quite insane, rather, and was now quite dead.

She treated Justice Goetz to a ferocious grin. "I'll get the transfer squad ready and join your team in the interstitial insertion laboratory. Give me less than thirty minutes."

Goetz pulled out and checked his pocket watch (an affectation which the Archdirector found both ludicrous and endearing). "Very well," he agreed. As she walked briskly away, he added: "By the by, where's Robert... Flanagan, I think you said his name was? The young man you introduced me to the last time I graced Mount

Elbert. Seemed like a bright young man – and sturdily built. Might help to have him along."

"Mmm," she answered neutrally as she walked away without looking back. She realized with a twinge of superstitious discomfort that the noncommittal, monotone syllable, spoken in her voice, sounded eerily like her sibling's habitual nonresponse.

Twenty minutes later, Dr. Freund's monster was prepared for his first trip to the King's Pockets. The figure that emerged from the labyrinthine holding area was straitjacketed and shackled. He shuffled forward with his head swathed in an all-obscuring black bag. The Archdirector led his steps herself, holding a man-catcher pole wrapped about his neck. She steered him as casually as if she were taking a terrier out for his morning constitutional. To either side of her, and somewhat *less* casually, a team of four armed ICON guards kept shotguns trained on Kinsey's hobbled man.

Honorable Justice Goetz laughed when this procession entered the interstitial insertion laboratory. "My goodness," he exclaimed, "isn't that a bit *much*, Kinsey?"

"Allow me to introduce VSOSeSa-A01," Dr. Freund said, offering a wan smile at the gentle gibe. "Back when he was talk of the territories, his name was William Guillebeaux. I believe the ducat dreadfuls called him-"

"Bloody Billy," Goetz breathed, interrupting Kinsey as he stared at the chain-bewebbed prisoner with newly burning fascination. To the credit of his troops, none took a backward step – but all tightened their black-gloved grips upon their guns. There was an audible, if subtle, creak of leather against steel as all four did so in the sudden silence. This drew a slow, sardonic smile from the King's Prosecutor. "I had the editor of the *New-York Gazetteer* hanged for leaking your insanity. Your *filth*," he said, his voice hot. He shifted his eyes back to the Archdirector. "The letters, you know, and how he signed them."

"I remember," Kinsey said.

"I had no idea he'd been remanded to ICON. Remarkable. You'd think I would remember that."

"It was kept rather quiet," Kinsey said, carefully leading her prize down the laboratory steps and to its grim concrete floor. *No beauty in my sibling's work,* thought Archdirector Freund. *The power of a god at their fingertips, and no sense of beauty whatsoever. Not even in the way in which they designed their hells.* She smiled at that. Could a hell be beautiful? She didn't see why not.

The strange, half-fleshy smell of freshly forged Pocket Protector filled the air of ICON's insertion point. This flat, unappetizing odor blended with the bright smell of ozone and the high-pitched reek ofr burning wires; a blend Ketch sometimes called *Eau de Interstice.* Gouts of retina-pocking sparks rained dreamily from loci on the chamber's tall, cylindrical field transformers as the technicians made their final preparations. All the personnel on hand were the Archdirector's pet technicians. While Kinsey might tell herself she'd trapped Ruzi in unplanned reaction to the Executioner's inspection, to tell herself her hand had been forced, the bare-boned, grinning inner Kinsey knew her preparations had preceded Ketch and had been long and careful.

For example: why train her own teams of technicians to perform the same tasks as Ruzi's staff, unless Kinsey had seen a day when she would have to bar her sibling's scientists from ICON's labs and set a band of trusted loyalists to work instead?

When Dr. Freund's and Honorable Justice Goetz's teams reached the exterior of the interstitial transport pods, the Archdirector handed Bloody Billy off to an anonymously-masked guard and joined Goetz. The jurist stared up at the slab of translucent gel enveloping their chariot like some behemoth's aspic. The semi-organic smell of it became a stench this close to its great, mucilaginous bulk.

"There's a lot about this whole affair that I don't understand," he confided, turning his fishy, Baby's Breath eyes to meet hers. "I comprehend the moral dimensions of the technology, the socio-legal implications of the technology, and the statistics regarding the technology's costs, benefits, and effect on crime rates and the stability of moralpol." He sighed. "But the technology itself? It might as well be magic, Archdirector. So much of what we take for granted works that way." He gestured at the concrete box of Dr. Gayle's laboratory, ending the wave in a halfhearted flap at the pod before them. "I know as much about how lightbulbs work as I do about *this* godforsaken thing."

Kinsey Freund smiled, a rare display of genuine warmth. "Why, Honorable Justice Goetz," she said with teasing consternation, "it almost sounds like you're *afraid* to climb aboard!"

"I'm not afraid," Goetz replied, his own smile rather more arctic, "but I am *uncomfortable*."

The insertion pods had been designed to hold guards and prisoners alike in their capacious innards, a layout crafted in anticipation of the day that work at ICON would proceed from experimental technology to run-of-the-mill carceral policy. In such a situation, transports would hardly be efficient if they only held a single prisoner per trip. Thus Archdirector Freund, her pet monster, Honorable Justice Goetz, and their combined armed personnel fit comfortably in the confines of a single pod. It even had a set of heavy steel loops bolted to its floor. Once the group had boarded the conveyance, a guard linked SeSa-A01's shackles tightly to an anchor point, and Kinsey radioed control to power up the reification engines for interstitial insertion. Though its walls were thick and armored against the atmospheric strain of transfer, everyone aboard the pod could feel the air vibrate and thicken as the charge of exotic, overlapping energies enveloped them.

Kinsey glanced at Goetz, whose wheyfaced visage was paler than ever. His beetle brow was crowned by gleaming laurels of cold sweat. *The Caesar of the Luddites*, Dr. Freund thought fondly, and took his hand. He glanced at her, startled, but Kinsey merely smiled and gave his hairy digits an affirming squeeze.

"I hate this too," she said softly. "It's one of the reasons I reached out to you in the first place. The first time Ruzi took me into one of the interstices, I knew that this technology was *wrong* on a fundamental level."

This was a topic they'd discussed before, and Goetz, reassured by this reminder, nodded.

"If ten millennia of jurisprudence have taught our species anything, it's that incarceration is, at best, a half measure." The Honorable Justice warmed to his subject, and Kinsey was glad. The jurist was too wrapped up in his own oratorical gyrations to note the unsettling vibration which began to permeate the pod, shaking everything from Bloody Billy's jingling shackles to the restless air itself.

Goetz went on. "Lock an evil person in a box. What then? The best that one can do is to tend them, feed them, and keep them fenced off from the flock. There's just no rehabilitating human nature. Or, at least, not the way that Dr. Gayle and His Majesty, noble as his intentions are, believe in rehabilitation. You, Dr. Freund. You have made enormous progress in the praxis of moralpol. A place for everyone, and everyone in their place. That philosophy is the foundation of our new, eternal order. But what sort of place is a box, for killers?"

"It's a trash bin," Dr. Freund said, recognizing the Honorable Justice's rhetorical prompt and delivering her line accordingly. The vibration in the pod became a tremor, and a few of the armed guards, inured to combat as they were, betrayed their queasiness through the taut strain of their body language.

"A trash bin," Goetz said, satisfied, and continued to hold forth. "What Abyssus offers is a recycling program. Take our good friend Bloody Billy here. He butchered, what, 60 people?"

"67," Kinsey answered flatly. A flash of Flanagan's eyes, drunk with mortal pain and molten lust, floated through her mind like a silk veil borne upon a breeze. "67 proven victims who were subjects of the Kingdom. But he took a sojourn south. Bypassed our border control somehow. We know he hunted…" Kinsey caught herself and turned the word into a cough, correcting herself as smoothly as she could. "We know that he murdered others while he was there. VSOSeSa-A01 will only say, and I quote, 'I don't care to count,' but there's reason to believe his number of victims is in the triple digits."

"A monster," breathed Honorable Justice Goetz, but Dr. Freund could hear the edge of grudging admiration in his voice. She didn't blame him. She felt much the same. Goetz turned to his coterie of masked and black-clad guards. "Show of hands. Can any of you claim a hundred kills?" None of them moved. "My point exactly," Goetz concluded triumphantly. As these words left his plump, anoxic lips, the transport pod's tremor, which had steadily intensified, disappeared completely. Kinsey braced herself, recognizing the last steps of the insertion sequence.

"All the monsters, Kinsey," Goetz said fervently. "They don't belong in cages in the zoo. We'll leash them and we'll train them, and we'll set them at our enemies' throats. The era of the soldier ends with Abyssus, Dr. Freund. The era of the sanctioned sadist can begin."

The insertion was a subtle but unmistakable sensation; a piercing or a penetration, soft and vaguely sexual. Kinsey was reminded, again, of her night of red passion with Flanagan; of the feeling of a blade as it met eager, teasing resistance; as it parted flesh and penetrated secrets only known by the elect. She glanced up at Bloody Billy, hunched inside his straitjacket, black hood, and shackles. She saw his taut frame shiver. She knew it wasn't fear; she'd spent more time inside of VSOSeSa-A01's mind than anyone beside the prisoner himself. No, William Guillebeaux was incapable of fear, organically speaking. It was the sex-death tide that surged inside of him, anticipating the delights to come.

Kinsey was certain that, beneath the hood, Bloody Billy wore the secret smile he showed to those the Archdirector fed to him within her private labyrinth. Dr. Freund's attention meant she heard the single word that Bloody Billy breathed as they left everything behind and pierced the veil between realities. It was a puzzling word, and though she dismissed the word itself, she caught the burning longing in those five syllables. *It sounds*, she thought distractedly, *a little like a prayer*.

"*Pandemonium*," murmured Bloody Billy reverently.

112.01.01
FROM THE ROYAL HAND OF KING CLEON III,
ABSOLUTE MONARCH AND PROTECTOR OF THE REALM,
A DECREE:

To our beloved subjects: It has come to our attention that moralpol and our subjects' sense of personal safety have been adversely affected by recent news coverage of criminal activity by mentally deranged and degenerate misdemeanants. It is our will that such sensationalism cease.

FIRST: Any reportage on criminal activity must pass through our Moralpol Office before distribution through the Royal Press.

SECOND: Any person found in violation of this decree shall face penalties up to and including ultimate sanction.

SIGNED: KING CLEON III

11.
A Subsequent Death of JR

The judgment of the black shed was harder to watch when Skunk Pussy and the Jolly Rancher were being meted. Though Executioner Ketch was physically incapable of sympathy (another cognitive adjustment which accompanied the office), her brief acquaintance with both men had made them ad hoc comrades in arms, if not companions. "I understand," said Mystery Morrison Spare, reading her discomfort. "But all must be judged according to their desires."

"Says who?" asked Ketch.

"Says me," replied Frank Blank. His voice was just a quiet, stony rasp, but it brooked no dissent.

Skunk went first. For him, the black shed opened on a different tiny wooden shack; a tumbledown hovel of swamp wood boards that wore a perforated tin roof like a crooked hat. The drumming of spring rain against that tin filled the cobweb-shrouded, dark interior with an artillery barrage of sound. Merle Martin, known to Arsonists as Skunk, and to the Kingdom's carceral authorities as subject SOCV-A101, didn't mind. Spring was a special time for Merle, a time that stirred strange longings in him. He'd fostered them within the bony eggshell of his skull since he was just a blonde, pug-faced boy, growing up half-feral in Roeville, Florida. Stench, rot, dissolution, and decomposition held a place of primacy in Merle's desires, and the fertile, fetid soil in which his lineage had lodged itself offered up an alligator's banquet of these things.

Merle's first run-in with the deep water swell of sensation that would come to govern him arrived by happy accident. A haunter of the swamps since he could walk upright, a seven-year-old Merle had come upon what Royal Police referred to as "a floater;" a flyblown human body found in water. The sexless thing was bloated with a mortuary treasure-house of scents, textures, secret sights, and haunting, surreptitious flavors. Merle had burned for years until, grown enough to wield a pick and spade, he'd embarked on an adventure one warm spring night.

Later, then-King's Subprosecutor Goetz would mark Merle's file with the CV code due to his incursions into many of the numerous, secluded graveyards of the territory once called north Florida. These cypress-choked cemeteries were the haunting-grounds where Merle dug for his buried treasures. Eventually, the Royal Police located Merle's shack, though he'd found it off the beaten track on Munson Highway where it met a sluggish stream called the Bucket Branch. The RPs pried the door loose of its rotting frame with little effort, and a gale of late-summer stench hit them like a booby trap.

In his shed, Merle had collected rotting heads, whole torsos, limbs, denuded skeletons, and the other sweets. His collection marked his file with "necrophilia," "mysophilia," and the simple criminal code "Grave Robber." Ketch watched Skunk react with mild disgust on seeing his indulgences through eyes unclouded by his predilections. Offered the fateful choice between keeping his unspeakable delights or giving himself to the Pit, Merle "Skunk Pussy" Martin chose to keep his foul delights. Even half-hypnotized by Mystery Spare's eerie touch, Skunk displayed the same intelligence which few in his benighted life had noted. Skunk said simply "I didn't hurt anybody." The Executioner thought the families of those despoiled in death by Merle might argue with that statement, but she wasn't the jury trying Skunk: *he* was. He emerged from the black shed exhausted, but enriched by newfound self-awareness.

Would the Jolly Rancher prove as lucky? Ketch had her suspicions. All his friendliness and shallow surface charm were wasted on her. Ketch had already familiarized herself with his file before her trip to Arson. There had been good reason for JR's impromptu execution, to Ketch's choice to test Dr. Gayle's regenerative subroutines on him specifically.

The Rancher's former expertise with chemicals had not been part of ICON's shriving of JR, though the man himself had no idea how he knew such useful things about improvised chemistry. The Jolly Rancher, known by the Kingdom's carceral authorities as SOCV-B1, had once been someone else (as had they all). The Jolly Rancher had been Jeremy Rose. Rose had been a manufacturer of illicit drugs of remarkable variety and potency. He'd been a poet with his -mines and -ates, just as true as any wordsmith with a pen. The origins of his steep fall into Gayle's clutches hadn't been this talent with chemical manufacturing, however. His troubles with the Royal Police sprang from Rose's *other*, even *less* public career.

A monster had spread fear from California's Inland Empire through Phoenix down to Matamoros' way. The

Sun Belt Rapist, he'd been called by press and journals at the time. Like many predators, he reveled more in terror, degradation, and control than he did in sex itself. He'd spoken of it one night, in his cups, to a fellow (though relatively minor) miscreant. "Why, sex," JR had slurred in a drunken swerve into total honesty, "sex is no big deal at all, much as I've got my weasel wet over the years. On the other hand, if I can make a woman *weep*, or better yet, get backed up to the gosh darned *wall*, well then. *Now* you're talking. Nothin' on God's green earth makes a man feel stronger. More ferocious. Well," he'd added slyly, "*one* other thing, am I right?"

When he'd seen only blank incomprehension in the other fellow's eyes, he'd smoothly changed the subject. It was too bad, really. He'd been eager to talk about the other ones, the ones he hadn't left alive. They'd sentenced him for over forty counts, but had the Royal Police connected just a few more dots, they may have learned about his private plot of ranchland outside Matamoros; the one left fenced off, bare but for the treasures cached beneath the ochre soil. Twelve treasures, each neatly stowed within an oversized plastic storage tub.

Like any number of his morbid make and model, stamped from one of nature's vilest molds, Rose kept trophies. He didn't live near Matamoros but made a special trip each time he took his hateful passions to their bleak endpoint. He thought of these trips as his "pilgrimages." He hung his hat – a tasteful cowboy number much less silly than the whimsy worn by Frank Blank – in Bisby. The town in what had once been Arizona had been hammered to a flat and half-dead smear of cinder block and battered siding by the brute force of the summer sun. Like Frank, Rose also was a creature of the endless and endlessly deserted highways. He trawled the

Kingdom's lost, vast, dusty reaches. He'd hunted, trailed and followed. He'd always retrieved trophies from these extra-special hunts, and he'd reverentially preserved them in a basement room he simply thought of as "the temple." The question of to what or whom this temple might be dedicated had not crossed his mind.

Now he found himself in Frank's black shed. No longer did he stand in Arson, in a strange Möbius refrain of monstrous acts performed and punished; of monsters placed in charge of monsters making even more degraded monsters yet. Jeremy "The Jolly Rancher" Rose instead stood with Mystery Morrison Spare and Executioner Ketch in the shed, but *also* in the temple of his modest Bisby home. The basement's seeping pipes had drawn strange, feather-legged centipedes out of the walls. This was where he would go to succumb to arousal and violent fantasies, his black eyes dilated while he relived the chilling clarity, the vortex of depravity from which he'd stepped freely to the Pit's edge and leapt in many times. The Pit (though he didn't call it that): the blank and vacant ecstasy of a monster's secret heart.

Mystery Spare asked the grotesque of the Sun Belt if he'd like it back, the passion or the Pit, and for the first time since she'd found Frank, Ketch said simply "No."

"No?" repeated Spare

"No," said Ketch. Her voice was placid, like her plastic murderer's eyes. "This one doesn't get a choice." Ketch paused, considering, then asked; "This place, this 'shed.' It's not in Arson, is it?" Mystery Spare simply nodded. Ketch turned to the Jolly Rancher and said "Kneel."

The Jolly Rancher turned from his obscene, meticulously-maintained trophy shrine; the candles, Polaroids, torn clothing, bloodstained bits of rag, and other souvenirs. He had a feral look of desperate charm in his oil-colored eyes. The grin of a conniver gripped his clenching lower jaw.

"Hey now," said the mask of Rose's Jolly Rancher. "Golly. Wait just a second, Executioner. Now, I think we'd both agree you've gone off half-cocked on me before, right? Luckily the consequences weren't-"

Ketch's matte black, steel-toed boot took JR in the side of his knee and broke the complicated mechanisms there with a crunch as bright as the sound of a snapped celery stalk. JR screamed and fell to the shed's floor, a carpeted simulacrum of the floor in his long-demolished Bisby home. The predator managed to arrest his fall with both hands and then voiced a secondary grunt of pain as the carpet skinned his palms.

The Executioner still held Frank's axe. Its smooth, wooden haft felt warm and supple in her grasp. The weight of its beaten steel head was comforting; the gleaming smile of its bright edge a welcome symbol of the root simplicity of her life's purpose. She lifted it and hefted it, well pleased by its balance.

"Jeremy," Ketch said flatly, "look at me." When he lifted streaming eyes to meet hers, she grasped her cowl by one edge just beneath her jaw and pulled it free.

JR stared up, uncomprehending, at her face.

"No," she agreed, "you don't know me. We'd never met before I landed here. I want you to see a woman's face while you die, Jeremy. The cowl is off. This isn't for King Cleon. This is personal." Here Ketch dropped the cowl to grip the axe in both hands as she raised it high above her head. Its murderously mirthful edge smiled brightly in the dead light of the Sun Belt Rapist's trophy room. Ketch lowered her voice to a confiding murmur. "You're not the only one whom Frank set free."

The axe head fell in a brief, brutal blur; a flash like an

ephemeral steel rainbow. The blow struck true, guided by the Executioner's enhanced cognition and augmented strength. Her axe slid cleanly through the Jolly Rancher's neck with almost no resistance. Ketch didn't pull the blow, and the slick, sharp edge continued downward into JR's right hand and split it midway through his metacarpals, severing his right thumb as it did.

The Rancher's head dropped to the carpet and rolled once, then halfway back again. The final look on JR's face was made up of surprise and horror. His truncated right hand gave out a half-second before his left one did, sending JR's body – pumping blood in thick gouts from his severed neck – into a lopsided slide.

The instant that the fetid little lights in JR's eyes went out, the Bisby lair vanished like a dream on waking. The Executioner was once again in Arson, standing just beside the black shed with Spare's smooth, cocoa palm pressed lightly to her shoulder. Jeremy "the Jolly Rancher" Rose was gone. Ketch still held her cowl between her fingers, which were wrapped around the haft of Frank Blank's axe. The dull, starlit gleam of its head was partly masked by a smear of fresh blood. Ketch hurriedly re-donned her cowl and turned away from the shed to face Frank and the others.

Skunk Pussy's squashed and filthy features were screwed up in a strange configuration. Ketch knew fear better than most and saw it clearly in his eyes. Ketch wasn't surprised; nothing in Skunk's record indicated that he was especially prone to violence (not compared to baseline criminality for the Florida Panhandle more generally, at any rate). His assaults on Eichmann had been just like any morbid form of release in Arson's never-ending death-in-life; a brutal game of whack-a-mole, where clobbered fellow travelers upon the fabled mule would reawaken with the same discomfort as a normal hangover. Hell, the highly toxic local libation cooked up by the late proprietor of the Open O Ranch had claimed men's lives through violent neurological reactions every single night, from what Ketch had been told. The patrons' corpses merely woke up stuck to the unspeakable floor of the Woodpile, or in whichever warren they had crawled into to die the night before. In their situation, both protracted and purgatorial, murder had become no more immoral than a fistfight. The interminable status quo had changed, though, with the coming of Frank Blank's black shed; and that meant that the rules had changed. Skunk's eyes told the Executioner he might not like the new rules much.

"Well god *damn*, Executioner," said Frank Blank with a faint note of reproachful surprise. He was perched on the outsized loading ramp to his enigmatic truck, and studied Ketch with unseen eyes and creamy cowboy hat brim pulled down low. "I had plans for that fellow when I pack the whole rig up. Deal is, usually we take whoever wants to hitch a ride. This place isn't proofed against its own illogic anymore. Arson is an hourglass, Executioner, and the grains have started to run. We've got…" Again, Frank looked with invisible eyes at a watch that didn't exist, a strange piece of burlesque. "…two hours before Archdirector Kinsey Freund arrives here with a pretty sizable team of heavily armed and armored assholes. Their mission is to subdue you all and trigger an interstitial collapse on their way out. Of course, the best laid plans of deities and doctors are often pretty wry."

Ketch shouldered the axe and squared off before Frank. "None of these prisoners are going anywhere."

"'Prisons are built with stones of Law, Brothels with

bricks of Religion,'" Frank recited. Then shrugged. "Or the bricks of moralpol, I suppose. At any rate, *you* can't stop me. And more importantly, you *shouldn't* stop me. Your pissant little Kingdom wanted these marvelous deviations removed from the very substance of your universe? Fine. Pandemonium offers sanctuary to anyone who seeks it from any law. We'll take them off your hands."

This gave Ketch a moment's pause as she mulled the truth of the outsider's statements. If what Frank said was true (and thus far he had shown remarkable candor, whatever he was), then what choice was there? And hadn't Archdirector Freund already made *one* attempt on Ketch's life, a successful one at that? The fact that she'd returned to life did not erase the unpleasant memory of that experience.

"'Tell me what you need me to do," Ketch said quietly, and Frank Blank did. When he'd finished, and she had agreed to her part in it, he added an odd caveat.

"Make sure to catch the puppet show outside the Woodpile. Uncle Funny's really onto something there." Frank's grunted mirth was as dry and avuncular as the hollow chuckle of falling rocks. "It figures that ICON would stick a puppeteer *here*, where *I'd* run across him. There's irony and humor in that, don't you think?"

"Frank," Ketch said, "I have no earthly goddamned idea what you're talking about."

After a few moments of sullen silence, Skunk grumbled, "I *liked* JR. He was good to talk to, and he let me play with his blumpkins. And everyone's going to be in some serious shit when they run out of mule vinegar." Ketch ignored him. If Skunk had half a brain (and that was a topic up for debate), he'd realize that he was lucky she hadn't split him like a stick of kindling with her executioner's axe. At some point, she realized, she'd stopped thinking of it as *Frank's* executioner's axe.

The sky was ruinously rent by a thunderclap of sound. By now, a sonic boom's signature was growing all too familiar: authority, at least in some form, had arrived again. At night, the sunburst of the Pocket Protector's entry felt twice as bright, and every Arsonist who saw it shielded their eyes against the glare. A chill fear gripped the heart of all beneath the light of that nocturnal sun. Outsiders had come to interrupt their revelry. Faster than the fear had blossomed, it was transmuted into hot, hard hate.

From pit to pinnacle, and now back down to pit? *Oh no*, said Arson as a body. *No, we don't think so.* The thought took different forms in every mind but the content was, at core, the same. Filthy hands retrieved crude weapons, ugly things made from scraps of metal or papercut-thin plastic blades impregnated with the toxins of the Open O. Some had halfway-decent improvised short swords; all at least had cudgels or, as Skunk would no doubt approve, large stones.

Dr. Gayle, their tormentor and the architect of Arson's desolation, was dead. The Jolly Rancher, Arson's leading citizen, was dead. *Maybe*, Skunk thought as he hauled his iron beartrap on its long iron chain from where he'd buried it beneath his filthy bedding, *we'll all be dead before long. It's about fucking time.* He possessed religious leanings, though not in a form that CGP analysis would recognize as such. These inclinations had been what led him to make his charnel chapel of the sundered flesh in the first place. He swung his makeshift mace experimentally. A pleased smile festered on his face. Ketch had told them (and had told them to tell others) to gather near Frank's truck, past the blacktop's edge and on the strip of the uncanny highway.

Skunk fled his shanty in a crouching run, headed for Frank's truck. The sky's forever-night now shone with ample starlight, but still offered little comfort.

The Prosecutor, upon his arrival in the Area for Registered Sex Offenders: North, was at first only capable of speaking in unanswerable questions. Decent questions, the Archdirector allowed, but unanswerable nonetheless.

"Why is it *night?*" had been his first. The diurnal cycle in ARSO:N was keyed to daylight at Mount Elbert, and as such it should have been a bright, unsightly morning. "Are those stars?" had been his second. This, too, troubled Kinsey; night within the Area in daytime was unsettling, but this was worse. The Pocket's night had been designed to be as black as its day was inescapably and poisonously radiant.

The truly unpleasant surprises began shortly after they disembarked from the transport pod. Both teams of guards proceeded with guns held ready, moving in a loose ring around Honorable Justice Goetz, Dr. Freund, and Bloody Billy. SeSa-A01 was still straitjacketed and shackled, and Kinsey steered his hobbled, jangling steps by catch-pole. The Archdirector figured it was best to get the worst out of the way first, and that meant her sibling's worst abominations. She directed both teams to don filter masks (and even thoughtfully placed one on SeSa-A01 herself, drawing his black hood up to nose level to do so. She didn't want to see his eyes, nor did she care much for the lethal smile that creased his lips. She stuffed the mask in place as quickly as she could, then reaffixed the hood.

Kinsey led the team straight to the noisome edge of the Open O Ranch. On the short walk there, she outlined for the Justice what her sibling had been up to with the so-called Jolly Rancher. His reply, of course, had been another question.

"The Sun Belt Rapist?!" Goetz barked, eyes flaring briefly with glacial Teutonic wrath. Kinsey nodded, and the Justice shook his head with grim disgust. His last question – the one, Kinsey suspected, which had finally revealed to him that questions posed to madness would never obtain a satisfactory answer – came when the group reached the Open O and, not encountering its "owner," ventured inwards. They treaded carefully past bubbling crater pools with crystal rims and shrouds of toxic, varicolored fumes until they found a long, low, chicken-wire enclosure. The mesh was half-submerged in a vile stew of corrosive, septic slop. Dr. Freund gave her team the signal, and freezing white light bathed the scene in nightmarish clarity.

"What," asked Kerik Goetz in a shocked, hollow voice, "in God's holy name *are* those things?"

"The Sun Belt Rapist's assistant named them. They're called 'blumpkins.'"

Goetz's moue of puritanical disgust was visible beneath the hard plastic faceplate of his filter mask, and it told Dr. Freund that she didn't need to explain the creatures' name. "How..." the Honorable Justice began, but the unasked portion of his question withered on his tongue. Spotlighted by the piercing lights of the combined swarm of guards, two of the blumpkins were engaged in a sloshing, skin-scorched grapple. At first, the Archdirector took it for combat, but the thrusting, prehensile penises seemed determined to find and penetrate the varied, raw, red orifices of their partner/pugilist.

Quietly, in the same lightless place where her sweetest memories of Flanagan were kept, Kinsey Freund rejoiced. This demonstration of her sibling's madness could not possibly have been more visceral or, as a result, more effective. *ICON is yours*, the lightless place inside her whispered. *All the King's Pockets, and all the King's prey; the prey he'll give up into ICON custody. Think of all the hot, red, jolly times you'll have! Nothing quite so...* baroque *as these monstrosities of Ruzi's, certainly, but still a good, sharp time.*

Kinsey came back to herself and noted that Kerik Goetz had fixed her with a curious stare. She realized that she'd lost herself in thought as he had posed his half-voiced question.

She cleared her throat, the sound rendered vaguely mechanical by her filter mask. "The Area for Registered Sex Offenders: South," she said slowly, "was populated by CV offenders. Most of them were guilty of repeated violent crimes, some of which were quite thoroughly unspeakable."

"'*Was* populated?'" Goetz now condescended to the realm of the answerable query.

Kinsey nodded, staring meditatively at the blumpkins' flailing progress through the muck. "I don't know where Ruzi- where *Dr. Gayle* got the idea. I *certainly* don't know where they got the specialized surgical equipment. They removed..." She gestured distastefully. "...*certain portions* of the offenders' anatomy in ARSO:S, along with portions of their cerebrum. Then they knit the whole thing together here, in ARSO:N, where the regenerative algorithm no doubt assisted in a frankly physically impossible act of abominable animation. That stuff they're bobbing around in is highly acidic, and I'd imagine it's rather *unpleasant* on the, ah, exposed membranes. Another punishment intentionally instituted at Dr. Gayle's behest. If you'd like more information on their, ah, antics, I believe I have some of my sibling's notes…"

That was when Honorable Justice Kerik Goetz, King's Prosecutor East, finally lost his grip on his disgusted, outraged wrath and swapped it for a firm grip on the nearest guard's shotgun stock. The guard, as masked and anonymous as all their number, passively surrendered the weapon and the Justice opened fire. His first blast shredded one of the copulating blumpkins into boiled and turgid chunks of shiny flesh. The blast transformed the thin soup of toxic, piss-stinking fluid into thick, meaty porridge, which only thickened as the Justice's guards followed suit and loosed a fusillade. The roar of annihilating gunfire and the strobing muzzle flashes made a thunderstorm of the already-floodlit chemical cesspool, complete with rolling storm clouds of gun smoke.

In the space of less than a full minute, the sizzling, ammoniac liquor of the hutch's pond became a chunky bisque of blood reds and unpleasant purples. One of the guards clawed at their mask, pulled it free, and turned, vomiting profusely into a different, smaller crater; one which had evidently been used to cultivate a crust of shimmering purple crystals.

"*God damn it, Lopez,*" barked another of the guards through their own filter mask, "*you had your fucking orders! No food or drink after midnight before this mission! Just like a colonoscopy! You're familiar with those, I take it? Since you're such an* asshole?" The nauseated guard – Lopez, presumably – waved a hand in weak acknowledgment as they grappled their filter mask back into place. Kinsey was quietly pleased that her suggestion had actually been passed onward.

"Now, now," clucked Honorable Justice Goetz, handing the shotgun back to its rightful owner. Bloody Billy hadn't so much as flinched during the ruckus; his head was cocked to one side as he listened voraciously to the goings-on. If Dr. Freund hadn't been feeding him victims for the preceding decade like an amateur herpetologist feeding crickets to a pet iguana, she would have suspected he was having more fun than he'd had in years.

Goetz bent at the waist and examined the stew of lead shot and shredded organic refuse with genuine interest. "If I were a betting man – which I'm not, you understand," he said, "but if I were… I'd want to place a wager on just how strong your sibling's regenerative algorithm is. Not to mention what it does when presented with the famed Ship of Theseus."

"That's Greek, isn't it?" teased Dr. Freund. "I thought the King considered them a degenerate culture. Made quite a deal of smashing the Aphrodite of Milos himself, when we took the Louvre."

Goetz shrugged dismissively. "Think of it this way, then. Will Dr. Gayle's monsters grow back? If they do, will they have to locate all the bits scattered in this stew, or will each bit grow a whole new beast? Why, we might have just multiplied our problem a hundredfold."

Dr. Freund's mouth felt very dry; a state which was a known side effect of the Area's ambient toxicity, but which she suspected had little to do with the air and soil's exotic minerals and gases.

"Oh, don't worry," laughed the Honorable Justice when he saw the Archdirector's face. "I can't imagine we'll leave this place here, after everything we've seen and everything we know. Can you? Once we're done here and we make our way back to the real world, we can collapse this wretched Pocket like a popped balloon." His moist, round eyes, blue as spring skies underneath his filter mask, glittered merrily. "Speaking of which, I think the time is right, don't you? Whatever derelicts are still hunkered down in this hell, they're *prey* now. Let's see about the, how did you phrase it? Ah, yes: the 'practical military applications of chromatic-geometric psychogrammar.'"

Kinsey had anticipated this moment. On some subconscious level, she now realized, she'd been anticipating it since the discipline she'd mastered was still in its infancy and she'd first heard of Bloody Billy. She reached into her satchel and removed a CGP interface unit that had been outfitted with a black nylon strap so that she could carry it like an accordion player. A series of stubby antennae protruded from one end of it, and the CGP, which had been augmented with extra controls that were meaningless to the guards or Honorable Justice, but which would have raised the eyebrows of even a first-year CGP student. They weren't for altering a texture-color projection to elicit a response. By the semi-intuitive layout of the interface, they appeared to be controls for transmitting entire psychogrammar sequences straight to a linked subject. Admittedly, the surgical modifications required for such a link were still invasive, but the Abyssus Project prototype as so presented *worked* just fine.

What Archdirector Freund held could broadcast to the very core of a subject's prerational impulses. In this case, that subject was Bloody Billy.

Kinsey pressed a rubberized stud on the unit's side, and it came to life in her hands with a gentle, thrumming vibration. Lights played over the controls as she gripped them, manipulating the complicated haptic controls with squeezes, strokes, and flicks. SeSa-A01 jerked upright. The movement made his shackles jangle and the guards surrounding him hold tightly to their shotguns.

"Easy," said the Archdirector, and Goetz nodded at the teams. The guards only hesitated slightly before lowering their barrels.

She dug her digits into the coils of the interface; a sensation, she had reflected before, not unlike digging into A01's living, thinking brain itself – but thankfully less wet, or so she would assume. Bloody Billy took one convulsive step, then another. His motions, hindered by the shackles, were also intensely unnatural. The movement wasn't the least bit human-looking.

"Like a goddamned puppet," the guard named Lopez muttered, and with no further ado the guard captain who'd previously upbraided him threw a vicious punch directly into the center of Lopez's face, cracking his mask and dropping him to the piss-stinking hardpack trail that wound between the crater pools. Lopez, presumably chastised, slowly and silently got back to his feet.

Archdirector Freund, though, beamed at the remark behind her filter mask.

"Oh, yes," Kinsey said. "He's going to be our Mr. Punch."

ROYAL STANDARD PRAYER BOOK, 2ND Edition
PRAYER FOR KING AND KINGDOM

Dear Heavenly Father,

We thank Thee for this day, and for all our many blessings.

Bless the King, who art Thy earthly patriarch. Grant him long life and many sons.

Bless the Kingdom, which has worked Thy will by making safe Your children.

Bless that we can remember this lesson and apply it in our daily lives,

And bless that we be vigilant for treachery against King and Kingdom.

In the name of Jesus Christ, amen.

SECURITY PERSONNEL EDITION | MORALPOL CONTROL FIELD AGENT NOTE: MCVAs should carefully note observance of this prayer in district stake centers and the gathering-places of approved sects. See MICROEXPRESSION ANALYSIS (MP2.1) and BODY LANGUAGE ANALYSIS (MP2.2) to see which indicators to look for and refer for CGP processing.

12.
WHAT SKUNK LEARNED

"Make sure to catch the puppet show outside the Woodpile," Frank had said to Executioner Ketch. "Uncle Funny's really onto something there. It figures, that ICON would stick a puppeteer *here*, where *I'd* run across him." Ketch had thought herself inured to the uncanny and the frenetic churn of depravity even prior to her life as Executioner. Maybe it had happened in the trenches somewhere outside Palo Alto, where several squads, including hers, had been bombarded with psilocybin-derived gas before the Cyberdelic Assault Associates made their final, blistering assault.

The gas was made to bypass the Royal Army's filter masks by acting on contact with exposed skin. The lingering effects, like shrieking nightmares, grim delusions, and, in many cases, eventual dissociation, drove many a veteran of the Battle for Palo Alto to the point of full mental collapse: or worse. Ketch, who then answered to Singh, was the rare exception. She had always credited her steady mind to strength of will. Other, less charitable veterans said that it had been a lack of creativity and flaccid imagination which had saved the lucky few still who survived still fit for duty afterward.

Ketch wasn't sure what was implied by "lack of imagination." Could anything imaginary match the meat hammer of reality? Could anything be more uncanny than the horrors *she* had wrought and all the desolation which had followed, eager, at her heels? Ah, but would she – *could* she – do those things again? Certainly. Though many lacked the courage to accurately comprehend the atom-deep and universal horror of the godless and uncaring cosmos, Jacqueline Ketch was never such a person. She found the concept-image of such vast indifference liberating.

Her trip to Arson had revealed to her that there were larger forces than mere chance in the vastness of the all, and obviously *they* weren't uncaring. Their incomprehensible agenda didn't put the Executioner at lease. While Ketch's thoughts rolled like black marbles, Uncle Funny swilled his mule vinegar, prancing his preternatural plush puppets over the Woodpile's makeshift stage. Funny screamed his awful and uncanny voices to a roaring audience of half-dead, poisoned exiles from the saner universe that made humanity bereft of purpose. Here in Arson, there was purpose. There was art; the art performed by Uncle Funny, yes, but wasn't he just one component of the greater artwork that was Arson? Bespoke damnation had, by way of petty tyranny, been taken to a literally cosmic level. *Puppets making puppets making puppets*, thought the Executioner, and for a moment she could almost *feel* the very real and quite unsettling sensation of phantasmal wires buried in her flesh, rising to hallucinatory heights. She felt them not just in her flesh, but also strung to every atom of the corpus haunted by her soul. Cold and irresistible, those wires, connected to the withered digits of King Cleon.

And who pulled *his* strings? Ketch could only entertain dark suppositions.

Morrison Spare walked her to the Woodpile. The Mystery was a silent and serene presence just behind her. After they'd walked clear of Frank ("I need to pack things up for phase two," he'd said, adding: "You'll *love* phase two. Sort of a grand finale."), she saw fit to break the chilly stillness.

"So, Pandemonium," she said with skeptical precision. "Would you care to expand on that theme, Morrison?"

"Expand like a balloon?" asked Spare. "Or expand like an accordion?"

"Morrison." Ketch kept her voice level, but she stopped and turned to face him. Her unreadable eyes met his naïve, mazy stare. In it, she saw Frank Blank's smiling, eyeless visage looking back.

"Royal Subject Spare." Ketch's tone had dropped in temperature. "I am ordering you to divulge what you know about Frank Blank and this Pandemonium business. What is it? A government? An entity? A religion?"

"You're wrong," said Spare.

"About what?" Frustration led Ketch to grip the cryptic Mystery by his papery uniform lapels. They nearly dissolved in her gloved grasp. "*What* am I wrong about?"

"I'm not a Royal Subject anymore. They revoked my status when I fled my own assassination. I'm not subject to *any* king. I'm Pandemonium, now."

Not "I'm with Pandemonium," she thought, *but "I'm Pandemonium."* Spare had lain more steel into his statement than Ketch had heard up to this point. She gnawed the gristle of that observation.

"So," said Ketch, as cold as winter's rind of bacon

grease left in the pan, "you're a traitor, then."

Morrison spared the Executioner a catching laugh. "*Traitor?* I was cast out. I didn't leave of my own free will. What was I supposed to do, surrender peacefully and let your friends butcher me?"

"Yes."

He shook his head. "You're likable enough, Executioner, for what you are. There's not much *who* to you, is there? But for *what* you are, and for the sake of peace, let's keep this cordial. Yes?"

"Fair enough," conceded Ketch. She released his meager uniform lapels. He nodded, and the two resumed their walk. Ketch began again. "*Please*. Explain Pandemonium."

"I can't," sighed Morrison. "You asked if we were a government, an entity, or a religion. We're not a government. A religion? No, not that either. An 'entity?' That's vague, and the answer's complicated. Is an ant an ant? No. To understand ants, the individual is the wrong scale to consider. The colony – the superorganism – is the essence of the thing. More accurately, the essence is the networks such colonies establish and the offspring colonies they spawn, but superorganism is close enough."

"So, Pandemonium is what; an anthill?"

Morrison smiled. "Pandemonium is like the *drive* that pushes ants to build, or vines to strive and stretch. It's pre-elemental. It's the spark of sacred mischief inside of our magnificent, curious, intemperate species; ours and many others. It's the tongue of fire that drives the saboteur, the rampart firebomb-flinger, and those among us who oppose the metastatic growth of a dread god-cancer. The enemy call the collective existence of their utopian realm 'Wolfaria.' Before our cosmogenesis, Wolfaria appointed themselves the guardians of license and allowance. They thrive on hierarchy and punishment, discipline, pain, and subjugation. Their technicians of stricture and renunciation feed the dreams of tyrants everywhere – and I do mean *everywhere*. Individually, Wolfarians are small potatoes. In combination and conspiracy, they can be very *big* potatoes."

By now, they'd reached the fringe of Uncle Funny's raucous, mule-bitten audience. There were about a dozen people there; damn near the entire population of Arson. Uncle Funny's performance had, but for long, gurgling draughts of the mule, continued since he'd launched the endeavor earlier that morning.

"I killed the shit out of that corpse-thing from Wolfaria," Ketch noted, neither pride nor modesty in her matter-of-fact appraisal.

"That was an emissary, built out of the raw stuff of this place." Morrison Spare frowned. "Not a thing *from* Wolfaria."

The Executioner shrugged, and the axe she held back over one shoulder caught the starlight and smiled slyly. "Do you think an actual Wolfarian will show up here?"

Spare smiled sadly as he shook his hairless head. "No," he said.

"Because they're cowardly?"

He laughed; the bitterest sound he'd voiced in Ketch's presence.

"Because, Executioner, none of them are simple or stable enough to fit into what we consider 'reality.' Certainly not Arson. They have a hard time traveling, though I've heard that it can be done. Wolfarians are cogs in a single, vast machine. And they *hate* realities that aren't their own." Spare sighed. "Pockets are a terrible metaphor for these little worlds. They're more like plates of food left steaming on humanity's metaphorical doorstep. The doorstep of a house located in a deep wood full of starving things. And, regrettably, our little house has no doors."

"What have we got to worry about?" Honorable Justice Kerik Goetz declaimed.

He said these words with boastful nonchalance to the guards he sent to secure and make fast Arson's populace. They didn't seem particularly reassured as they trudged off. Goetz considered disciplining them for cowardice, and weighed their disgraceful reluctance against the fact that all of them were bottled in a place so utterly foreign to the proper universe. Magnanimously, he decided to let the lapse slide. The team he'd brought with him were efficient butchers, and would soon realize that ARSO:N held no challenges.

Nearly instantly – as though it were a punishment for hubris dealt to him directly by the gods – his radio implant sprang to shocked and shrieking life.

"They're resisting the goddamned pacification effort!" howled one ICON guard. His next transmission was a bubbling, liquid scream. *Resisting? Really?* wondered Goetz with genuine surprise, but his question was put to bed moments later when another pair of guards managed to report for thirty full seconds before they were overrun. That was time enough for the Honorable Justice to divine the nature of their foe. The passive, moping perverts of the Area, it seemed, were not as passive as he had been told. Reports were sporadic: bands of the tatterdemalion guerillas bludgeoned and stabbed the guards they caught with effervescent savagery. Not all were killed, but the carnage was enough to push the guards back to their

safer vantage near the transport pod.

"The regenerative algorithm," Goetz assured the harrowed, bloody survivors. "Any one of us those rat-fucking psychopaths hurt will be back on their feet and kicking ass again soon, rest assured."

"Sir," began one ICON guard hesitantly. Her uniform distinguished her from Goetz's crew.

The King's Prosecutor whirled on her. "Obscenity, yes, I know, bad for moralpol, yes? *Fuck* moralpol, at least until we get out of this fucking cosmic sewer you lunatics built."

"No, sir," the ICON staffer stated, steeling her voice as she consulted readouts on a portable monitor with a thick, rubberized handle. "It's not that. The regenerative subroutine. It's… not functioning, sir. These numbers are – well, they're bad. Local reification is faltering. ARSO:N has become unstable. And sir, it seems like there's something… *external* to the subroutines at work here."

Goetz stared at her. In his fishy corneas, irises like ice-blue drill bits bored into the ICON guard. Unsatisfied with her as an adequate receptacle for his incipient wrath, the Honorable Justice whirled and scanned the ranks of armed and wild-eyed personnel. *"Kinsey!"* he barked. *"Where the fuck is Archdirector Kinsey Freund?!"*

In fact, the Archdirector was still within earshot. She was too engrossed in her own journey of unspooling mysteries to hear Goetz's shouted words, let alone respond. When the guards had first departed, Kinsey added a bulky monocular goggle to her getup; a thick, opaque lens set within a leather skullcap stretched over her close-cropped scalp. Dr. Freund was, quite literally, inside the mind of SeSa-A01 (previously preferred appellation "Bloody Billy"), and it was intoxicating.

Years before, A01 received that designation because he was the first subject of the first generation of a new order of being, one which had been conceived with Ruzi's assistance, but which Dr. Freund herself had played sole midwife to. *Homo interfectorem*, she'd decided, might be a good designation, once further tweaks had been made. She'd wrested custody of Bloody Billy's mind from him, but this was just the start. Billy was a man of rare athleticism, energy, and homicidal *joi de vivre*, and Kinsey had such terrible plans for him. The augmentations of a Royal Executioner, to start with. *I'll have to recruit a human enhancement technician,* Kinsey thought, *but this is the first chapter. This is where it starts.* And the end point? Well, that was the thing. Perfection was a journey that never reached its destination. She could spend the rest of her long days refining this new, weaponized unhuman.

Dr. Freund kept the eye not occluded by the monocle half-focused, taking in the flat and noxious landscape. Once under her control, A01 had been stripped of chains and canvas and nudged to the Archdirector's directions. He was far ahead of her now, his lithe nude form as silent as the shadows as he loped toward his prey. Once, when she'd conducted interviews with him before his implantation, Kinsey asked the killer to explain his tracking skills, which had won him horrified renown when word of their near-preternatural sharpness reached the press. He'd answered that he could smell human souls. He'd hesitated, then corrected himself: "I can smell *souls*. Not all of them are human."

It was the type of macabre, ridiculous braggadocio she'd come to expect from him. Everything was one part legend, one part lies, and one part serviceable data. Weren't locked skulls like his what drove the pioneers of the abnormal psychosciences; the difficulty of prizing off the lid of such a monster's living skull to render his disturbed mind legible?

Whatever the source of his uncanny hunting instinct was, his skills had yet to fail him. He'd proven their existence through clinical trials within the Archdirector's private labyrinth. Her working theory was based on pheromones, but unsettling data had emerged from trials in which she'd blocked airflow between locked rooms. Bloody Billy found his quarry nonetheless, in half a second less time than his record to that date.

Where was he going now, though? To Kinsey's knowledge (and this wasn't her first visit to the Area), the habitation cluster was far from where A01 seemed bound. The only thing that lay this way was a crumbled patch of useless blacktop, one too windswept and raw to make good cover for any prey her puppet might pursue. Kinsey was so focused on her monster's strange behavior that she almost tripped over her sibling's corpse.

She paused. There lay the remains of G. Ruzicka Freund, her last surviving blood relation. She felt… nothing. A memory flitted through her mind: the cold clarity of the Pit on her CGP display, her red-stained hands, and the soundless, echoing murder-song the Pit sang, sweet enough to render all else flavorless. She pushed the memory aside and leaned to take a closer look. She'd known that Ruzi was a loose end she would have to tie up *some*time; clearly her beloved sibling had lost their fucking mind. Better, then, that Kinsey didn't have to wield the blade, even by proxy. Better that another beat her to the punch. But the way that Ruzi looked in death made Kinsey queasily uneasy.

In her happy fantasies, the end always came quickly for her sibling. She didn't hate them, after all. By the look of it, whomever – *what*ever – had killed Gayle hadn't been as merciful. Her sibling's eyes were artificial, which surprised the Archdirector. Multifaceted and repellant, the lens-pocked orbs stared up at the night sky and its inexplicable stars. Every single tiny lens was shattered. The flesh socketing these glass-and-plastic orbs had been burned down to the gleaming bone. Worst of all was Ruzi's face, which wore the twisted, silent shriek of one who's known the full, fathomless profundity of horror.

"Oh, Ruzi," Kinsey breathed. She wasn't grieved, but filled with the long-expected sadness of one who loves a person whose incaution merits grief rehearsal. Finally, when tragedy at last arrives, its sting is blunted.

She kept walking. Some of her colleagues, she knew, would consider this an act of singular callousness. Those "colleagues" were unfit to serve His Majesty in a scientific capacity, in Dr. Freund's opinion. She was in the middle of an unheralded advance in moralpol and psychogrammar. Taking time to snivel on its first field test would be unconscionably weak. ICON didn't value sentiment unless it was being vivisected or induced.

Kinsey paused far longer when she came across the body parts. If they *were* body parts; they certainly lay in pools of what could be, perhaps, blood. Their cheesy skin and malformed shapes made the Archdirector discomfited and vaguely ill. Soon, she had to look away. She noticed that SeSa-A01 had ventured well ahead of her. When Kinsey spotted him, Bloody Billy was halfway down the slope to where his quarry waited. Kinsey cursed softly and began to jog to catch up, nimbly dialing through data and digging her fingers into the rubbery folds of the specialized CGP control unit as she did.

There was a truck, a goddamned *truck* on the blacktop.

Who had authorized this madness, and how had Ruzi transported it here? It certainly looked like the type of thing that would infest this lowest, saddest sewer of her sibling's mind. Nevertheless, its sheer impracticality offended the Archdirector. Something in the thing's shape was too organic, even for some new iteration of the Pocket Protector. An entirely unpleasant chill swam through Kinsey's bowels as she realized that the words she'd been groping for were foreign and, even more unsettlingly, alien.

She reduced A01's frenzy-kill activation and lowered the pleasure threshold in his stalk-hunt-kill, causing her subject to shift from a ground-gobbling lope to a low, slinky stalk. Bloody Billy, thus leashed, prowled the very periphery of where his human target was likely to detect him. Even at this distance, Dr. Freund could make out the prey; a lone man, solidly built and of no little stature. Not to worry; men almost twice the mass of this lone target had been the work of red and blissful moments for Kinsey's pet killer.

Unless, Kinsey mused, she modified Bloody Billy's reward structure just a *bit*. To prolong the experiment, say, and test her fine-motivation control. *And because you want to watch*, Flanagan gurgled in her mind, breath a bloody bubble-bath. *You want to watch from up close. And maybe do* other *things, while you're here alone with Billy.* She silenced the unwelcome interloping thought, drawing nearer to where SeSa-A01 paced like a wolf beyond a camper's firelight.

At last, Kinsey was close enough to take stock of who the target was. Someone clad in a ridiculous white cowboy hat, it seemed. Was he a test subject? What might he tell Kinsey about the tumorous transport rig? The Archdirector didn't have long to mull these questions before the hatted man called out to her by name. It froze her in her tracks.

"Dr. Kinsey Freund! And… why, is that *Bloody Billy*?"

With a terrible, lead-gut feeling that she'd stepped into a trap she didn't understand, Kinsey bore down on the controls in her grip, sending KILL-KILL-KILL pulses to her weapon. Her controls, sadly for her, seemed unwilling to live up to their moniker. When the man in the white cowboy hat addressed him by name, Bloody Billy cocked his head to one side and half-rose from his hunter's crouch. He hesitated, shook his head as though trying to dislodge water from his ears, and swayed in place. Kinsey checked the output in her monocle and signal readout on the control, and was quite confounded by the data that she read, despite having designed and built the interface herself.

"Oh no," said the man – little more than a black silhouette beneath his creamy hat. "Don't bother yourself with *that*, Dr. Freund. I've snipped your reins." He slowly strolled closer. "Name's Frank. Frank Blank. I'll be taking Bloody Billy off your hands. Thanks for nothing, by the way. We know your species' anatomy better than you do, and it's *still* going to take us a while to dig all of that bullshit out of Billy's beautiful, broken brain."

"Who the hell *are* you?" Though she asked, Kinsey wasn't sure she wanted to know.

"Pandemonium," Frank answered simply. He lazily grasped the brim of his great, creamy hat and slowly tipped it downward in a cowpoke's salute. "Nice meeting you, Dr. Kinsey Freund. I've got to get along now; got some packing up to do. And would you believe it? *I'm* going to meet the *King*! I mean…wow!" This last was said in such a naïve way that Dr. Freund was briefly unsure if he was being mean-spirited or genuine. Her answer came a moment later as Frank, strolling to the rear of the unsightly pink contraption, spoke back over his shoulder.

"Billy, would you please rip Dr. Kinsey Freund's rotten fucking lungs out for me?"

He had crept up behind her, silent as a shadow. As he circled around to face her, Bloody Billy's eyes met Kinsey's. She saw a terrible intimacy in them.

"Frank," breathed Billy; SeSa-A01 no longer, now again an unnumbered thing of pain and feral darkness. "I'm going to take that literally, if you don't mind."

Skunk Pussy was discovering that the corroded length of iron chain and the iron beartrap that dangled from it were an astonishingly effective weapon. Why, he wondered, had no school of martial arts developed around the implement? Or maybe one had; he'd never watched that many karate movies. He'd liked to watch autopsy instruction videos, the ones you could order if you pretended to be a student at one of the Kingdom's medical schools. In all the peaceful time he'd spent in his shack of treasures, in all his graveyard ramblings and late-night excursions, he'd never killed a soul in the real world, though he had certainly liked to look at the result of killing. Arson had awakened something in him; had kindled dormant violence in them all. How could it not, with its eternal reset switch and carefully-designed awfulness?

Did Skunk, deep down, like killing people? Maybe. Skunk had discovered that he goddamned sure liked killing *cops*, and he'd tell you that free of charge. In fact, if you were one of these assholes in the fancy uniform onesies, he'd *show* you free of charge. Call it an exhibit. That's what they'd called all those glorious photos they'd dragged into a courtroom, where they didn't belong. It had been his *private life*; wasn't those the words they'd used? "Mr. Martin, could you tell the Prosecutor why you needed these dissection tools in your private life? Exhibit A, if you please."

What happens when you take a peaceful, rot-loving creature and damn him, strip him of his private life; of any life at all? *Exhibit A*, he thought, and brought the beartrap gripped in his chain-wrapped fist down on a guard's face with a layered crunch and a thick gout of blood and vitreous. By the time he'd finished, Skunk was breathing hard, and guess what? Evidently he *did* have a taste for hands-on brutality. *Exhibit B*, he thought, cradling his erection through his tattered uniform pants. Had he always liked this sort of thing? If he had, why hadn't he fantasized about it, let alone gone through with it? He wondered briefly at the paths life can take, and where his inclinations might have taken him or not taken him, had they been allowed to bloom like the bodies in his special shed. Squashed-up face contorted with perilous philosophy, Skunk rose to his feet. He'd heard something.

Skunk didn't bother to wipe the clotted blood, jellied brains, bits of bone, or other biological detritus from his makeshift bludgeon. He *did* drop the trap, allowing it to dangle on a length of chain. As he swung the flail, it cleaned itself: the centrifugal force of its accelerating head threw blots of gore to the four winds. As Skunk got the whirling flail worked up to full steam, the chain and its projectile began to emit an intoxicating *WHUM-WHUM-WHUM* of displaced air. *Hot damn*, Skunk thought joyously, hunting for the source of the sound he'd heard, *I hope there are still some of those cops left.*

The gods of murder smiled on Skunk that day. There were, in fact, no "cops" left (they had actually been privately employed, state-sanctioned security personnel, but "cop" was close enough). Instead, like a sweet slice of pie at the end of a savory meal, he found a man with forget-me-not blue eyes and a snub-nosed pistol in one hand. Merle "Skunk Pussy" Martin would have known him anywhere (at least, once he'd gotten it all back thanks to Morrison Spare). The man was Judge Goetz, the very fellow who'd remanded Skunk to Arson. The very one who'd dragged him into court like a gaffed gator.

Goetz was injured. One of Skunk's fellow merry pranksters had taken a pretty good whack at the man's leg with a sharp implement of some kind, and His Honor had been reduced to a rapid backward crawl for the safety of the transport pod. His frightened movements reminded Skunk of a crawdad, which tickled the former swamp ghoul.

"Hey there, fuckface!" called Skunk with genuine good cheer. He grinned at Goetz, who kept up his retreating scuttle on the hardpacked dirt. His finger kept convulsively squeezing the trigger of his pistol, which produced an impotent *click-click* and nothing more. Skunk's grin widened. He had no way to know it, mirrors being spare in Arson, but his grinning face was spattered with a layered, dappled coat of blood and brains. With his slick, slimy uniform, troll's face, and whirling flail of gore-soaked and corroded iron, he looked like a woodcut from another, darker age.

"You probably don't remember me," Skunk said to Goetz, and this was true. The former lower circuit judge did not try to deny it. Though most violations were handled in concrete boxes by Prosecutors, the caseload which had warranted Goetz's attention had been vast. Utopia's glorious garden required that a great many undesired weeds be removed.

WHUM-WHUM-WHUM went the whirling beartrap on its length of iron chain. "You know," said Skunk to Goetz in a comradely, confiding way, "a lot of us here, what we've been through… can you fucking *believe* it? We thought we *deserved* it!" He gestured with his free hand at the omnidirectional desolation of the Area; a desert wrought not by nature's vast indifference, but a stage for human cruelty's petty melodrama.

"This. Fucking. *Place!*" Skunk barked a bitter laugh. "Turns out, most of us *don't* deserve this place. Or didn't at the start, anyway. That's the thing, Judge. And you ought to know it; it's an old story." *WHUM-WHUM-WHUM* "This place taught me how to hate." *WHUM-WHUM-WHUM* "It taught me how to suffer." *WHUM-WHUM-WHUM* "And you know what else, Judge Goetz? What *really* gets to me?" *WHUM-WHUM-WHUM*

The Honorable Justice was too afraid to blink, and his burning blue eyes streamed with tears like cliffside seeps. Goetz shook his head, perhaps in denial, perhaps in answer to the awful man's query.

"Maybe the seed was there, but Arson made it sprout. It taught me how to *murder*."

*WHUM-WHUM-***WHOKCHT***!*

The effect was every bit as satisfying as Skunk had hoped.

When the new visitors had all been dealt with, Frank Blank took leave of his stitched-together wasteland congregation. He made his way to the derelict blacktop and its brightly colored line of sheds. When Frank was involved, structures tended to be more complicated than the human mind could cope with; meta-hyperobjects were one of his many specialties. Pandemonium enjoyed a jape at nature, had had learned a sort of dimensional origami. For Frank, it was the work of moments to fold each shed into a cube the size of a sugar lump, weightless, massless, and yet unimaginably dense. He folded all the sheds up more quickly than a seasoned circus crew could tear a big top down, and soon only the black shed stood. It did not stand in the same place, exactly; Frank took the time to move it from the blacktop to one hardpacked edge where it would not obstruct the truck's long loading-ramp.

The night was starting to cool down, and its gentle nips at exposed skin grew toothier. Frank watched his stars and contemplated adding more; a galaxy, perhaps, or the dim, deathly outline of an onrushing black hole. Shortly, Ketch approached and stood beside him.

"You did it?" asked Frank.

"Hours ago, when you first asked. I didn't believe what you said, but I should have. You're right. The King has his own interstitial control facility. He just responded to my single-use transmission code." She exhaled and flexed her fortified, enhancement-riven hands and forearms. "It's confirmed. He's coming, Frank. The King is coming to Arson himself."

"You did well," Frank said, and offered Ketch a sandstone-like palm. She hesitated, then removed a glove. Beneath it, there was not much flesh. Her wrists attached to armored, crushing claws: far gone beyond the boundary of human; though scraps of muscle here and tendon there remained. She took Frank's palm in hers and shook his hand.

"You're out of your fucking mind," Ketch told the desert smuggler.

He shrugged. "No offense, Executioner, but you aren't my peer. You can't make a judgment like that."

"I can assure you that when King Cleon drops in, it will be in force," Ketch said. She didn't sound particularly alarmed at this. "Soldiers. Weapons. Probably sneaky little tricks they thought up after I left the RA. And they'll be here *soon*. The encrypted response made that clear. Inside of an hour from now, I'd say."

"I thank you for your concern." Frank sounded amused, and that irritated Ketch.

"I don't understand what Pandemonium wants with us, Frank," said the Executioner. "With this place *or* the weirdos locked up here. If you're supposed to be some sort of, I don't know, cosmic order of liberation or whatever, why sink so much into saving the people of one Pocket?"

"There used to be a warband in part of your Kingdom called Texas. They called themselves the Rangers; a generic name, from what I gather. Anyway. They had a saying, those fellas: 'one riot, one Ranger.' Who says that I'm the only one at work, or that Pandemonium only seeks to liberate one swollen little boil in your cosmos?"

Ketch processed this behind her shallow eyes. Surely she would know if things were that dire. Necessarily, they would have briefed her in. The idea of such a monumental series of breaches was terrifying, but it made her a little giddy. *Why* it did, she could not articulate.

Frank strutted to the top of the big, unpleasantly organic truck and threw the cargo doors open wide. He swept aside the drop cloth with a flourish. Ketch couldn't bear to look inside. There was movement, and things among the movement that seemed inside out and outside in and sideways at the same time; a gibbering and crawling tunnel made of eager, playful angles, populated by a million whirling portals to a hundred million gleaming worlds. *If those techies at the Network Society had blared* this *at us*, came Ketch's disjointed thought, *I think we would have died that day.*

"*TIME'S ALMOST UP,*" Frank bawled to the sky and (presumably) the citizens of Arson. "*Time to climb aboard, if you've a mind to! Hell, if you've a mind! The Pandemonium Express is getting the* fuck *outta here for the last time, and he who hesitates disintegrates!*"

The Arsonists began to line up. They shuffled to the truck with wide-eyed, freshly unscrambled wits, and liberated but disorienting memories and urges. Frank was gentle, leading each aboard to their impossible, collapsed, and quasi-geometric bunks. Ketch kept a loose count as they came. Now that she had joined the team, as it were; now that she'd seen what Wolfaria would wreak.

The last Arsonists to climb aboard were Uncle Funny and his plush menagerie, locked safely in their rolling travel case. "My best, my truest friend," said Frank with genuine and unexpected warmth, and kissed Funny full on his mustached lips. Funny flushed as red as rouge and both men had a laugh to see each other once again. "I'm ready," the puppeteer and sometime onanist declared. "I'm Pandemonium now, Frank."

"You always have been Pandemonium, Funny," said Frank as tenderly as any lover, and the prim and balding man made his way up the platform and into the swirling madness of Frank's truck.

"Well," said Jacqueline Ketch, swinging her executioner's axe to rest on one black-clad soldier, "I believe your audience with His Majesty is about to begin."

The sky was rent by thunder and a crown of flaming cracks upon the night. The flames were bright and pretty in the starlight, up above the darkened hovels of the settlement. Descending in a pillar of patriarchal purity and purging flame, King Cleon, Third of His Name, came to mete or meet a final judgment.

**TCON INTERNAL MEMO | TECTONIC CONTROL
!URGENT! | DO NOT REPRODUCE | DO NOT
TAPENOTE | DO NOT KEEP**
FROM: Tasha Clarke PhD TCON Senior Regional
Engineer
TO: ICON General Staff
CC: GEN. RUTHERFORD ULYSSES BRIGHAM, Royal
Army att. FORT CARSON

Dear Dr. Freund and Dr. Freund,

After my attempts to contact you, I've initiated emergency procedures. Tectonic activity at the summit of Mount Elbert is not only extremely unlikely to have been triggered by natural processes, our inability to raise you by emergency wire call leads us to believe that some sort of situation has developed at ICON's facility there.

The scale of tectonic activity leads me to believe that something is transpiring that will have widespread effects beyond your facility. I am not pleased at your refusal or inability to answer our urgent contacts regarding developments there.

Regards,

TC

REDACTION ORDER | RANDY REGIS Acting
Regent of Communications:
Belay this order, General. Special
units from the Royal Guard and Royal
Army based out of Fort Douglas are
en route. They have the clearance
to deal with matters pertaining to
the situation at ICON. Redact and
destroy this message and any traces
of communication.

13.
A FACET OF A VAST, IGNOBLE BROTHERHOOD

King Cleon, known before his coronation as W. Cleon III of the line of Skousen, was enraged.

This was hardly an unusual state for the aging monarch. His subjects, from the lowest lowborn filth up to the highest-favored courtier, knew his reputation as a man of icy anger. The source of His Majesty's opprobrium always had the veneer of legitimacy. He'd rage about a failed economic plan, a war (and there was always at least *one* war) not proceeding as he would prefer, or, often, a perceived insult of some kind. The true source of King Cleon's constant displeasure was known to only one soul; the honorable Noah Christiansen, Groom of the Stool.

It was Noah's solemn duty to clean the royal anus after Cleon's kingly shits, a job he had enthusiastically performed for more than a decade now. It was a task which required more finesse than many would suspect. The King's brown rosebud was afflicted with a case of chronic hemorrhoids. His piles bloomed and receded with a tidal rhythm all their own, one in which they never *fully* disappeared.

Life was a pain in King Cleon's ass, and he treated life accordingly.

He didn't like the Freund siblings, whom he considered little more than useful aberrations. He didn't like the fact that he didn't understand the technology or philosophy behind the creation of his Pockets. If he were honest with himself (a rare event indeed), the very concept of the power at his disposal terrified him. It was one thing to rule a landmass, one well-whipped into servility by his predecessors. It was another thing entirely to inherit hand-made universes. Cleon III was a devout man, and though the idea of limitless cosmoses governed by godlike, virtuous men slotted neatly into the revelations of the Church, the practical realization of this divine plan made him feel scared and small. And fear? Well, that made Cleon angriest of all.

Fear is unbecoming to a King, Cleon mused as he assumed the padded throne in his interstitial transport pod. He'd received an urgent, coded message from his Executioner informing him that all had been made safe in ARSO:N. Furthermore, his presence was required to dispense the justice of the Crown. This was rare, but hardly unheard-of. On occasions when a particularly high-ranking official had earned his terminal disfavor, they might request that he be present at their execution. It was at the Executioner's discretion which of these appeals had merit.

His Majesty was hardly overjoyed at Ketch's choice. He'd been dragged from the plush interior of his winter palace to watch the distasteful sausage-making of his justice. He was doubly irked that this required him to visit one of the Pockets. It was not his first trip, nor his second, but he tried to visit them as infrequently as possible. The air, the soil of those places… it never felt right, never gave Cleon the same sense of his Heavenly Father's sculpting hand that his native universe provided in such abundance. The King scowled and tried to shake off his discomfort by redirecting his anxiety as irritation at the pod's pilot and engineer.

"Well?" Cleon demanded. "Are we leaving or aren't-"

Perhaps it was innocent mistiming and perhaps it was subservient passive aggression, but the King was halfway through his reprimand when the pilot activated the insertion protocol. The pod slid through the flesh of God's creation like a dagger through a ripe peach, and the King gagged mid-sentence. His hands clamped, claw-like, to the arms of his throne as they breached the foreign atmosphere. The pod's descent pushed the King forcefully back in his throne. A roar like the breath of a vast dragon wreathed the pod as its pseudorganic shell (another abomination Cleon cared for not at all) burned away.

Their plummet didn't take long, but to Cleon it felt like an interminable age; a roaring chaos of shaking surfaces and varicolored flame glimpsed through the cockpit's forward windshield. The air crackled with the atmospheric charge of static gifted them by interstitial friction. Eventually, the pod's cord drew taut and their descent slowed, first gently, then abruptly as the pod was brought level with the surface of ARSO:N. The King unhooked his restraint harness, ran a hand over his bald, spotted pate and ermine cloak of office, and strode to the front of the capsule. There, he boxed the pilot's ear so hard that the man cried out and blood flowed.

Cleon, satisfied that he had burst the man's eardrum, instantly forgot him and returned to his complement of guards and courtiers. One of them bore the King's crown on a velvet cushion, Cleon was glad to see. *At least* one *of these miserable bastards knows how to do their job*, His Majesty thought. Sweet Heavenly Father, but his piles were paining him. He'd have to speak to his religious counsellor about it, he decided. A direct anointing of the ailment with consecrated oil from a fellow member of the Melchizedek Priesthood would no doubt provide some relief.

King Cleon, Third of his Name, placed the glowing silver coronet upon his big bald brow and adjusted his oversized spectacles. He readjusted his ermine robes and forced a smile for his assembled Royal Guard and Royal Army troops. He'd brought twelve of them, just to be on the safe side, and all were equipped with automatic rifles and flak gear. ARSO:N might be a small settlement whose boundaries were delineated by his Royal will, and all reports suggested that the population of prisoners had been properly beaten into servility, but Cleon was not a trusting soul.

"Let's see what Executioner Ketch has to say for herself, shall we?" he asked with cold and mirthless cheer, and the Royal Guard near the door snapped a smart salute and punched the open pad. The pod door opened with a frictionless and graceful extension of its ramp, unveiling a rectangular chunk of one of his Royal realities.

Six guards swarmed one pair at a time to scan and secure the landing site. Once they'd signaled their confederates, the remaining soldiers marched in a close rank behind the King as he descended to the subtly sick-smelling soil, whereupon he cast a dour eye upon the lifeless landscape of the prison colony. *Since Heavenly Father's plan for His faithful is for us to be like unto Him,* the monarch thought with glumly fatalistic brutishness, *needs must we make an outer darkness for the sons of perdition.* The span of God's design was no utopian's painless stroll into eternity; His (and thus His humble servant Cleon's) justice was defined by punishment.

Of course, the Interstitial Control projects had never tried to craft a *proper* universe for the sealed and anointed to govern over. Not yet. As it came to pass, it was more efficacious to construct ten thousand hells than one realm of divine and perfect governance. King Cleon breathed deeply of the foul and faintly ozone-haunted air of the Pocket and fixed a scowl in place as his aging eyes adjusted to the gloom of night. Despite his frowning jowls, the King was pleased. *At least*, he thought, *this shouldn't take long*.

The half-dozen Guard units already outside had their guns raised, barrels trained on three figures who stood at the limit of the doorway's wedge of light. Two of them were unfamiliar to the King, but one he knew well. He made it his business to know his Ketches, Jacks and Jacquelines alike. Had he lined them all up, incognito in their garb of office, the nuances of form and body language were like fingerprints. This Ketch was flanked by two men, each lowered on both knees with necks exposed. Absurdly (and discourteously), one still wore a silly hat as he genuflected. Outrageously, the other man was bare down to the lean cheeks of his ass. The naked man, like Cleon, had a crown, of sorts: a sculpted steel cap with short, protruding rubber antennae. The cap appeared to serve as the top of his skull. Cleon shuddered slightly as he recognized the handiwork of Archdirector Kinsey Freund.

"Executioner," barked the King, striding down the ramp with the vigor of a man half his age, despite the terrible toll this took on his aging joints and poor, beleaguered asshole. *"Report!"*

Ketch knelt, then rose back to her full height. As she

rose from genuflection, she tossed a hefty-looking object halfway to the King. It rolled to a stop, and Cleon paused to cast his eyes down at it. It was the saggy-fleshed head of Dr. G. Ruzicka Freund, severed at the neck. The evidence of the late Dr. Gayle's disregard for King Cleon's edicts spoke for itself. Gayle possessed fused, flesh-and-melted-plastic nodules where prohibited cognitive implants had blown out. Their staring, lens-blown artificial eyes spoke eloquently for the dead technician's guilt, as well.

"I believe you know Dr. Gayle?" inquired Ketch in an unsettlingly neutral way. The King did not respond, marveling at the awful expression frozen on the dead Moral Philosopher's awful face. While he still considered Dr. Gayle's decapitated head, a greyish-red and veiny bundle flopped bloodily beside the head, tossed to the dead dirt by the naked, crouching stranger with the steel cap (and, the King could not help but note, hands stained almost black with blood).

"Lungs," supplied the cowboy helpfully, his head still bent. "Those belonged to Archdirector Kinsey Freund." Cleon didn't know the man, but if he and the naked beast had helped his servant sew up this unpleasant mess, a little eccentricity might be overlooked. Not the beast – on that topic, he and Ketch would have to have words.

"Well," allowed the King, poking with interest at the lungs with the tip of one crushed-velvet slipper, "*that* much went well enough, then. Well done, Executioner, but I expected nothing less. Nor would I have accepted anything less."

"Thank you." The way she said it, she may as well have been saying *your services will no longer be required.*

The cowboy burst into a low, throaty chuckle, and rose to his feet. Unbidden. King Cleon was too flabbergasted to order his Guard to shoot the lout. As the cowboy rose, the King saw that he was garbed in desert-tinged jeans and a checked shirt bleached by a thousand all-day drives. The man's eyes were obscured by the brim of the cream-colored hat.

"Forgive me," said the man in the hat. "It's just that you were right on target there. 'Your services will no longer be required,' that's good."

King Cleon felt a thrill of religious fear run up his spine with a serpent's-scale touch and stared at the man in the hat. "Yes," the man said, "I *am* reading your mind. Billy, you can get on up now. We've had our joke." He chuckled again, and as he did the lean, naked man with the silver mechanism crowning his skull obediently rose. Cleon found his eyes drawn against his will to the metal-capped man's bare, circumcised, and slowly-swelling cock. He barked an inchoate sound of outrage; a cough of surprise and offended propriety. The naked man noted the King's discomfort and repaid him with a slow, sly smile.

"*Executioner!*" King Cleon finally managed in a strangled, high, and breathy voice. "What in the name of *decency* is going on here? Who *are* these men?"

Instead of Ketch, it was the man in the cream-colored hat who replied. The King was achingly aware that he couldn't see the man's eyes; a distasteful habit in a grown person, and no doubt indicative of narcotics use. "Narcotics? Absolutely!" said the cowboy enthusiastically, plucking Cleon's thoughts out of the air. "Though I'm not really into anything you kiddos have in *your* native neck of the woods. Although, from what I can gather, the late Dr. Gayle and their late associate have been cooking up exotic treats right here in Arson."

The man went on. "I'm Frank Blank, and this is my friend Bloody Billy. Billy, say hello to Cleon."

"You've got the greedy little eyes of a born fuck-pig," said the naked, bloody man. He now sported a good-sized erection. He purred the words in a low, predatory leopard's voice. "I'll make you *love* it before I gut you, fuck-pig." The purr gave way to a nerve-shredding, deafening pig squeal, an uncanny performance which the naked man delivered at full volume.

"Now, Billy," said the man named Frank in a mild, parental, scolding tone, "that's no way to talk to such an important man."

King Cleon, Third of his Name, had heard quite enough. "*KILL THEM!*" he screeched at the Royal Guard more shrilly than he would have liked. "*KILL THEM ALL!*"

Silence from the Royal Guards to his left, though their guns were still raised in ready postures. Silence from their fellows on his right, and from those stationed just behind him. The King was poised to scream his order once again, but stopped as he noticed the strange, static uniformity of his troops. None shifted weight from foot to foot. Not a one appeared to breathe, in fact. Cleon was more astonished than frightened or furious, and strode to the nearest soldier. The King gripped the man's shoulder, intent on shaking him from the unsettling stupor which the Kingdom's enemies had evidently unleashed.

His hand did not meet flesh and blood. It met unyielding, lightweight plastic. As Cleon turned the soldier by the arm, he felt very much like a child caught in a nightmare; well aware of the boogeyman behind a door, but unable to prevent himself from opening it. The soldier had, moments ago, been a long-serving, elite trooper of the Kingdom, loyal to King and Kingdom, and well-hardened by battle. Something *else* had hardened him now. Whatever had beset the soldier had hollowed him and recast him in a sculpted simulacrum of the living article. Beneath the King's ungentle hand, first one, then more "Royal Guards" collapsed, revealed as naught but mannequins.

"*What! What!*" The King barked the word as objection and interrogation, appeal to Arson's manmade heavens and to the malignant cowboy himself. He whirled to face the architect of this most unwelcome miracle and froze.

Against the black, improbably starry sky of Arson's night, the cowboy's accomplices – the bloody man, and that rancid traitor Ketch – were slowly ambling away, over a low hill and out of sight. The cowboy, on the other hand, had stepped closer until he was nearly within arm's reach of Cleon's royal person. As though to emphasize this travesty, the dusty xerocole extended one tanned finger and gently pressed it into Cleon's bony chest.

"I came an unimaginably long way to be here," the man who named himself Frank Blank declared. "I had plenty to take care of here, but then I heard about *you*, Your Majesty." He poured more scorn into these last two words than Cleon had ever heard. "What a happy coincidence! You see, I *collect* kings. Your kind is thinning out, Mr. Third-of-his-Name. Mere anarchy has gobbled you up one by one, *yum!*" Frank removed his leathery finger from the royal chest. He reached for the crown of his improbable white hat. He lifted the chapeau and dropped it to the sand. When Frank Blank spoke again, he spoke from everywhere around the King. His voice rang like a revelation from on high, though Cleon – eyes gummed up with fearful tears – suspected that wherever this thing came from, it was not "on high." Not in a spiritual sense, anyway.

Counting only ears, nose, lips, teeth, tongue, and everything from there down, Frank was as human as a man could be. His skull, however, stopped just above his nose. This truncation was compensated for. From the place where eyes, forehead, and scalp should be, Frank played host to a spectacle. He bore a cloud beneath his hat; now released, it stretched its way up to the starry heavens. Its convolutions flickered with varicolored lightning, coruscating with a beautiful, internal light. The King's mouth dropped open; he couldn't help it.

"How many kings?" Frank's lips no longer moved. His voice seemed to come from the quaking air of Arson itself. "Have you ever wondered that, little king? How many of your kind have tried to stem the flow and flux of chaos, the only *real* truth? Little shards of hierarchy and miserable 'order,' that's what kings are. That's what you are, Cleon, a facet of a vast, ignoble brotherhood, and you never even knew it!" Frank's human half-face smiled a broad, satisfied smile and the directionless voice gave a brief, dry chuckle.

"You've had a good run, little king. Little puppet. You're a lost piece of something much bigger and more terrible, though, and it's time to take you home." The shimmering, living pillar of smoke pulsed and roiled. King Cleon was riven by an insight like a lance made of cognition: those coiled shapes in the gas, those flashing bolts of colored lightning? They were thought and language to the stranger. It called itself Frank Blank because a human name was necessary. Its own name was composed of a poetic dance of light and smoke, a phenomenon as pretty as it was devoid of phonemes.

Frank's voice was as gentle as a sidewinder's sidle. The cowboy-doll-man's lips did not move out of their fixed idiot grin. "On behalf of Pandemonium, allow me to invite you to be part of an adventure. We're going on a journey, Cleon; out beyond the narrow walls of order.

Down where the gleaming coils of chaos forever roil the waters." *No,* the King wanted to say, *you can't, I won't let you, I demand!* Not a word came out. Try as Cleon might, he couldn't stir his sluggish, fuzzy tongue or move his soft and nerveless jaw.

"Oh, but there's a bit of a hitch, little king. Did I forget to mention that?" The voice was like the glorious boom of a desert deity whose imminence Cleon III had often fantasized about. He found it wonderous and terrible. The fact that this was not *his* god filled him with a stew of fear and desire, revulsion and attraction. Frank Blank towered over the King. Was it Cleon's imagination, or was the whole scene's scale subtly *bigger* now, pulled out of true to render everything gigantic? Frank's pillar of smoke and lightning loomed larger than ever and the starry sky seemed vaster than it had. Something felt very wrong to Cleon. Something was *funny* – yes, that was the word exactly.

"You see," Frank said, his soft, thunderous voice shaded with patriarchal pity, "you wouldn't be able to make it where *you're* headed in your human form. You're going further than Pandemonium. Into story. Into madness. Into dreams."

King Cleon realized that he couldn't move. His flesh felt sensual and foreign. His whole frame felt luxurious and soft, though unresponsive to his mind's commands. The great Leviathan, the King, the Body of the State, had been unstrung. Snipped from his autonomous control, he'd been restrung as something new. *This isn't happening*, Cleon's mind shrieked, unable to summon tongue or throat. *This isn't real. I'm in control: of my own destiny, and the destiny of a nation! I'm not… I'll never be… I can't be…*

After all his careful efforts, Frank felt almost weary.

Soon, he'd have the chance to rest. But there were words that needed to be said, and choices yet unmade. Blissfully, like rotating a well-stretched human limb, the coils of Frank's more esoteric, gaseous body compacted and compiled until they stacked as neatly as a tiny thunderhead inside his hollow human-suit. He plucked his voluminous cream-colored hat from Arson's toxic soil. Frank blew a nearly invisible film of rancid dust from its immaculate surface, then placed it back atop his head where it masked his cranial truncation.

Frank whistled a little tune as he slowly sauntered toward the King. It wasn't much – just a spry little slice of madness he'd picked up in a dream he'd passed through once. The hendecatonic anti-melody felt good. It often struck Frank as rather tragic that so many entities took so little pleasure in the simple things. Like whistling. Or the feeling of clean, well-stitched puppet flesh between your fingers. Frank enjoyed that sensation quite a bit as he grasped the felt marionette King Cleon had become. This was not the Kindly King of Uncle Funny's Hoboken broadcasts. This was a much more accurate effigy: cruel, black dots of eyes, intricately-stitched scowl, plastic spectacles, and dour, jowly face.

"Your Majesty," said Frank Blank with unfeigned respect as he gently gathered up the fragment of the King of Marionettes. Puzzle pieces. Scattered fragments. One more gleam of Wolfaria's monarch captured in the name of Pandemonium. When they all were gathered, Frank's fellow travelers would build the first and only prison in their realm, and it would hold – eternally – their first and only captive. Once assembled from constituent components like King Cleon, the King of Marionettes could finally be chained, and chaos could dance free among the many worlds.

A single instance of Executioner Jacqueline Ketch had ceased to be. Ophelia Singh had shed the name along with her black cowl of office and tight black gloves. In the incomprehensible starlight glimmering from Arson's false night sky, Ophelia examined her mechanical-organic hands. They were the instruments that had defined her life for what felt like ages. Originally the rich color of tea brewed from a black leaf's golden buds, her hands had been overtaken, over time, by bands of matte black metal. Her knuckles clicked almost inaudibly as she stretched her fingers, examining the reinforced and semi-mechanized phalanges.

"I can smell it, you know," someone said.

Singh's training suppressed her startlement at the rich, cultured voice. It was Bloody Billy, naturally; who else could have stalked her with such unearthly stealth? Singh turned mild eyes on him and raised one eyebrow. Billy wore a smile and nothing else. Perhaps his nudism had been part of his persona prior to the meddling of Dr. Freund; perhaps he had developed a distaste for clothing in whatever laboratory-prison Freund had penned him in. "The blood," explained the murderer, sinking to a crouch before her. "You've done a bit of killing the old-fashioned way, haven't you?" He raised his own hands – caked in blood – and pantomimed a wrenching, clawing act of vague but terrible violence.

"More than a bit," Singh confessed. "More than you." She sighed. "I suppose I ought to feel some sort of respect for you, one professional to another."

The steel-capped man began to nurse one digit, then another. With fascinated revulsion, Singh (once Ketch) observed that Bloody Billy was sucking the filth from his fingertips. He battened on some unspeakable amalgam of blood, Arson's evil soil, and mass spectrometry alone knew what else.

"That's a very stupid thing to say," Billy said, pausing in his nursing to reply in his strange, melodic way. He searched Singh's face with eyes more human than her own. "'One professional to another,' what do you think you mean by that?"

"I…" Singh fumbled to expand.

"Oh, I'm not insulted," said the sadist in a mollifying tone. He moved on to the next finger, licking it clean of its unholy cargo. "But make no mistake, Executioner, I've never been a professional. Obviously, you aren't familiar with the extensive dossier the Kingdom has compiled regarding my frolics. I never stooped to robbery when I played my funny games. It's one reason it took them so long to find me, even though I gave them my real name in the first of oh so many letters. I never used anyone's credit chips, never took their valuables. A profession is a *job*, Executioner, as you well know. Killing is my art, my politics, and my religion – but never my job. Never that."

They sat in silence, side by side, and looked at the depraved and desolate landscape of Arson: Ophelia "Jacqueline Ketch" Singh (who, in the King's name, had claimed 512 lives) and William "Bloody Billy" Guillebeaux (whose desire, as William Blake had put it, was not weak enough to restrain, and who had tortured and killed 341 human beings). Leering down, the perverse stars made no distinction between murderer and executioner; killer for the Kingdom or for killing in and of itself.

When Billy finished nursing the last of Kinsey Freund's scabby blood from beneath his fingernails, his hands looked remarkably clean. From wrist to elbow was another, redder story. Even so, Singh was impressed with his impromptu, waterless tidying in spite of herself.

"Well," said Bloody Billy, standing up and stretching his crackling back, "it's certainly been…" He trailed off and, with a shrug, walked down the slope to Frank Blank and his truck. To Frank Blank, his truck, and the black shed. The crude, ebon-hued structure stuck in Singh's awareness like a thorn. She'd seen horrors in that locus, though she'd never stepped beyond its threshold for herself. Mystery Morrison Spare had been her medium of perception. Had he needed a witness? She didn't think that this was why he'd shown her so much of so many.

I can smell it, you know, he'd said. *The blood.* Singh looked down at her metal-woven digits. and allowed that, given his proclivities and sharpened senses, it was possible that Billy *did* sense an arterial aroma rising from the knuckle gears and mechanisms. To the right nose, her hands would always reek of blood. When she'd been King Cleon's Executioner, that had never crossed her mind. If it had, she would have thought of it as an advantage; another way to wield fear for the Kingdom's benefit. Now, though. What now?

"Now comes a choice, Executioner," said Frank Blank from just behind her.

"Not Executioner anymore," said Singh, "and not Ketch either. I guess you could say I've thrown that name back into the sea. You can call me Ophelia, if you like."

Frank stepped into the starlight before her. Even after all the monstrous miracles she'd seen, she felt a thrill of disembodied strangeness at the sight. In one hand, he held a doll of sorts; a felt marionette of the exact variety that Uncle Funny had employed in his coprolalic puppet show at the Woodpile. It bore a comic fabric version of

King Cleon's face. She didn't need to ask, nor Frank to answer, for Singh to comprehend the monarch's fate.

Singh pointed one metallic, flesh-spare finger at the puppet. "That," she said with genuine warmth, "is fucking *hilarious*, Frank."

Frank Blank didn't smile. He turned the puppet head to face his own. "Do you think it's funny, Your Majesty?" The felt head shook in firm negation, and Singh had an uncanny feeling that the doll was moving Frank's hand, not the other way around. She shivered. Frank shrugged. "I'm on your side," he said to her, "but humor's a subjective sort of thing, isn't it?"

He studied Singh in silence for a moment. Finally, he said; "I said you had a choice to make, and you didn't ask me what it was."

"I assume it's the choice between joining your cosmic carnival or going back to the reality where I was born. The retrieval sequence in the King's pod will override any sort of restriction, and I can ride that back if I want. I'll probably be executed."

"You probably would," agreed Frank, "if that were an option. But it's not."

Singh stared at him.

"You're not Pandemonium," Frank said bluntly. "A servile killer? Why would we want anything to do with a creature who'd do the dirty work of hierarchy and punishment? You belong to Wolfaria, Ophelia. Every executioner before you, and every one that will come after. And as for your home on the old cosmic range, I'm surprised you aren't more observant." Again, Singh had the strange sense that the puppet lifted its floppy little arm to point, rather than that Frank lifted it to make his point. The puppet pointed, and Singh looked.

Where once had loomed two holes in everything with

two dependent pods on stretched retrieval cables, the dome of Arson's heavens was unblemished by rift, crack, or crevice. At some point, the cords had been cut and the ruptures in reality had healed. Arson was as cut off from the universe where ICON was as it had ever been. "No way home," Frank said, "and you're not Pandemonium."

Singh had already started to put this last formulation together for herself. To her surprise, she felt betrayed. Yes, Frank was some sort of *other* in the purest possible sense, and yes whatever faction or force he served or was part of evidenced an ethos that was far from anodyne. Even so, hadn't she done as he'd asked?

"You did," Frank answered, "and that's why you get a choice." He dropped something onto the ruined soil beside her: a matte black key. She didn't have to ask what door it opened.

Frank began to walk away and called over his shoulder; "I'd wager you have the equivalent of a day to think it over, though I turned off Dr. Gayle's sun, so don't expect a dawn or dusk. After that, this interstice will cease to exist; will, technically speaking, never have existed at all. So, former Executioner, it's up to you. Oblivion... or the Pit. The pendulum is swinging." He paused in his steps for a moment. "It might be worth noting that I'm not *actually* sure what's down there. In the Pit, that is."

Frank picked up the pace again, striding to the waiting cab of his pussy-pink truck. All the souls embarking with him had been safely taken on, the trailer's gate was closed and locked, and Frank was itching for the desert road, *the* road, the one blown by the burning wind between the worlds.

"Goodbye," Frank called in his voice of sand and shed snakeskin, "and thanks again!"

The awful engines of his vaguely obscene transport

came to life with a disorganized riot of sound. By both the racket and the shuddering of Frank's transport, the roar seemed more explosion than ignition. The mechanism shook atop its outsized tires, and at a distance – vaguely, through Frank's window, past his cumulous cowboy hat – Singh could see the face of Morrison Spare, now properly asleep and dreaming the strange dreams born in the minds of dreamers of the real.

With a lurch and an ear-splitting, painful hiss, one pilot in the fleet of Pandemonium released his air brakes and weighed anchor. He drove the monstrous rig in reverse for a short stretch, then pulled a massive, looping U. The truck's mutated tires crushed rocks and disregarded gullies and potholes alike. Seconds later, Frank's truck's lights came on. Singh was unsurprised (was, in fact, almost amused) to see that the light blazing from the grille was the same pornographic shade of pink as the rest of the truck. The high beams lit the impossible road before them, past the ring of bone dust, up, up into the mountains where it led to next stop on Frank Blank's route.

Ophelia watched the stars. She felt the black key on the naked, all-too-human flesh on one patch of her palm, and she pondered her next move.

ROYAL NEWS WIRE | TUESDAY EVENING TRANSMISSION

COLORADO TERRITORY (Royal Press) – Tuesday afternoon at 3:23 PM, a massive volcanic event occurred at the summit of Mount Elbert, the highest peak in the region and one of the highest in the Kingdom.

"We're still attempting to determine the nature of what transpired," said Royal Army Spokesperson Wen Sarle, "but we know it was an unprecedented volcanic event. The peak is still emitting an ash cloud that is preventing transportation in or out of the area, but wired communication with local authorities has been established."

Sarle was able to confirm the tragic news that all evidence indicates the destruction of the Interstitial Control facility there, as well as the deaths of Archdirector Kinsey Freund, Doctor Gayle Ruzicka Freund, and on-site personnel. ICON spokesperson Randy Regis assured the RP that this regrettable disaster will not affect the future of the King's Pockets carceral programs.

As of this time, His Majesty King Cleon III has been privately mourning the events of Tuesday morning, but public comments have been delayed until an indeterminate future date.

Who is
Charles R. Bernard?

Charles R. Bernard is a writer who lives in Salt Lake City, Utah. His work has been featured in publications like Thuggish Itch and Cosmic Horror Monthly and has appeared in anthologies like American Cult, Peaks of Madness, and Deadman Humour: 13 Fears of a Clown. He is a contributor at Madness Heart Press, where he co-hosts the podcast Wandering Monster and blogs about horror culture. He resides next to Salt Lake City Cemetery; a sprawling necropolis whose tombs and markers stretch out over a square kilometer of grounds. Charles is lively enough company, though. You can find him at tinyurl.com/charlesrbernard.

More Books from

Madness Heart Press

By Charles R. Bernard

- He Led us Into the Wilderness and Spoke to Us
- Baptism for the Dead
- Congratulations on Your Hatred
- Baptism for the Dead
- Black Sunrise on Piss Earth

By Other Authors

Extinction Peak by Lucas Mangum
You Will Be Consumed by Nikolas Robinson
Curse of the Ratman by Jay Wilburn
Trench Mouth by Christine Morgan
Encyclopedia Sharksploitanica by Susan Snyder
The Television by Edward Lee
A Psalm Sung in Spores by John Baltisberger
Gush: Tales of Vaginal Horror by Gina Ranalli
City of Spores by Austin Shirey
Trip Chainsaw by Christian Smith
Pure Hate by Wrath James White
Mercy Kills by Jeff Oliver
The Reattachment by Douglas Ford
The Home by Judith Sonnet
Lights Out by Nate Southard
Kennel by Garrett Cook

9 781967 517008